# Husbands May Come and Go but Friends are Forever

*a novel*

## Judith Marshall

Kelso Books

ISBN: 0982504608
ISBN-13: 9780982504604
Library of Congress Control Number: 2009905907
Kelso Books

*To the Wilson Family, with love*

*With special thanks to the loving and supportive women in my critique group, "Women Who Write"*

*A good friend will come and bail you out of jail, but a true friend will be sitting next to you saying, "Damn that was fun!"*

— ANONYMOUS

# CHAPTER ONE

## *March 7, 2000*

Morning sunlight sliced through the dark canopy of clouds, but the rain continued to pummel the pavement, and I was on a tear. Stacks of manila envelopes, stamped Confidential in blood-red ink, covered every surface in my office. My company had recently completed a major acquisition, and as Vice President of Human Resources, my job was to prepare separation packages for the 113 employees targeted to be laid off.

My black suit jacket hung over the back of a chair. I had shed my pumps so I could move about more quickly. Company dress code was casual. But that day my attire looked as if I were going to a funeral.

I was sealing the last envelope when I heard a knock. I slipped on my shoes and went to the door, a bloom of dread in my stomach. Over the next three hours, I would be meeting with each manager whose department was affected by the downsizing. In my mind, I could hear my best friend, Karen, saying, "Downsizing is just a nice way of saying you're firing people."

"Am I late?" Kim Webster asked, cheeks flushed and panting. I glanced at my watch. 9:05.

"Not at all," I said. "Please come in."

Kim had been with Tekflex longer than anyone I knew. A former Accounts Payable Clerk, she had started right out of high school and worked her way up to Director of Accounting, responsible for a staff of twenty-three (seventeen after tomorrow).

"Coffee?" I signaled toward the pot.

"No thanks. I've had my limit for today."

I could tell by the way Kim was fidgeting that she wanted me to get to the point. I sat down behind my desk. Kim sat across from me.

"We've chosen tomorrow to do the layoffs."

"So soon?" she said, her voice on tiptoes.

"I'm afraid so."

"I've never done a layoff before." The skin around her eyes wrinkled.

"There's a script in here that will tell you exactly what to say." I patted the top envelope on the stack marked

Accounting. "Look it over. If you have any questions, give me a call." I managed a weak smile.

God, how I hated this part of my job. Although I had nothing to do with the decision to reduce staff, I felt responsible. My signature graced every letter.

"I assume the list is the same as the one you emailed me?" she said.

"Yes, there were no changes."

Kim sniffed and pulled a tissue from the pocket of her jacket. She waited a long time before speaking. "I've worked with some of those people for more than ten years," she finally said. "It's just not fair."

I leaned back in my chair. My eyes wandered over to a snapshot of Sam and me that I kept on my desk. Taken years earlier, it showed us in bathing suits, laughing, and sharing a beer in a beach bar in Cabo San Lucas. How I wished I were there right now.

I turned my attention back to Kim and tried to resettle the composure that I knew my face had lost. "I wish there was another alternative, but with so many duplicate positions…"

"I know, I know," Kim said. She raised her eyes heavenward. "Lord, I just hope I can do this."

"I'm sure you'll do just fine, Kim. You have an excellent relationship with your staff, and they respect you. That counts for a lot." My pep talk seemed to work. Kim gave me an appreciative half-smile.

"I'm so sorry," I said. I couldn't think of anything more to say.

Kim heaved herself out of her chair and picked up her stack of envelopes. She hovered for a moment before turning to go, then straightened her back and marched out the door.

Each of the other eight managers reacted as Kim had. "So soon?" "So many?" "But he is one of my best employees."

My response: "I'm so sorry."

—⁂—

Drained, but also relieved to have finished my last meeting, I sat in the blue-gray glow of my computer, scrolling through my daily deluge of emails. My assistant Rita rapped on the open door.

"I'm going to lunch," she said. "Would you like me to bring you something?" Dear Rita. She knew I often worked through lunch and worried about my health.

"No thanks. I've got some yogurt in the fridge."

"Okay," Rita said. "Sam wants you to call him." She tapped the door jam twice, and left.

I reached for the phone. He answered on the first ring. The sound of his voice was as consoling as my morning coffee.

"So, how did it go?" he asked.

"Worse than I expected," I said, toying with my cup.

"In what way?"

"It's one thing to put together packets with people's names on them, and a whole other thing to learn who they really are. This one is a single parent, that one has a wife who's three-months pregnant. Everyone's got a story."

"I'm sure they have," Sam said. "But you can't take this personally."

"I know." I breathed out a weary sigh. "I wish you didn't have to leave tomorrow."

"I wish you were coming with me."

"Me too," I said, picturing myself in Geneva strolling down Mont-Blanc Avenue, stopping for a coffee, or nipping in for a Swiss chocolate treat, while Sam attended his conference. On the weekend, we could take a train trip to St. Moritz; maybe go skiing or submerge ourselves in the healing waters of the mineral springs I'd read about.

"Sure would beat stripping employees of their livelihood," I said.

"There's still time to change your mind, you know," Sam said in a buttery baritone meant to persuade me. "It would do you good to get away, reenergize, get a clear perspective."

"No. No. I couldn't possibly."

"I know," Sam said, as if he'd like me to understand that this wasn't all he knew. "I'll see you tonight."

One of the nice things about our tenured relationship is that Sam and I no longer have to argue everything through. We each know what the other will say.

That doesn't mean we don't communicate. One of the reasons I fell for Sam was that he was nothing like my ex-husband, Ricky, who could sit in front of the television for hours without saying a word. Sam always has something to say.

Moments later, I was making half-hearted progress on a turnover report when the phone rang.

"Hey Liz, it's Taco Tuesday at the Cantina," Karen said with a burst of eagerness. "Two dollar margaritas and all the mystery-meat tacos you can eat."

I smiled for the first time that day. "Sounds delightful," I said. "But I can't."

"Oh come on. Jo's meeting me, and Gidge is coming by after work. It'll be fun. A night out with the girls." The girls. No matter how old we get, we'll always be "the girls"— Karen, me, JoAnn, Gidge, Rosie and Arlene—six women who have been friends since high school.

"I'd really love to, but I'm meeting Sam for dinner," I said. "He leaves tomorrow for the International Sales Conference in Switzerland."

"Oh shoot, I forgot. Well, give him a big smack for me." Karen had long been a fan of Sam's, always eager to point out what an overall good guy he was, unlike the parade of disappointing husbands she'd had.

"I will. Tell everyone hi, and don't wreak too much havoc over there."

"Who, us?"

The rain had stopped by the time I left the office, and the air was so fresh and sweet, I started to feel cleansed of doing the company's dirty work. I hurried across the parking lot as if dismissed from detention, hesitating briefly to ad-mire my Porsche—a gift I had given myself upon my pro-motion—before clicking the door open. It wasn't worth feeling bad about today. The important thing was to know I'd done my best. And to remember who I was, a woman with no college education, who began her career as a part-time Personnel Assistant, and now through years of commit-ted hard work, wore the proud mantle of Vice President of Human Resources.

As I drove west from San Ramon toward San Francisco, the lighting on the Bay Bridge cast a golden glow over the water. I'd made this trip often to see Sam, or to go to the airport, and each time I passed through the toll plaza, I thought of my Aunt Vi. A lifelong resident of the city, she loved to tell the story of the day the bridge opened in 1936. "We were all so excited. It was the biggest traffic jam in San Francisco history," she'd say, waving her cigarette in the air for affect. "Every auto owner tried to crowd his machine on the bridge." Till the day she died, she referred to a car as a machine. "Be careful in your machine," she'd warn each time I left her apartment.

Spiedini's restaurant was located two blocks from Sam's condo in SoMa, the area South of Market made trendy by the dot-com boom. It had become our "go-to" place, not only for its close proximity, but also for its intimate atmo-sphere and mouth-watering Northern Italian cuisine. By the time I parked in the underground garage of Sam's building, I realized I was starving. My breath quickened as I headed up the street in a trot. After almost twenty years, I still looked forward to being with Sam.

I entered through the double glass doors into the marble entry paneled in rust-colored suede. The softly lit bar to my left was a sea of dark browns and black. A group of business people was gathered around two tables near the windows, clutching bottles of designer beer. As I passed by, I heard a man ask, "Did you get pre-IPO stock? What's the lock-up?" I smiled. Every twenty-something in the tech industry dreamed of cashing out with a bundle, enough to travel the world, maybe buy a little vineyard in the Napa Valley. Good luck.

Sam was seated at the far end of the bar, engrossed in conversation with young, sweet-faced Dimitri, the week-night bartender, probably discussing the latest international soccer scores. Both were compulsive soccer watchers.

I shrugged out of my raincoat, hung it over my arm, and arranged my face in what felt like my most appealing look: a careful, pleasant smile, not too wide, just enough teeth showing.

"How are two of my favorite men," I said, stepping up behind Sam. Dimitri flashed a welcoming smile and reached for the martini shaker.

"Hello darling," Sam said, turning to plant a kiss on my cheek. Even his five-o'clock shadow couldn't hide his finely chiseled features. As I hoisted myself up onto the barstool, my skirt hiked up to my thigh. I left it there.

"You're early," Sam said, a hint of surprise in his voice. He took my coat, and laid it across the stool next to him.

"I couldn't wait to get out of there."

"Ah," Sam said with a nod.

"But I've made my peace with it," I said, reaching for the bowl of mixed nuts. Sam shot me a look of disbelief.

"I mean it. What's that poem about God giving you the strength to change what you can and know what you can't?"

"You mean the Serenity Prayer?"

"Yes. That's it. I'm making it my new mantra." I popped a cashew in my mouth in a gesture of finality.

Sam leaned over and caressed my thigh. "Whatever it takes," he said, reaching for his Heineken.

Dimitri served me a cold shimmering martini in a cool misshapen glass. I knew I hadn't convinced Sam. He knew that I really meant I couldn't do the job if I let myself care too much.

As I sipped my drink, I allowed my mind to dwell only on good things: the pleasure of Sam's company, his voice soft and strong, the relaxing warmth of the alcohol, the promising smells of roasted garlic and simmering marinara sauce. We talked easily, Sam and I, about his upcoming business trip, and my plans to catch up with my children and my friends while he was gone. And in the last pale light of what had been a stressful day, things didn't seem so bad.

# CHAPTER TWO

*March 7, 2000*

Half an hour later, we were seated in our usual booth at the back of the restaurant. It was still early, and there were only two other tables occupied. Dean Martin crooned in the background as a waiter with shiny, wet-looking hair took our orders: Veal Piccata with extra vegetables for me, and Veal Marsala with mashed potatoes for Sam. Not very imaginative, as we ordered the same thing most times we ate here.

I was half way through my Caesar salad when I noticed Sam wasn't eating. He was staring off in the distance, tapping on the table with restless fingers.

"What is it?" I asked, lowering my fork. "What's wrong?" Sam looked up, and when our eyes met, I realized he had been waiting for me to ask.

"There's something I need to tell you. I didn't want to bring it up while you were under all this pressure at work, but I don't think I should wait until—"

"What is it?" I blotted my lips with my napkin. "Tell me."

"I've been offered a promotion."

"That's wonderful," I exclaimed, reaching across the table for his hand. "It's about time they recognized you. What's the position?"

"VP of Sales."

"Leo Straussman is finally retiring?"

"Yes."

Leo was one of the founders of Western Pharmaceuticals, a man in his eighties who still put in a full workweek. Sam and his co-worker, Steve, often joked that they'd have to take Leo out of his office feet first.

"But, he's based in New York."

"Yes," Sam said. He paused to let me contemplate what this meant.

My stomach wrenched. "They want you to transfer to New York." It was a statement, not a question. I withdrew my hand from Sam's, and fell back in the booth. For a long moment we looked at each other.

Sam leaned forward, both forearms on the table. "I've accepted the offer, and I want you to come with me, Liz."

When I didn't answer, he continued. "Look, I'm fifty-five years old. My time's running out. This is my last chance."

"And I'm on the cruel cusp of sixty. What's age got to do with your moving three thousand miles away?" I could feel myself bristling. "How could you accept without discussing it with me?"

Sam rolled his eyes. "I didn't discuss it with you because I knew what you'd say. 'I can't leave my job. I can't leave the kids. I can't leave my friends.'" I could tell that there was no stopping Sam now. He was on a rant. "Tell me something, this job you seem to love so much, does it love you back?" he said, unable or unwilling to keep the anger out of his voice.

"You're being unreasonable Sam."

"I'm being unreasonable? You know the reason we've lasted so long? Because the whole arrangement suits you. Dinner once or twice a week, weekend trips, sleepovers when you can fit me into your schedule."

"Well, it must have suited you, too," I shot back, tightening my grip on my napkin.

"Maybe so. But it doesn't anymore."

"What does that mean?" I asked, aware of the edge in my tone.

"It means something has to change." He waited a beat. "We're either together or we're not." My ears pricked up at Sam's last words.

"So you're giving me an ultimatum?"

It was Sam's turn to fall back in his seat. "No, I'm not giving you an ultimatum." He closed his eyes for an instant, as if trying to find the right words to make me understand. But I understood completely. I didn't need a brain scan to know that I was a person who didn't like change. I'd lived in the same house for thirty years and had the same friends for forty years. My natural tendency was to avoid uncertainty at all costs. And Sam was right about our relationship suiting me. I liked it just the way it was.

The waiter arrived with our entrees. I picked up my fork and began pushing the food around on my plate. My stomach was still churning, and I wasn't sure it would be wise to eat anything right then.

Sam filled my wine glass, and then his, giving us both a little breathing room. I could feel the anger leak out of me gradually, like a tire with a tiny puncture.

"When do you have to be in New York?" I asked.

"The end of next month," Sam said. When his voice fell, I let silence fall with it. But in the end, I was more comfortable with the silence than he was. "Just promise me you'll think about it while I'm gone." Hope shone in his eyes.

I said I would. But thinking about it would be a wasted effort. I couldn't imagine myself abandoning my job, my children, and my friends to move to New York, nor could I imagine Sam going without me. Both options were impossible.

The rest of our dinner conversation occupied a delicate space as we danced our way back to neutral ground, snatching at any subject to avoid revisiting Sam's life-changing proclamation. But soon the banter became too heavy to lift, and silence took over.

We declined coffee and dessert. Sam paid the check, and we set off down the street. Head down, I concentrated on putting one foot in front of the other. Sam carried our two raincoats over his arm. With his free hand, he reached for mine. We continued our silence for most of the five-minute walk.

Steps from the entrance to his building, Sam stopped and turned to look at me. "Can you stay?" he asked in a gentle voice.

"It's been a really long day," I said.

I wanted to bury my face in his neck, inhale the lime fragrance of his skin deeply into my lungs, and tell him how much I loved him. Instead, I chose to kiss him lightly and wish him a safe trip. He stood looking down at me, disappointed, as if he knew full well the choice I'd made and why I'd made it. If he understood why, he was ahead of me.

# CHAPTER THREE

## *March 8, 2000*

I awoke before dawn, tired and pissed off because it was pouring again, Sam was moving away, and 113 people were getting laid off today.

Unable to go back to sleep, I drove into work. This early, the office building was dark except for a few security lights. I sat behind the wheel in the empty parking lot, staring through the rain at the place where I spent most of my waking hours; my second home. I thought back to the question Sam had asked the night before: "This job you seem to love so much, does it love you back?" At the time, I had found his question profoundly irritating. But this morning, I saw his point.

I stepped out of the car, snapped open my umbrella and made a dash for the back door, dodging the biggest puddles on the way. Fishing through my purse for my key card, I considered calling Karen with the news about Sam. We often talked early in the morning, before I became immersed in my workday. But she was probably suffering from tequila poisoning and wouldn't be up for hours. Besides, I knew what she'd say. She'd tell me to go.

I inserted my key card and pulled open the door. The building was eerily quiet. The only sound was the faraway rumble of traffic on the freeway half-a-mile away. As I passed the Xerox machine in the hall, I jabbed the start button. The sudden rush of energy triggered by the familiar surroundings propelled me toward my office.

Once inside, I flipped on the light, switched on the coffeemaker, and decided to clean out my filing cabinet; a chore I'd put off for months. After hanging my coat and umbrella on the rack, I pushed up my sweater sleeves, and yanked open the top drawer.

Rita was surprised to see me sitting on the floor amidst stacks of Pendeflex folders and loose paper. It was only 7:30, and I wasn't due for another hour.

"Good Morning," I said. "Look what I'm doing." I gestured at the mounds of files around me.

"Aren't those your new Armani slacks?" Rita asked in horror, a variation on the more traditional 'good morning.' I looked down at my pants.

Rita shook her head. "Honestly," she said.

I struggled to my feet, and dusted myself off for Rita's benefit.

"Let's go out to lunch today," I said, pouring myself a second cup of coffee. "My treat." I had a good reason for my invitation. Managers would be meeting with the employees to be laid off between eleven and twelve. Soon after, the office would be bedlam with the news, and I wasn't up to defending the company's position or worse, sparring with a disgruntled employee.

"No sense risking life and limb," I said, feigning frivolity.

Rita gave me a disapproving look as if to suggest what I already knew, that no matter how lightly I tried to play it, this did not promise to be a good day.

We spent the rest of the morning focusing our attention on the purging project, me sorting through files, and Rita shredding documents and processing new labels. The phones were strangely silent. Our only visitor appeared around 11:30. Devin from Communications, a wire-rimmed, young man in camouflage pants and a ponytail had a question about his 40l (k) plan. Rita directed him to Patti, our Benefits Administrator, who sat him down at her desk and patiently went over the distribution options noted in his packet.

"Goodbye, Ms. Hayden," Devin said, stopping for a moment in my office doorway. He smiled pleasantly.

"Goodbye, Devin," I said from behind my desk, toughness falling away for an instant, then returning almost immediately. When he'd gone, I turned my attention back to the screen full of emails.

Rita and I returned from lunch around 1:15. The rain had let up, and a few long golden pencils of light angled through the trees that lined the parking lot. I couldn't help noticing the number of empty spaces, evidence of the mass exodus that had taken place an hour earlier.

"I still don't see why they couldn't have tried some other types of cost controls like a hiring freeze or reducing the travel budget before letting so many people go," Rita said, as I pulled into my space. We'd managed to avoid discussing the layoffs during lunch, but the subject hovered around us like the odor of last night's fish dinner.

I switched off the engine and turned to look at her. There was more gray in her hair than I'd noticed before, more than there should be for a woman in her mid-thirties.

"We may have to do those things as well," I said. "I don't think the belt tightening is over yet."

Rita let out a sigh and reached for the door handle.

Back in the office, Patti reported no catastrophes had occurred while we were gone, only a few drop-ins with benefits questions. The message light on my phone was blinking. I was pretty sure I didn't want any messages, but I picked up the receiver and punched in my code anyway. Six voicemails, two from my boss' assistant, Keri. I dialed her extension.

"Warren would like to see you," she said.

"Now?" I asked in a pleading voice. The beginning of a headache pulsed behind my eyes.

"Sorry, Liz. He said it was urgent."

I sighed. "I'll be right up."

I plopped down in one of the chairs reserved for people begging an audience with Warren Steadwell, General Counsel. Keri Amato, a petite dynamo who presided over the second floor, sat across from me, head down, tapping on her keyboard. By the way she was avoiding my glance, I suspected she knew why I was there. Assistants to senior officers always knew everything.

When she'd finished what she was typing, she looked up. "You can go right in, Liz" she said. "He's expecting you." Whatever she knew, she wasn't letting on.

I knocked, then opened the door to find Warren standing in the middle of his spacious office. In his hard-finish suit, wing-tip shoes, and slicked-back hair, he looked like he belonged on Wall Street instead of in a West Coast high-tech company, where the Chief Technology Officer sported a neon-green Mohawk, and the CFO wore a diamond stud in her nose.

"Elizabeth, please come in and sit down," Warren said, looking over the tops of his glasses. A newly sprouted moustache concealed his thin upper lip. He waited until I was seated. "First of all, I want to thank you for all the hard work you and your staff have done in the last few weeks."

I didn't reply, but my interest was piqued. Warren wasn't one for compliments. In fact, he hadn't had much to say about my performance one way or the other since becoming my boss a year earlier.

"As you know, the corporate offices of the company we are acquiring are in Atlanta," he said, walking to the window, his hands clasped behind his back.

Of course I knew. Hadn't I spent two weeks out of every month for the last four months in Atlanta, stuck twice a day in traffic jams four lanes wide? And in an effort to bond with my new female colleagues, hadn't I spent Friday nights at their invitation eating Buffalo wings at the local Hooters, watching guys who drove pick-up trucks with shotguns mounted in the rear windows drink themselves into a stupor?

Warren turned and fixed me with a steady stare. "I'm sorry to inform you that as a result of the acquisition, your position is being eliminated."

My brain stalled on eliminated.

"Since there is a fully-staffed HR department in Atlanta, we feel there is no need for a duplicative function here." He paused to let the words register with me. And register they did. My God! They're giving my job to that nimrod, Stan Perkins, the ex-IBMer. I pictured him in his white short-sleeved shirt and clip-on tie, sitting at his metal desk, the wall behind him plastered with stupid motivational posters, pretty pictures with snappy statements like Strive for Excellence and Teamwork Works that are supposed to solve all your problems. Wait until he gets his first call from the lesbian in IT, claiming the mail girl is stalking her.

"What about my staff?" I asked, when I could gather my thoughts.

"They will be offered other opportunities within the company."

I slumped back in my chair, my head throbbing.

Warren walked to his gleaming mahogany desk. "I took the liberty of preparing your package myself," he said. He leaned over and opened his top right-hand drawer. Out came a large manila envelope stamped Confidential. "I think you'll be very pleased with the severance."

I stood up on wobbly legs and hung on to the back of my chair to keep from keeling over. I was rooted to the spot. Warren stepped around his desk and pushed the package into my hands. It was heavy. His eyes were trained on mine for an uncomfortable moment before he lowered them to stare at the package in my hands.

My throat tightened.

"Thank you," I croaked. I turned and forced my legs to move, afraid that if I stayed another minute, I'd break down and cry.

Keri was no longer at her desk, most likely by design. None of the other assistants were around either. Probably couldn't stomach seeing a dead woman walking.

I made my way down the stairs, clinging to the banister for support. I had always thought of myself as young for my age. Suddenly, I felt like a decrepit old woman, someone who should voluntarily turn in her driver's license.

Stay calm. Breathe. Remembering my yoga principles, I inhaled through my nose and blew the air out hard through my mouth.

As I rounded the corner, two young men dressed in jeans and T-shirts came toward me, the rubber soles of their athletic shoes squeaking on the tiled floor. I quickened my step, trying to look as though I was on my way to an important meeting, flashing a confident smile as I passed.

The initial shock quickly turned to anger. Rage spiked through me as I hurried down the long hallway that led to my office. For nine years, I had helped Tekflex grow from a small company to a major technology services firm. And this was the thanks I got? How many nights had I skipped dinners with Sam, or nights out with the girls, because I was either too exhausted or had an early meeting the next day? And how many times had I played telephone tag with my now-grown children, trying to touch base, while I was between planes or meetings, never having the time for a real conversation?

I slipped into my office, shut the door and sank into my chair. The plush leather made a hissing sound under my weight. I rested my elbows on the desk, my head in my hands. My thoughts fell helplessly back in time, to a particular evening during my fourteen-year marriage to Ricky. I'd had dinner waiting when he came home from the oil refinery, where he worked as a pipe fitter. Despite having a job of my own, I never ignored my "woman's work;" a lesson that had been drilled into me by my mother.

Our son, Kevin, had baseball practice, and his sister, Kristen, was at her weekly piano lesson. As a special treat, I made meatloaf and mashed potatoes, two of Ricky's favorites.

After a shower, he took a seat at the kitchen table. "I've given it a lot of thought, Liz, and I want a divorce." He unfolded his napkin and placed it on his lap.

"What?" I said in a voice barely audible.

"A divorce, I said. I'm moving out." He was wearing the new plaid sport shirt I'd bought for his birthday. His muscled arms stretched the sleeves tight. "You know we haven't been happy for a long time." His eyes held mine. I knew nothing of the sort.

The plate of food in my hand began to teeter.

"Let me help you with that," he said, jumping up and taking the plate from me. He put his palm under my elbow and escorted me over to a chair as if he were a Boy Scout and I an elderly lady.

I stared into his face, waiting for him to shout "just kidding" or "gotcha," like he did so often. But the way his jaw was set told me he wasn't joking. He mumbled something about being sorry for not loving me anymore. Then he salted his food and began to eat.

Panic rose in my throat. Maybe a good old-fashioned fight was what we needed. It had always worked for my parents. Maybe if I screamed and threw something. I opened my mouth to speak, but no sound came out.

After Ricky left, I promised myself I would never again be caught flat-footed. In every aspect of my life, I'd watch for the warning signs, see the red flags, strike before being stricken. Now, twenty-five years later, I had once more been blindsided.

I don't know how long I sat there wallowing in the past before I heard the knock at the door.

"Come in."

Rita cracked open the door a couple of inches. "I thought maybe you had someone in here with you," she said, her face barely visible. "What did Warren want?"

"Why don't you come in and sit down for a minute."

The blood drained out of Rita's face when I told her. She reached for the arms of the chair as if she were afraid she might fall out. When she'd gone, I realized there was a lot more I could have said, expressions of gratitude for overseeing my personal, as well as professional life, buying birthday cards for my friends and family, sending thank you notes and flowers on my behalf. But that would only have made her uncomfortable, as always.

I turned and looked out the window toward the parking lot, staring at leaves soaked with rain stuck to the car windshields, my mind sorting through alternatives, avoiding that cold place where desperation takes over, where my spirit could leak out.

What to do? The simple answer was to see today as an omen, the nudge I needed to put an end bracket on this segment of my life, pull up stakes and move to New York with Sam. That's how Karen would see it. But something about having a decision that important made for me seemed wrong. Nothing should be that easy.

I leaned back in my chair, closed my eyes, and sent a silent prayer to my Aunt Vi asking for her guidance.

I pictured my mother's sister, Violet—one of two daughters of Scotch-Irish immigrants—as she looked when I was a child. Slender, almost birdlike, she always brought a touch of pizzazz to the slouch of her hat, the wrap of her scarf. To me, she was the true measure of womanhood. Unlike her younger sister, my mother, she never apologized for her accomplishments or downplayed her intelligence. Despite being turned down for a job at the telephone company five times during the 1930s, she kept going back until they hired her.

"I just wore them out," she had said.

I felt a burst of clarity. I'd draw upon that unshakable optimism, a kind of sticktuitiveness that I had learned from Aunt Vi to help me find an even better job. I wasn't ready to pack it in and call it a career. I reached for my Rolodex.

Terry Winslow was one of the best headhunters in Northern California. We'd known each other for years.

"Hi, Terry, it's Elizabeth Hayden," I said into the receiver.

"How nice to hear from you, Liz. What's up?"

"You know that HR position in the Valley you called me about a while ago?"

"Yeah."

"Is it still open?" I tried to sound nonchalant.

Terry paused before answering. "I don't know. Why?"

"Well, it seems my position's been eliminated." I waited for a response from Terry, an "I'm sorry to hear that," or something similar. When none came, I went on. "I've just been told that the HR function is moving to Atlanta. You see, we've been working on this acquisition, and the company we're acquiring has more employees than we do, so I guess it makes sense to have HR where the majority of the people are." I had a penchant for babbling when a subject made me uncomfortable. I shut up.

"Let me check and get back to you," Terry said.

"That would be great. You have my home number."

I hung up the phone. Sam's words about this job loving me back echoed in my head. Had I believed in such things, I might have attributed his question to the helping hand of some higher power, some god of forewarning watching over me. But I didn't believe in gods, not even if they channeled themselves through Sam; I believed only in myself.

I glanced over at my computer screen. Eighteen new email messages; two marked urgent. I was tempted to forward all of them to Warren with a message saying, "Fuck you!" Instead, I snatched up the manila envelope, grabbed my purse, and stomped out.

# CHAPTER FOUR

*March 8, 2000*

As I unlocked the front door to my house, I felt scattered and shaky, not quite rooted in my own feet. I couldn't remember driving home. Had I run a red light? I had no idea. But by the grace of whichever saint it was that protected distracted travelers, I'd made it.

Inside, the smell of Pine Sol mixed with furniture polish reminded me that it was Flora's day to clean. I pitched my car keys into the bowl on the entry stand, hung up my raincoat, and stepped out of my shoes. The demands of the working day often required me to attend brain-scalding meetings where pigheaded executives kept the pot boiling, or to intervene between small-minded employees whose hidden agendas clashed and banged like bumper cars. Those things only heightened the joy of my returning home. And on such a harrowing day as this, my fondest wish was never to leave.

I carried the bulging envelope into the family room and sat down on the couch. With the packet in my lap, my eyes traveled around the room: the custom-built entertainment center, the 19th century Italian sideboard, the remodeled kitchen with its buffed granite countertops and gleaming stainless steel appliances, all rewards reaped from my success. Ricky and I had purchased the house new in 1970 with the help of his GI loan. For more than a year, sheets covered the windows, and a picnic table and benches served as our dining room furniture. But we didn't care. It was ours.

As I sat there, hushed and still, I could almost hear music coming from Kevin's bedroom, and Kristen shouting for him to turn it down so she could hear on the telephone. I envisioned Ricky sitting across the room in his battered leather recliner, the paper spread before him, oblivious to the noise.

What is it about the past? It pops up like a Jack-in-the-box and wraps its arms around you, squeezing so tightly sometimes that it takes your breath away.

"Enough," I said out loud. I ripped open the flap of the envelope in my lap and removed the contents.

The next morning, feeling fierce and proud in a black pants suit and white dress shirt, my hair in an updo, I strutted into the offices of Stevenson & Glick, the outplacement firm that had been retained by Tekflex to help me find work. Having read through the materials in my exit package the night before, I was shocked to learn the company had sprung for the highest executive level pro-gram for me. At $15,000 a pop, it didn't happen often. Most laid-off employees were offered a one-day workshop on how to write a resume, and a few networking tips. Warren must have felt extra guilty. The bastard.

I waited in the rich, well-upholstered lobby, thumbing through the Wall Street Journal, Business Week and Time, pretending to be interested in their contents. I stared at a page, and tried not to think about Sam. I felt relief in his absence. With Sam gone, I didn't have to explain what I was doing.

"The market for senior HR executives is fairly tight right now," Mr. Glick informed me from behind his imposing desk. Every inch of him was polished to a high sheen. His glossy charcoal gray suit was beautifully cut, and his light blue shirt and tie with a subtle pink stripe had been carefully chosen.

"Oh." I knew what he said was true, but I couldn't keep the disappointment out of my voice.

"But I'm sure a woman with your skills and experience will have no trouble finding a suitable position." He smiled. I appreciated his attempt to make me feel better. "Your out-placement package includes group meetings, as well as indi-vidual counseling. You'll have a private office, a computer, and all the support services you'll need."

"That sounds perfect."

"When would you like to begin?"

"How about right now?" I said. Pleased with my show of enthusiasm, Mr. Glick shook my hand and showed me the way to my new temporary office.

While I waited for the computer to boot up, I looked through the desk drawers: pens, paper clips, sticky notes, a yellow pad, all the basics. I retrieved a pen and the yellow pad, squared my shoulders, and began making a list of to-dos: 1) update resume 2) call Rita and ask her to send my Rolodex (remember to ask her to include the picture of Sam and me) 3) make a list of contacts 4) slit my wrists.

The light on my answering machine was blinking when I got home. I hoped it was Sam calling to tell me he'd arrived safely.

"Call me," my best friend Karen's voice said. Quickly dismissing the ripple of disappointment I'd felt that it wasn't Sam, I hit speed dial.

"Hey, what's up?" Karen said. "I called your office this afternoon, and Rita said you were at home."

"It's a long story," I said.

"What? Tell me."

I paused and rubbed my forehead. "I can't, really. Not tonight."

"I can come over there." I heard the concern in her voice.

"No, no. That's not necessary."

"Tell you what, I'm going to Tahoe to do some skiing, and I need some new sexy underwear. Meet me at Nordstrom tomorrow around eleven. We can talk over lunch."

"You're going to ski in your underwear?"

I set out to meet Karen the next day wearing a high-collared white shirt, slim jeans and boots. The rain had blown through, and the air held the aroma of freshly laundered sheets. As I

33

pulled into the multi-tier garage, I allowed a slow wave of delight to break over me. Spending the day with my best friend offered me a quick snippet of relief from my burden.

Nordstrom Department Store was unusually quiet. But then, I wasn't used to shopping on a weekday. I felt like one of those rich ladies who lunch.

"Liz, come here a minute," Karen called from across the aisle. She beckoned to me with her long arm, kept flabless by thrice-weekly weight-bearing exercise sessions at the gym. Her hair was blonde-streaked caramel, while her eyes seemed positively backlit by the fluorescent ceiling lights. She was literally glowing.

As I came up beside her I caught an over-powering whiff of the Chanel perfume she'd just sprayed from the tester at the cosmetics counter, misting herself as if she were an African Violet. She commented that it made her feel like Catherine Deneuve.

"What do you think of this?" she said.

"What is it?" I asked. I waved the strong smell away from my nose and squinted at the thin beaded chain she had draped over her manicured fingers.

"It's a decorative chain for your glasses," she explained. "See these? They're Austrian crystals." She fondled the tiny beads that looked like cheap glass to me.

"You've got to be kidding," I said.

"About what?"

"You would actually hang those dime-store glasses you bought at Thrifty from that thing?" Karen refused to invest in prescription glasses. That would mean she'd have to admit her eyesight was failing, which could only mean one thing— she was getting old.

"How much is it?" I asked. I reached for the tiny price tag that hung from the clasp. "$85.00," I exclaimed.

She shushed me.

"Are you nuts?" I whispered.

"I'm always misplacing the damn things and I thought—"

"If you're so worried about losing your glasses, why don't you get laser eye surgery?" I said. "Everyone's doing it." She ignored me and continued to inspect the chain. The diamond cocktail ring made from her various wedding sets, caught the light and sparkled as she rolled the chain between the pads of her slender fingers. "Karen, do you want to look positively geriatric?"

That got her attention. She frowned.

I put my mouth close to her ear. "If you buy that thing, I swear I'll send your picture into Glamour magazine and have them put you on the dreaded 'Don't' page."

She turned to look at me.

"I swear to God," I went on, crossing my heart with my forefinger. "You'll be there with the black tape over your eyes right next to the seasonally-confused woman wearing socks with her sandals." Karen's large blue eyes crinkled at the corners as her lips turned up in a grin. I knew I had her; there was no greater feeling, no achievement so great for me as making Karen laugh. "Or maybe next to Ghetto Granny in her mini-skirt, fishnets, and white patent leather boots."

Karen let out a sputter that turned into that full rich laugh of hers, a laugh that made me want to break out the balloons and confetti.

Out of nowhere, a saleswoman appeared, her face with skin drawn tight across her cheekbones, eyelids stretched smooth, forehead shiny and line-free – all the signs of recent cosmetic surgery. Her dyed-too-dark hair was pulled into a tight bun, and she was dressed all in black, accentuating her pale complexion.

"May I help you, ladies?" she asked, looking at us like we were breathing in some of her air.

"No thank you," Karen replied, composing herself. "We're just looking." The woman turned and walked away.

Karen nudged me, her favorite conspiratorial gesture. "I wouldn't let that surgeon cut my lawn," she said behind her hand. "You could set a table on that forehead."

With her big Six-Oh birthday only months away, the topic of plastic surgery crept into every conversation. She had gone for several consultations with doctors all over the Bay Area, but she was too afraid to go under the knife.

"I've told you a hundred times," I said. "You don't need surgery." I was filled with the desire to tell her I loved her just the way she was.

"Come on," I said, wrapping my arm through hers and steering her away from the counter. "Let's go have lunch before the bus full of old ladies from the retirement home arrives and we can't get a seat."

The bistro across the street was set back behind a wrought-iron railing that enclosed a small patio where patrons dined in warm weather. Each table was adorned with a single fresh daffodil.

Women in spring dresses and minimal makeup emitted little bursts of social laughter, their hands fluttering as they talked. I would have done anything not to break the mood.

"I lost my job," I said into my Cobb salad. The words came out in a rush.

Karen's face clouded over. She lowered her glass of iced tea and reached for my hand. "Oh honey," she said, her voice heavy with sympathy. "I know how much your work means to you."

"Silly, isn't it?"

"No, it's not silly."

"Sam thinks it is."

"No, he doesn't," Karen said in a tone meant to scold me. "I know Sam, and he would never think such a thing."

I shrugged my shoulders.

Karen squeezed my hand. "You should be proud of what you've accomplished." This was pretty much what I had been telling myself for the past two days. Without success. "You've worked very hard to get where you are."

"You mean where I was."

"Tell me what happened," Karen said.

I reiterated the details of my termination. By her expression, I could tell she was listening, hanging on my every word, a talent Aunt Vi also had.

Since Aunt Vi's passing, if I had a problem, I went to Karen. If I had a success that warranted celebration, she was the one I called. And if I failed, I knew Karen would love me unconditionally, the way we had loved each other since we were fifteen.

"Listen to me," Karen said, pushing aside her bowl of soup, so she could lean close. "Recently, I've learned that you can't shoehorn life into preconceived tidy little boxes. Life is messy and riddled with surprises."

I blinked. I'd never heard Karen sound so profound. She looked like she might say something more.

"What?" I asked.

"Nothing," she said, leaning back in her chair. "It just is."

"Speaking of surprises," I said. "Sam is moving to New York."

Karen clutched her chest. After a pause she said, "Excuse me?"

"That was exactly my reaction. I couldn't believe it." I shook my head. "But it's true. He's getting a promotion to a position in New York."

"When did he tell you this?"

"The night before he left for Switzerland."

"Does he know you've lost your job?

"No, he hasn't called."

"Why haven't you called him?"

I sighed heavily. "Because Sam wants me to move to New York with him, and I promised to think about it while he was away, and now if I told him I was unemployed, he'd say 'Great! Now there's no reason you can't come with me.'"

I was babbling again. I clamped my mouth shut and began fiddling with the salt and pepper shakers.

Karen's eyes never strayed from my face. "And that's bad because?"

I considered how to answer this.

"Be honest," Karen urged.

"It's bad because I know if I went, eventually I'd resent him. And he's much too good a man to be put through that."

Karen stared at me for a long time, then said, "You're really screwed up, you know that?"

I couldn't help smiling. "I know," I said. By what magic did this woman insult me, and in so doing lift my spirits?

"So what's next?" Karen asked, reaching for her glass.

"Well, I figured I'd take advantage of the outplacement package they gave me and try to find another position. I've got the kitchen remodel to pay for, and I promised Kevin I'd help him with a down payment on a condo he wants to buy. We'll see what happens."

Karen nodded.

"By the way, I haven't told the kids. I don't want them to worry. You're the only one who knows."

"That makes me feel very special," Karen said, fixing me with a caring smile.

I felt my lungs expand.

"But you really need to tell Sam," she said.

# CHAPTER FIVE

*March 13, 2000*

In spite of the feeling of dread in my stomach, I made myself attend the group meeting at the outplacement center on Monday morning. The conference room was thronged with people half my age, milling around, coffee cups in hand. Looking at them I felt as outdated as a vinyl LP.

At the stroke of nine, a thirty-something woman strutted into the room in a suit designed for the boardroom, minimal makeup, and just the right amount of chunky gold jewelry. A Diane Sawyer look-a-like, she oozed self-assurance. We took our seats. I sat at the back, near the exit.

After introducing herself as Kate Whitcomb, and giving her credentials as an outplacement counselor, she asked us to spend a few minutes reporting on what we had done the previous week to further our job search, and what we had scheduled for the upcoming week. I couldn't help feeling a pinch of resentment at having to account for my activities to a woman who was young enough to be my daughter.

One by one, people hopped up on caffeine shared their horror stories of rejection and fears of long-term unemployment. As I listened, I could feel my resolve begin to crumple. My woes were complicated by the fact that I'd still had no word from Sam. It had been our practice to touch base daily when either of us traveled, if only to leave a brief voicemail or dash off a quick email. Part of me was grateful that he wasn't pressuring me for an answer, while another part of me wanted to strangle him.

At the break, before it was my turn to share, I opted to go back to my temporary office. No sense wasting valuable time being demoralized by a crowd of whiners. As capable Kate had pointed out, "Life is 1% what happens to you and 99% how you react to it." I knew if I wanted to find a new position, I'd have to do more than just some serious finger crossing. I reached into my briefcase for the list of contacts I'd compiled over the weekend and picked up the phone.

Because I like to finish everything I start, I went to my temporary office the next day and the day after that, wobbling back and forth between the tough determined stance of a female executive, and the fragile insecurity of a woman who had lost control over her life. But it didn't take many more visits to the outplacement center to quash what little optimism I had left. Warren had destroyed my confidence as if he had wadded it into a ball and thrown it into a wastebasket.

Although I couldn't explain or even understand it, the idea of stopping work terrified me. I could see how some people looked forward to retirement with plans to play golf, travel, or write a book. For me, it meant a huge chunk of my very self would fall away. Who was I, if not the Vice President of Human Resources for a $2B Fortune 100 company?

When it had become clear that I didn't have a Sno-cone's chance in hell of having a job offer, or even an interview by the time Sam returned from his conference, I called him in Switzerland.

"How's the conference going?" I asked, lying on my bed in my pajamas, staring out the window through the dripping trees, at the gray sky.

"Good. Fine," Sam said.

"Are you stuffing yourself with Weiner Schnitzel?" I grimaced at my lame attempt at humor.

"No."

Sam wasn't making this conversation easy. I dared myself to get on with it. "I got laid off," I said. Sam didn't answer for a moment. The phone line crackled. "Did you hear me?" I asked.

"I'm sorry to hear that." I could feel the barrier between us.

"Well, I just thought you should know," I said in a hard, cool voice.

"Is there anything else you want to tell me?" Sam asked in a level tone.

"Just that I don't know what I'm going to do. I haven't made any decisions."

"I see."

Oh God. We sounded like two characters in a bad movie. This couldn't be an exchange between Sam and me. We were intimates; I'd breathed his breath, my skin knew his skin.

I waited, but he didn't say any more. We said our good-byes without the standard "I love you," and "See you when you get home."

I heard a click on the other end of the line. I sat there in a sweat of uncertainty with the phone to my ear for a couple of seconds before clicking the off button, and placing it gently on the bedside table.

# CHAPTER SIX

## *March 20, 2000*

Just as the last glimmer of light was wrung out of the sky, the phone rang. I heard Karen's voice on the recorder. My momentary impulse was to run to the phone, but I could barely move, my limbs as heavy as sandbags.

As I sat in my robe staring numbly at the television set, I found myself envying the people in the news buried by avalanches or swept away in flash floods. How nice for them. I hadn't thought much about death up until then. Oh, there were times when I developed more than a light case of the "mean reds," as Holly Golightly in Breakfast at Tiffanys called depression. But never, not even after Ricky walked out, had I felt such a painful emptiness.

Days and nights had trudged by, dragging me with them. I became a case of nerves, patience rubbed bald. When Rita called to check on me, I'd snapped at her like a high-strung Chihuahua.

For as long as I could remember, I'd believed I could survive whatever life threw at me. I ticked off the tests I'd passed: The lonely childhood spent watching my parents' civil war rage on; dinnerware shattering, doors slamming and windows rattling. The bitter quarreling I heard from under my cave of covers late at night. Fights about money. Sex. The marriage itself. And then there was my own failed marriage – forced into couplehood by an unplanned pregnancy only to be left with a ruptured heart and two children to support. I had helped a friend survive the loss of her only child, and saved another friend from a violent husband. I had faced the uphill battle of proving myself in the corporate world, working twice as hard as my male peers to earn my place at the executive roundtable.

Big deal. I wasn't the only woman to sustain a three-aspirin headache from bumping her head against the glass ceiling only to be knocked off the ladder. And I had come to terms with the ancient shadows cast by family and love. Or so I thought.

Curled up in the dark, clutching my remote control, some rational voice in my head told me that it was ridiculous to be thinking like this; so self-indulgent and repulsive in the face of genuine suffering, not to mention diametrically opposed to the way I'd always valued myself. What was wrong with me? Despair had somehow taken root slowly and firmly, even in my most reticent heart. That's what can happen when you cut yourself off. Messages from friends who couldn't reach me at the office were piling up on my machine. Karen had already called twice before, inviting me to join her at Tahoe. No word from Sam.

I hauled myself off the couch, cinched up my robe and shuffled down the hall.

"I must be crazy," Karen's message said. "Skiing is the only sport where you put on as many clothes as you can, only to proceed to take them off because you have to pee." I let out a laugh. "Anyway, I know you're there, ruminating. It's not good to think too much, you know. Call me."

I raked my fingers through my unwashed hair. My awareness began to crystallize. I needed to make a connection with the outside world, get things back into perspective. Karen was the one I wanted to speak to. Maybe I'd take her up on her offer to join her at the lake.

The doom I'd felt minutes earlier shifted slightly into a kind of hopefulness. With the decision made to call her first thing in the morning, I fell into the first restful sleep I'd had in days.

The shrill ring of the portable phone woke me with a start. I squinted at the red illuminated numbers of the clock on the bedside table. 4:45 a.m. Sleep-fogged, I needed a minute to recognize Arlene's voice on the other end of the line.

"Dead. What do you mean? Who's dead?" The phone crackled with static. "Let me get to the other phone, Arlene."

I scurried down the hall toward the kitchen, the portable phone pushed hard to my ear, my heart racing as time took on that strobe-light quality it does when the mind is trying to register that a bad thing has happened. A strange internal chatter started up. Like when I had heard my mother's shaky voice on my answering machine early that one morning, telling me that my father had suffered a stroke and to get to the hospital right away. Or when Arlene had called that Christmas Eve to tell me a drunk driver had killed her son, Timmy. No, no, no, the inner voice chanted. Over and over.

I flipped on the light switch in the kitchen and rushed to pick up my reliable wall phone.

"Arlene? Arlene, are you there?" Silence. Where the hell is she? I was so frustrated I thought my head would explode.

Not knowing what to do with myself, I went to the stove and turned on the burner under the kettle. With the phone clamped between my ear and my shoulder, I reached for a tea bag. My sleeve caught on the corner of the cardboard box and pulled it off the counter. Tea bags scattered all over the floor.

"Shit!" I kicked the empty box as hard as I could with my bare foot, sending it flying across the room.

"Liz, you there?" Arlene's voice came through.

"Yes, I'm here. Where were you?"

"I went to get my cigarettes out of the freezer," she said, as if I'd asked a stupid question.

"Please, repeat what you said."

"I just got a call from the Reno police. There was an accident last night on Mount Rose Highway."

"Accident? What kind of accident?" I knew I was asking questions to stall for time, to postpone hearing the painful news that would follow.

"Something about a motorcycle and ice. Or gravel. And a man. He's okay, but Karen was pronounced dead on arrival at the hospital."

The mention of Karen's name nearly choked me. I gasped, fighting to stay above it. Quick. Think of something else. Greg has a motorcycle. She must have been with Greg. I conjured up a picture of the two of them on his shiny black Harley, swooping and gliding downward on the winding, twisting road, scenery racing by them like a fast-forward movie. Karen is wearing her new black leathers—tight pants and matching jacket. I can see her blond hair whipping in the wind from the bottom of her helmet as she sits behind Greg on the "queen seat," her arms wrapped tightly around his waist. She's smiling with uncommon brilliance, looking like a twenty-two-year-old instead of a woman about to turn sixty. They hit a patch of ice. The bike swerves. Karen loses her grip. She blows backwards. I squeeze my eyes shut. I can't watch.

"Liz? Liz?"

I let out my breath, not realizing I'd been holding it. "Yes?"

"I said I'd get in touch with Squeak." Squeak was the nickname Karen had given her daughter, Julie, who as a toddler had a voice like Minnie Mouse. "I think I have the number of her modeling agency in L.A. They should be able to reach her. Then I'll call the girls, and tell them we'll meet here tonight. After I get a hold of everyone, I'll call you back."

Struck dumb, I hung up the phone. The whistle on the kettle sounded. I walked over to the stove, taking careful steps, and turned off the gas. My head continued to ring with the sound of the kettle, as I sagged over the sink and stared out the window into the darkness. How could this happen? A few hours ago, I had a best friend. Why didn't I pick up the phone last night? We could have talked. Now, I will never be able to speak to her again.

That bone-chilling thought brought with it the full impact of what had happened. Karen was dead.

My legs buckled underneath me, sending me to the floor. I curled into a ball and crossed my arms over my head.

"Please, God. No," I wailed, rocking and sobbing, my lungs fighting for breath.

# CHAPTER SEVEN

## *March 21, 2000*

I waited until after eight to call Sam at his office. According to my daytimer, he'd returned from his conference two days earlier.

"Sam Steuart," he answered in a crisp businesslike tone.

"Hi, it's me," I said in a shaky voice. "Something terrible has happened."

"What's wrong? Are the kids all right?" It was just like Sam to be concerned about my children as if they were his own. It was one of the things I loved best about him.

"It's Karen. She's dead." The words sounded so strange, like someone else had spoken them. I waited for him to say something, something that would change what I had just told him.

"Oh, my God. How?"

"There was an accident near Lake Tahoe. A motorcycle accident."

Sam let out a deep sigh. "I'm so sorry, Liz." I pictured him sitting at his desk on the 30th floor of No. 1 Embarcadero, his blue oxford button-down shirt rolled into artful three-quarter sleeves, his tie loosened around his open collar.

"I called to ask if I could borrow your van." What I really wanted was for him to drop everything and come over, to encircle me in his arms and comfort me. But I wouldn't let myself ask for that.

"My van?" He sounded both surprised and disappointed, as if he wanted me to ask for more—to prove that I needed him.

"We have to go to Tahoe and I offered to drive."

"Of course you can borrow the van."

"Thanks." The strained silence that followed stirred in my chest. I sensed Sam was wondering why I didn't bring the conversation to a close. I just couldn't break this fragile link with him.

"Well, I guess I'd better go," I said.

"Elizabeth." He rarely used my Christian name. When he did, I knew it was meant to draw my attention.

"Yes."

"I can be there in an hour."

His words threw me into a muddle. I massaged my forehead with my fingers. Say yes. Why don't you say yes?

"No, no," I said. "I'll be all right." I tried to keep my tone light. "I don't need the van until tomorrow morning. This evening will be fine." I hung up and drew a ragged breath.

The rest of the day was a blur. I called my children to tell them the news. Kristen, a pediatric nurse at Children's Hospital, was about to leave for her shift when she answered. "Not Auntie Karen," she cried. I recounted what I knew and promised to call back when I had more information. Kevin was not at his desk at the engineering company where he did the payroll. I left him a brief message.

I moved mechanically through the routines of showering, flossing, creaming, and dressing. As I stood in my walk-in closet, in front of the procession of dresses and separates grouped according to color, I watched an endless loop of Karen's death. My head was crammed with questions; all jumbled up like a box of loose rubber bands. When she fell, did everything slow down like it does in the movies? Did it hurt, or did she lose consciousness right away? Did her life flash in front of her? If so, which parts? Did she have time to think at all? Did Karen know she was going to die? I shuddered at the thought.

All afternoon, I kept wondering what Karen and Greg, her much younger off-and-on lover, were doing on Mount Rose highway at night. The scenic shortcut to Reno from the north shore of Lake Tahoe was mostly a two-lane road with steep inclines and hairpin curves. In the dark it could be treacherous. It wasn't like Greg to take such a risk when the freeway offered a much safer route.

Sam showed up with the van at a little after five. "Do you need a ride home?" I asked, as we stood together in the entry hall. He was wearing the overcoat I'd given him for Christmas.

"No thanks. Steve followed me over from the office. He's waiting outside," he said, gesturing with his head.

I nodded, folding my arms across my chest.

"Are you sure you're okay?" Sam asked.

"I'm sure," I answered, avoiding his glance.

Out of the corner of my eye, I saw him drop the keys to his van on the entry stand. He turned and took a step toward the front door. Then, as if something just occurred to him, he turned back to look at me.

"Just answer me one thing, and then I'll go." He fixed me with a brown-eyed gaze. "Do you love me?"

I tightened my arms. "That's not a fair question."

"Why isn't it fair?"

"Because when I say yes, the next question will be, 'then why won't you come with me,' and it's not that simple," I said, struggling to stay calm.

Sam looked at me in disbelief.

"Look, I can't just pick up and follow you to New York, like some little puppy dog," I said.

"I never thought of you as following me. I thought we'd go together. As partners."

"Well, that's not how it looks to me."

Sam shoulders sank. He watched me for a while longer, and then said, "Steve's waiting." His voice was as broken and lonely a sound as I have ever heard. He turned and walked out, the smell of his Armani cologne trailing after him.

I went to the window and watched as he walked down the front path and got into the car. In the semi-light, I saw

Steve turn and speak to him. He said something back, and they drove off. I stood there transfixed, staring at the spot where the car had been parked. I could hear the neighbor's cat crying for food and the sound of a car door slamming next door. I was struck all at once how life was out there going on and I was in here on hold, suspended in time, barely breathing.

# CHAPTER EIGHT

## *March 21, 2000*

Later that evening I drove Sam's van to Arlene's through the center of downtown Parkerville instead of taking the freeway. The streets were quiet, and only a few of the stores that had survived the opening of the mall on Hwy 680 were open. I passed the Vietnamese Market that used to be Mr. B's Fountain, where Karen, Arlene, and I often had lunch on Saturdays as teenagers. On the corner was the pawnshop, formerly Keller's Five and Dime, which had boasted the largest selection of comic books in the county. I remembered going there with Karen when we first met to pick out some perfume for my mother's birthday. We chose Evening in Paris. I can still see the bottle tucked into the royal blue fake velvet cushion inside the midnight blue box. I don't remember us ever smelling the perfume. We bought it because it looked like something a movie star would have on her dressing table.

Across from the pawnshop was a brightly-lit Chevron station. I looked down at the gas gauge. Full. It was just like Sam to fill the tank for me. I knew I should feel gratitude, but nothing could get through the numb icy wall that had formed around me.

I took the familiar turn at the end of Main Street onto Cypress. As I approached the high school, I realized why I chose this route. I wanted to see the old place.

I cruised by as slowly as a cop. The ancient brick buildings we thought looked like a fancy Ivy League college appeared tired and worn in the dark. Floodlights pointed out the cracking mortar and flaking paint. The lawn that Mr. Ceilinski, the custodian, mowed faithfully each week was now mostly weeds and dirt. Obviously absent was the sixty-year-old oak tree that had once stood so proudly in the center of the campus; some kind of beetle infestation, I'd read. The place looked like a penitentiary without it. The only thing missing was bars on the windows.

—〰—

On a sun-dappled spring day, the high school campus was abuzz with students. Girls wearing crisp cotton dresses over starched stiff crinoline petticoats giggled and whispered, while boys in low-slung Levi's strutted around them, trying to get their attention.

None of us realized how lucky we were to be growing up during the fifties in a town still small enough for most of the residents to know each other. We were called "war babies," but we grew up in a prosperous economy, untouched by the Great Depression and barely brushed by the war.

As Arlene and I hurried down the steps of the Science Building, I noticed that the large gnarled wisteria vines surrounding the entrance were starting to bud. By early summer, the fragrance from the blossoms would waft through the open windows and hang heavily in the air, which could only mean one thing; the school year would soon be ending. I felt sad already.

An army brat whose family had moved five times before settling down in Parkerville, Arlene Shoren had learned to make friends easily. I had just turned fifteen and was in the middle of my sophomore year, when we met while standing in line at the bus stop.

"Hi, I'm Arlene," she said brightly. I nodded nervously, intimidated by her self-assurance. "I just moved here from Texas," she jabbered on, catching my eyes with hers. "What a hole. They have bugs there so big you can put a saddle on 'em and ride 'em." She let out a throaty, uninhibited laugh.

I felt a smile bubble up irrepressibly, like a beach ball popping out of the water. "I'm Elizabeth," I said. "Nice meeting you."

It didn't take long for Arlene and me to discover that we were both in love with John Saxon, the newest teen movie idol, and from then on we shared everything from clothes to classes. Before I met Arlene, I had shied away from making friends, afraid they would expect to spend time at my house, afraid they might see the screaming matches between my parents.

"There's Karen," Arlene chirped. She'd told me that Karen Christensen lived up the street from her, and how they'd become good friends. She seemed amazed that I didn't know who Karen was. Everybody knew Karen. "Come on, I want you to meet her." Arlene took hold of my hand as if I were a baton in a relay race, and headed across the quad at a half-run.

As we approached a circle of girls, Karen stood out from all the rest. She had a special shimmer about her. The sun bounced off her silky blond hair, which hung to her shoulders in a perfect "tootsie" roll, the coveted hairstyle of the time. She could have been one of those Breck girls in the shampoo ads.

"Hi, Karen. Meet Elizabeth Reilly," Arlene said, shoving me in front of her.

"Liz," I said, feeling shy. "Just Liz."

"Nice to meet you, Liz," Karen said with a smile that displayed chalk-white teeth, perfectly straight like a row of Chiclets. I noticed how clean and fresh she looked in her full skirt and scooped-necked white blouse with puffed sleeves. I was immediately envious to see that she possessed the most important physical attribute of the day, the badge of womanhood—big boobs! Those firm missile cones, encased even in sleep I later learned, by crisp white cotton bras with lots of circular stitching. I was still wearing my "training" bra, a little white number with pink ballerinas embroidered onto the cups. I wasn't sure what it was supposed to train my boobs to do, but I hoped they'd turn out like Karen's.

"Where did Jimmy take you on Sunday?" Arlene asked. Her favorite subject at school was boys.

"We went to Santa Cruz and boy, did my girls get sunburned." Karen hooked her finger into the elastic neckline of her blouse and pulled it down to show us a glimpse of red breast. I had a sudden urge to reach out and touch her skin to see if it was as soft as it looked.

"Hey, good-lookin'. How's it goin'?" I turned to see Casey Arnold, the varsity quarterback, coming toward us, his sleepy eyes locked onto Karen. He ran an awkward hand over his brushcut. A flush rose on my face, as a pang seized my heart.

"Hi Casey," Karen replied casually, as if he were just any passerby instead of the most popular boy in school, not to mention one of the richest. His family owned the only bakery in town.

She moistened her lips with her tongue like a fashion model getting ready for a photo shoot. "Anyway, I hope I don't peel." She shifted her stack of books from one hip to the other.

"Try some Noxzema," I said. "It takes the sting out."

"Thanks," Karen said. Then she smiled at me. If she had given that smile to Casey when he walked by, it would have signaled that she liked him, maybe even loved him. But she gave it to me. I felt that smile go down through me like warm honey.

"Are you coming over after school today?" Arlene asked hopefully.

"I don't know, I've got a U.S. History test to study for," Karen replied. "Remember, we'll be having a pop quiz on Wednesday, so you better have your ducks in a row," Karen mimicked in a nasal tone, shaking her finger. She sounded just like Miss Whittington, the old maid history teacher everybody hated for being so stingy with good grades. A "C" from Miss Whittington was like an "A" from any other teacher, but that didn't help your transcript if you wanted to get into a good college.

"We better get going." Arlene checked her watch. Leave? I didn't want to leave. I wanted to stay there, close to Karen and have her beam her radiance down on me.

"Nice to meet you, Liz," Karen said, giving me another flashbulb smile.

I left feeling flattered and a little bit in love.

It would be years before I realized that I had been in the presence of what is known as charm; that natural ease and responsiveness to other people, the ability to make others feel like their best selves. Trying to define it is like trying to scoop fog into a cup. Charm is what made Karen so darned irresistible.

# CHAPTER NINE

## March 21, 2000

Arlene lived alone with her two stray cats, Fibber and Molly, in a rented two bedroom Victorian. The house was old with a garage that flooded every winter, but it was all she could afford on the paltry alimony payments she received. She'd been there ever since she and Fred had divorced six years earlier.

I pulled into the driveway and shut off the engine. My stomach felt queasy. I never knew grief could feel like the flu.

The pavement was wet, and a mist hung in the air as I stepped down from the van. I closed my eyes and willed my stomach to settle down.

As I started up the path, I could see the newly planted pots hanging from the beam over the front porch. She'd started already. In another month or so, this yard would be a kaleidoscope of color. Golden daffodils with long trumpets, purple crocuses and fragrant white narcissus would soon be blooming in the window boxes under the two big front windows. Next would come a variety of bedding plants, sown tightly together for massed beauty along the stone path to the porch and in pots of all sizes on the back patio. Later, along the fences in the backyard, the taller perennials would come alive again: bearded iris with its swordlike foliage, dramatic stocks of delphinium in true blue and purple, and foxglove, the blossoms of which would smother each 4-to 6-foot stem. Each spring, the bouquet of sweet floral fragrances mixed with the musty smell of damp earth and rotting wood made me inhale deeply, with complete disregard for my allergies.

So many times, I had come to this house and others like it, where I would hear my friends laughing and shouting over each other through the walls. Tonight, it was so quiet I could hear the wind rustling the leaves.

As I made my way up the front steps, I saw them through the window sitting at the dining room table; JoAnn with a glass of wine in front of her, and Rose with her bottle of water. They were studying something on the table.

I knocked at the door and waited like a stranger. Taking a deep breath, I closed my eyes and exhaled slowly. It felt like some kind of protective seal had been broken. How could Karen be dead? When someone died, Aunt Vi would announce, "They come in three's." I dismissed the thought as foolish.

Arlene opened the front door. The pounds added by menopause, coupled with recent loss of sleep, left little resemblance to the sultry temptress who once drew men to her like fruit flies to an overripe peach.

"Hi Liz. Come on in."

As I stepped inside our eyes met; hers were bloodshot. We opened our arms to each other and hugged hard.

"Everyone's here but Gidge," Arlene said, when we'd parted. She wiped her nose on the dishtowel she had in her hand. "She had to take the dog to her sister's place first."

"Don't tell me she hasn't put the poor thing to sleep yet? I thought the vet told her to put him out of his misery." After four failed marriages, Gidge had turned her attention toward her pets. Frequent visits to the veterinary hospital culminated in a part-time job which, when coupled with a small inheritance from her grandmother, provided her with a comfortable living.

"He did, but you know Gidge. She won't give up."

"Let's just hope when Buster goes she doesn't have him stuffed like Oscar," I said, wiping my feet on the worn rug.

"Yeah, it's one thing to have a cat sitting on top of your TV, but a Cocker Spaniel?" I shook my head. Gidge's love affair with taxidermy was for me, the oddest of her whims.

"We're in here," Arlene said, leading the way.

The living room was cheerfully messy with newspapers strewn on the floor, plus an array of hardcover books perched on tabletops. Arlene was an avid reader who didn't own a television.

"Do you want some wine or a real drink?" she asked over her shoulder.

"If you have some vodka, I'll have a vodka tonic," I answered. "And go easy on the tonic."

As I slipped out of my coat, I thought back to when we were teenagers, and we used to speculate on which one of us would go first, never believing that any of us would actually die. Like insects caught in the glow of amber, we were perfect and would never change.

When I stepped into the dining room, I was pleased to see that the photo albums were out. Over the years, Arlene had become the unofficial historian of the group. Eight albums lay on the table, each with a label entitled "The Girls" and a volume number.

JoAnn looked up. Her small lined face was framed by close-cropped hair, every color between black and white. There was still something girlish about her slight, angular body.

"Hey," she said with a sad smile. There was no need to exchange pleasantries.

Rose turned toward me, and I could see that her eyes were puffy from crying. I walked up behind her and put both my hands on her shoulders. She placed her hands over mine.

"Ah, the wedding photos," I said, looking over Rose's shoulder at an open album. I smiled as my eyes fell on one particular faded snapshot taken when Karen married Charles

Wentworth, husband #2, a roguishly handsome and wealthy contractor, who had dated all the other beauties in the area before proposing to Karen.

There we were in those god-awful lavender sleeveless bridesmaid dresses with the unflattering empire waistlines and all those ruffles around the scooped neck and down the back. Karen stood in the middle of the group in her cream-colored wedding suit, hair piled high in lacquered barrel curls called "love locks." She was strangling a bouquet of white roses in white-gloved hands, her face lit with joy. Arlene, her matron of honor, was on her right in a pink version of the same god-awful bridesmaid dress. The ill-positioned darts made her breasts look like footballs. Her matching head-piece was slightly askew and her right bra strap had fallen onto her shoulder. I was on Karen's left, my right hand above her head, giving the obligatory V sign. How creative. The perpetually pregnant Rose was next to me, eight months along and radiant. The dresses were short to begin with and due to the size of Rose's belly, you could see the tops of her nylons and a hint of the white rubber garters attached to them. Next to Arlene was Jo, and next to her was Gidge, bla-tantly flipping the bird and grinning insanely at the camera like the village idiot.

"I thought I destroyed all the copies of that picture," Rose said, her eyebrows furrowed. "Look, you can see my garters."

"Hey, it was the sixties," I said, giving her shoulder a playful shake. "Mini-skirts were in."

"You didn't look any worse than the rest of us," Jo said. She studied the picture as she chewed on her fingernail.

Arlene appeared with my vodka tonic.

"Sit down, Liz." She pulled out a chair for herself and sat down hard with a sigh. "I was going to wait for Gidge so I'd only have to tell this story once, but since she's going to be late..." She began worrying a loose thread at the corner of the place mat in front of her. "I was able to get a message to Squeak through her agency, and she called me this afternoon. I told her what I knew about her mother. She took it real bad." Rosie let out a soft groan. "She's on location in Bermuda. I told her that we would take care of everything, and that she could meet us at Tahoe. She'll be there Friday." Arlene breathed deeply to steady her voice. "I spoke to Officer Duarte of the Reno Police Department. Wait a minute, let me get my notes." Slowly, she lifted her body up, her hands pushing against the table.

We sat there, each in our own thoughts, Jo with her eyes averted, and Rosie taking an awkward sip from her water bottle. It was not a time for words.

Arlene returned with a steno pad, her cigarettes and lighter. She dropped to her chair, lit a cigarette and blew smoke up into the light overhead. As she flipped the page, I could see that she had taken her notes in shorthand, a skill she had mastered in high school and still used today, even for her grocery list.

Adjusting her glasses, she began. "Karen was pronounced dead on arrival at the Mt. Rose Memorial Hospital at 11:52

last night." Rose's chin began to quiver. I reached for her hand.

"Death was caused by a severed vertebra. The vehicle involved in the accident was a black 1998 Harley Davidson motorcycle registered to Gregory Ronelli of Incline Village, Nevada." Arlene kept her place with her finger. "No evidence of any other vehicle being involved. Mr. Ronelli was treated for minor injuries and released. Cause of the accident is under investigation. Strong possibility the motorcycle hit a patch of black ice, causing the driver to lose control." Arlene dropped the notepad on the table. "That's it." She settled back in her chair, took a deep drag on her cigarette and watched us through the smoke, waiting for our reaction.

I felt a gentle bite of suspicion. "Greg losing control?" I said. "That's hard to believe. He's always so cautious. I remember Karen telling me he had all these rules about where and when he would ride. It used to drive her crazy."

Rose was openly crying now. She reached into her purse and fished out a wad of tissue. "I told Karen to stay off of that damn motorcycle," she said. "Everybody knows how dangerous they are. I won't let my boys go near one." She blew her nose with a loud honk.

"I asked Karen what the attraction was once," Arlene said, staring down into her wineglass. "I'll never forget what she said. 'Time doesn't exist on a motorcycle.' She had this kind of secret smile on her face when she said it."

I could almost hear Karen's voice.

"What were they doing on Mt. Rose that late at night anyway?" Rosie said.

"What was she doing with Greg, is what I'd like to know?" Arlene said, sounding like a harpy sister from hell. Rosie gave her a searching look. "Last I heard that was all over."

"I think he made her feel young," I said.

Arlene harrumphed.

I turned to Jo. The vertical line between her brows had deepened, and her dark eyes glittered as she leafed through the photo album, turning the pages slowly

"Well, we know what we have to do," I said. "I borrowed Sam's van. Tomorrow morning, we'll get up early and drive to Tahoe. Karen would want us to keep it together, and get on with it."

A thump at the front door made me jump.

"Son of a bitch!" Gidge had arrived.

I found myself welcoming her casual profanity, and looking forward to her reliable wackiness.

After more rustling sounds, the door flew open, hitting the wall behind it hard. Gidge entered the room like a physical force, displacing the air. Her arms were loaded with two brown paper bags overflowing with groceries.

"Would somebody take this shit so I can go get the rest of my stuff?" she called, out of breath. Arlene went to her aid. "Don't anybody talk 'til I get back," she yelled over her shoulder.

The screen door slammed behind her. She was gone just as quickly as she had come in, but a crackling energy lingered in the air where she had been; just like when we first met at the Bijou Theater.

—◦◦◦—

Growing up in a house full of verbal violence, I walked around on eggshells, never knowing when the tension between my parents would give way to an eruption. I grew guarded and withdrawn, spending most of my time alone in my room, playing with my storybook dolls and making up stories about them. I would pretend I was one of them, an orphan, and that some nice lady had come to adopt me. She would take me to live someplace where the birds outnumbered the people. We'd have a dog, a cocker spaniel, and maybe a cat. We'd do fun things, whether we had the money or not, and leave the housework for last. She wouldn't have a husband; there'd be just the two of us.

Often, I would sit on the edge of my bed, staring at the repeated pattern of tiny rosebuds on my papered walls and dream of the day I would leave. But until then, there was the fighting.

"I hate asking you for money," my mother yelled. "You make me feel like a beggar." A cupboard door slammed and although I was on the other side of the house, it made me jump.

"I gave you $20.00 last week. What happened to that?" my father shot back.

"How dare you ask for an accounting of every dime I spend," she said. I imagined her pretty face all pinched and fierce looking. "I won't have it!"

My father didn't respond right away, which probably meant he was counting to ten to keep from exploding. "You're crazy. That's what you are." The whole house shook with the vibration of his heavy work boots as he crossed the kitchen floor. I squeezed my eyes shut tight in anticipation. A door banged shut.

"Don't you walk out on me John Reilly," my mother screamed. Her words were followed by the sound of crockery breaking against what sounded like the back door.

Late that night, my mother's heartbroken sobs kept me awake.

Unable to drown out their voices, I escaped to the movies. In the theater slumped down in the dark, feasting on Juicyfruits and Milk Duds, I could retreat. My troubles rose above me and dissolved into the smoke caught in the light from the projector.

By the time I was a sophomore in high school, I was spending so much time at the movies that I begged my parents to let me get a job at the theater. After much pleading and with my mother's help, my father agreed so long as I would put half of my earnings away for college. Little did he know I had no plans to go to college.

I met Gidge Peterson on my first day at work.

"I hear you're a friend of Karen Christensen's," she said, snapping the Doublemint gum that had a permanent place in her mouth. I felt myself puff up. I had just met Karen a few weeks earlier and already my status had been upgraded.

"Me too," she added, the corners of her small mouth turning up.

Six months older and lifetimes ahead of me in experience, Gidge was a small bulldog of a person; solid, stocky and determined, with short hair dyed the color of my mother's glazed yams that was combed into a perfect duck's ass at the back, which made her look impressively cool.

"Let's get you a uniform," Gidge said. She walked toward the door marked "Employees Only." I'd never seen a girl walk that purposely before, as if she didn't think twice about making a move before making it. I, on the other hand, was clumsy—tall for my age, with a body like a stick bug. Despite years of ballet lessons, I was constantly banging my knee or stubbing my toe.

As Gidge helped me fasten the top brass button on my freshly pressed navy-blue jacket, she said, "Don't let them give you any shit, kid." She nodded toward the manager's office, her chocolate chip-colored eyes burning into me. I was afraid to ask who she meant.

"Watch this," she whispered that first Saturday afternoon as we stood together behind the candy counter. Her eyes sparkled with mischief. I looked on in disbelief as she explained to a little boy that he could have one box of Jujubes for ten cents or two for a quarter.

"Two please," he said, his wide smile revealing two missing front teeth. Gidge gave him the candy and quickly pocketed the extra nickel. Not that she needed the money. Her father owned a successful real estate company in town. It was the thrill of the scam. The next day, the boy's mother complained to Mr. Delvecchio, the manager, and if Gidge's father hadn't intervened, Miss Flim-Flam would have been fired.

Tired of minding my manners, it wasn't long before Gidge awakened my suppressed sense of fun.

"I'll have a hot dog with mustard, please," the heavy-set woman said, her head down as she rummaged through her purse for change.

"I'll get it," I said cheerfully, volunteering even though it was Gidge's job to serve the hot dogs that day. Turning my back to the customer, I picked up the metal hot dog tongs and retracted my arm up inside the long sleeve of my uniform, so that the tongs were where my hand should be. Giving Gidge a quick wink, I reached into the warmer, picked up the hotdog with the tongs, spun around, and presented it to the woman, my hand safely out of sight. The horrified look on her face was priceless. Gidge doubled over with laughter.

My father would have described Gidge as a "bad influence," but despite her tendency toward criminal activity, we became good friends. I had never met anyone like her; vulgar, rowdy and unafraid, the kind of girl you would want on your side if a fight broke out. Up until then, the focus of my childhood had been on my parents' painful groove of ongoing conflict. But thanks to Gidge, that was about to change.

# CHAPTER TEN

## *March 21, 2000*

I helped Arlene unpack the groceries Gidge had brought. Eggs, sausage, green onions, a bag of limes, a pound of Starbucks Coffee, crackers and a variety of cheeses in one bag. In the other, two fifths of Cuervo Gold Tequila, and Gidge's Mr. Coffee maker.

"I see you've got her trained," I said, holding up the coffee maker.

"She knows my cardiologist said I shouldn't have coffee, so she brings her own."

"What would he say if he saw you smoking?" I asked. Arlene frowned. "Sorry. I had to ask."

Arlene had worked so hard to quit smoking. When I visited her in the hospital after her second heart attack three years earlier, she begged me to smuggle in a pack of her beloved Benson & Hedges 100s. I was so mad that I grabbed her oxygen supply tube and threatened to pinch it shut.

I pulled out the cutting board and began slicing the cheese. "I've been meaning to ask you," I said. "How did the police get your phone number?"

Arlene brushed cracker crumbs from her hands over the sink. "The officer said they found one of those in case of emergency cards in Karen's wallet with my name and number on it." She pulled open the top cupboard door on the second try, and stood looking inside, as though she'd forgotten what she wanted. "I wonder why me?" Her sentence trailed off like a puff of smoke.

I knew why she'd asked. Arlene and Karen had had a blowup a few months earlier. Neither one would say what it was about, but it wasn't one of their typical quickly-over fights. Real damage had been done. They had barely spoken since.

Out of the corner of my eye, I could see Gidge had returned with her duffel bag under one arm, and because she never spent the night without it, her pillow under the other. She dropped her things on the floor.

"Oh God, not the albums," Gidge said. She grimaced, then reached over JoAnn's shoulder and slammed the cover shut. "I can't take any reminiscing tonight. Hey, Arlene, crack open that bottle of tequila, will ya?" she yelled, pulling up a chair. "Those fuckin' farmers. I don't know how my sister can stand living in Lodi. Everywhere you go there's nothing but two-lane roads and pickup trucks. All I wanted to do was drop the dog off quickly, and I get behind Fred Flintstone in his truck full of rocks. It's enough to drive you fuckin' nuts!"

Arlene and I returned with the bottle of tequila, some lime wedges, a saltshaker, and a plate of cheese and crackers.

Gidge leaned forward with both elbows on the table. Her cheeks were the same color red as her hair.

"Rose, you look like shit," she said. Rose dabbed at her eyes with a soggy tissue. Jo's hooded eyes were fixated on the cover of the album that Gidge had slammed shut.

"Hi, Liz. Your hair looks great. You're back to highlighting it again, huh?" I didn't answer.

"So, what's the plan, Arlene?" Gidge asked, as if we were arranging a fun getaway weekend. She picked up the tequila bottle and unscrewed the cap.

"You know, Gidge, I think you're way out of line here," Jo said. There's the look. The drill-bit eyes turned on Gidge.

"What?" Gidge asked, licking the back of her hand and shaking salt on it.

"First, you come in here telling us we can't look through the albums, and now you break out the tequila like it's some kind of frigging party or something. Don't you have any feelings at all?" Jo glared at Gidge.

"Oh, bullshit," Gidge responded, waving her hand in the air. "Karen would have been the first one to grab the tequila bottle if it were one of us that got killed instead of her." She licked the salt and took a swig from the bottle before clamping her teeth down on a wedge of lime. "Come on Jo, what are you gettin' all steamed about? Have a hit." Gidge pushed the bottle toward Jo.

I could see the heat come to Jo's face. I wouldn't have been surprised if steam started shooting out of her ears, like one of those Saturday morning cartoon characters.

"Do you understand what has happened?" Jo said slowly and deliberately. Gidge avoided her steady stare. "Show some respect for once in your life." The room went quiet. Rosie looked around for an emergency exit.

"Who the hell are you to tell me how to act?" Gidge snapped. "The woman who didn't even go to her own mother's funeral."

"Gidge," Arlene said, putting her hand on Gidge's arm. Gidge shook it off.

"She started it," Gidge said, sounding like a spoiled child.

I looked over to see Jo's shoulders drop in a sign of defeat. "I'm going to bed," she said. "It's been a long day, and I'm exhausted." She pushed back from the table, stood up and shuffled out of the room like an old woman.

"Who lit the fuse on her tampon?" Gidge asked, when Jo was safely out of earshot.

"Everyone's just upset," Rose replied, as she nervously folded a tissue into a tiny square.

"Rosie's right," Arlene agreed. She refilled her wineglass.

I turned toward Gidge. "So, how are Joey and his new bride?" Gidge's face softened at the mention of her son's name.

"Oh, they're doing great."

"Did they get settled in their new place?" Rosie asked, relieved to be talking about something else.

"Yeah, my dad gave them a set of living room furniture for a wedding gift." I couldn't get used to Gidge referring to her father as anything other than "the colonel." Over the years, her love for her father had worked its way to the surface like a splinter. In an unguarded moment she had confessed that she had forgiven him for being so peculiar and even found his once unacceptable eccentricities, such as insisting his three daughters learn how to march in military formation, somewhat endearing.

"I left two voicemail messages at your office last week, Liz. Why didn't you call me back?" Gidge asked, catching me mid-sip. I blotted my mouth with a napkin. I felt a hiccup of guilt for not having told my friends about my job loss in the beginning, but I couldn't stand the idea of them tsktsking over my misfortune. Now, it didn't matter.

"I was laid off," I admitted. I gave them the short version of the events of my last day, while Gidge drank and Arlene smoked.

Rosie sat wide-eyed, listening intently. "Wow," she said, when I'd finished.

"Corporate bastards," Gidge said under her breath. She licked her forefinger and began blotting up the salt granules on the table in front of her.

Lifting my glass, my gaze wandered over to Arlene. She was regarding me with a cocked head.

"Being laid off must have been devastating," she said. "I can't imagine."

Marrying young, Arlene never had an interest in having a job. She preferred the traditional partnership where the husband went off to work and the wife stayed home and ran the house. I, on the other hand, had always wanted to earn my own living, maybe work in a bank or at the telephone company like my Aunt Vi. Instead, I had ended up in the back seat of Ricky's Ford one night in early June of my senior year. In the light from the full moon, I remember counting the tiny dots in the vinyl header and noticing the smallest crack in the plastic dome light cover above me. Stretched out in the back seat, I worried about how I would explain the wrinkles in my pink satin prom dress to my mother. As it turned out, that was the least of my worries.

"So, what are your plans," Gidge asked.

"Sorry, what?"

"Jobwise, I mean."

It couldn't be avoided; I'd have to put something into words. I said the only honest thing I could think of. "I have no idea."

"You could always marry Sam," Rosie said expectantly. My stomach retracted with instinctual opposition. I knew if I disclosed the truth about Sam moving to New York, it could only lead to further interrogation, which I didn't have the courage to face. Instead, I trotted out my usual reply.

"Now, Rose, you know once was enough for me."

"Well, I'm sure everything will work out," Rosie said with no foundation whatsoever for her optimism. I looked at her and tried to smile.

"So, Arlene, did you find out any more from the police?" Gidge asked. As Arlene started to retell the story, Gidge downed another shot and sucked on a lime wedge.

Shutting out the sound of Arlene's voice, I reached across the table and flipped open the album. Before me was a faded black-and-white photo of the six of us jammed onto the front porch at the Petersons' cabin at Lake Tahoe on the last day of Gidge's sixteenth-birthday weekend—youth in full bloom. I could almost feel the weight of Karen's arm flung around my shoulders.

# CHAPTER ELEVEN

## *May 15, 1957*

The invitation to Gidge's sixteenth birthday celebration at her parents' vacation home at Lake Tahoe arrived in the mail the second week of May. I hugged the small canary-yellow envelope to my chest and closed my eyes. Three months ago, I thought excitedly, this would have been pure fantasy, me getting invited to a party with all the popular girls. I smiled to myself.

Heart singing, I rushed to my room and locked the invitation away in my diary for safekeeping. I would have to wait for just the right moment to ask permission. It came the following Friday night.

"But John, you promised we could go out tonight," my mother said in a disappointed voice. I could hear them clearly as I sat in front of the mirror on my flounced dressing table, brushing my hair the one hundred required strokes to make it as shiny as Karen's.

"That was before I knew I would have to work overtime two nights in a row, Catherine," my father explained, using a condescending tone. Twenty-three, Twenty-four, Twenty...

I could never understand why a fun-loving woman like my mother would marry an old fuddy-duddy like my father. It was as though she had been dared to choose someone as unlike her as possible. His plodding nature exasperated her and he mistrusted her thirst for excitement. Although she never said so, I guessed the only reason she stayed was because of me. Thirty, Thirty-one...

"Don't you talk down to me, John Reilly," my mother warned.

"I'm not talking down to you. I'm just telling you that I'm too tired to go out." I could tell he was trying to control his quick Irish temper.

"That was your excuse last week," she yelled. Thirty-eight, Thirty-nine...

"Who do you think earns the money that seems to slip through your fingers?" he yelled louder. Here it comes. I knew where this was going—there would be lots more yelling, and if it got really bad, some dishes would get broken.

I wished I had the courage to go out there and tell them to stop. If Gidge were there, that's what she would do. But I was too much of a wimp.

Instead, I leaned over and turned my radio up full blast to drown them out. A big-band version of Deep Purple blared out over the sound of their voices. I was now brushing my hair hard enough to bring tears to my eyes. Why didn't she leave him? Move back to San Francisco with Aunt Vi. They were always gabbing about the "good ole days," what fun they had learning the Charleston and drinking "bathtub gin." It was her own fault. She could be floating across the dance floor in the arms of some handsome man instead of spending her free time at the kitchen table, entering radio contests, mailing in postcards, writing advertising jingle lyrics that sang the praises of laundry soap and cat food, searching for some activity to hide in.

When my mother came to say goodnight, I saw the twinge of guilt in her red-rimmed eyes, the same sort I always sensed in her when she knew I had heard them fighting.

"Please, please Mother," I whined. She sat on the edge of my bed, the open invitation in one hand and a Camel cigarette in the other. Smoke curled around her high cheekbones and up over her carefully combed midnight-brown hair.

"Lake Tahoe...it's so far away," she said, picking a piece of tobacco off her full bottom lip. Her nails were freshly polished, in anticipation of a night out. "You'll have to ask your father." I felt my hopes plummet.

"Oh, Mother, couldn't you ask him for me? I mean when he's in a better mood?" My mother could talk a policeman out of a speeding ticket and coerce old Mr. Mattson, our milkman, out of his last pint of whipping cream even though it had been tagged for our neighbors next door. And when my father was in one of his rare good moods, usually after a couple of beers, she could even charm him.

She reached down and brushed my bangs off my forehead. Her eyes were soft and warm.

"Karen's got her driver's license, and her mother said she can take the car. Oh, please, Mama. I'll never ask for another thing." I pulled on her sleeve.

A few days later, when things had calmed down, she asked, and as I expected, he said no. I wanted to die. First, I wanted to kill him, and then I wanted to die. I moped around the house for a week, wallowing in self-pity. Each time I'd see Gidge at work and she'd ask if I was coming, I'd make up some excuse for not having asked permission yet.

As the party date loomed closer, seeds of rebellion began to grow inside of me. What would happen if I went anyway? Just sneaked off, jumped in Karen's car and left? Would my father drive up to Lake Tahoe, seize me by the wrists, and yank me back to Parkerville where I belonged? Would I be put on restriction for life? I called Aunt Vi for advice.

"Honey, you know your father only wants what's best for you," she said in a voice made husky by too many Chesterfields. "Even though he can be a bit unreasonable." I pictured my mother's only sister Violet when she came to spend the night, sitting at our kitchen table, her hair in perfect pincurls with bobby pins poking out at all angles, making her look like a Martian from outer space, face full of cold cream, lecturing my mother on how to better handle my father's "unreasonableness," while my mother wept into her coffee cup.

"But all my friends are going, Aunt Vi," I argued.

I heard a long sigh.

"God knows, when I was your age, I was already driving my father's Model T Ford up and down the hills of San Francisco." She let out a laugh. I waited. "Only you can make this decision, kiddo. I'm not going to tell you to defy your father." I let out a groan.

Aunt Vi had a way with my father. On her weekend visits, the two of them would watch the Friday Night Fights, each sipping Hamm's beer from the can and shouting encouragement at the TV screen. I wanted her to take my side, maybe even call up my father and plead my case. No such luck.

"Mother, I've made a decision." We were doing the dishes after dinner as usual, she washing and me drying. My father was outside in his workshop, where he spent most of his free time. A machinist by trade, he was a big man who loved small things: nuts, washers, screws, anything useful that fit easily in the palm of his huge hand. His pockets jangled as he strode about our cramped two-bedroom house on Sycamore Street.

"About what, honey?" she asked, not looking up. I'd rehearsed my speech over and over, in front of the mirror.

"I'm going to Gidge's party." I finished drying a glass and placed it on the shelf before turning to look into my mother's shocked face. Her rubber-gloved hands were poised in mid-air, soapsuds dripping into the dishpan.

"What?" she asked, as if she had misunderstood.

"I think I've been responsible. I've never given either you or Daddy a thing to worry about." Compared to Gidge's pranks and Arlene's habit of dating only boys who had a great big T for Trouble emblazoned on their foreheads, I was an angel. The week before, the military police had shown up at Arlene's house, asking questions about her relationship with a sailor who was accused of robbing a gas station. My parents didn't know how lucky they were.

I held my mother's gaze with mine. "I've given this a lot of thought and I'm going, with or without Daddy's permission." My back was straight in determination.

"But—"

"The only reason I'm telling you is so you won't be worried when I go," I added, sounding very grown up. Slowly, my mother resumed washing the dishes, as she stared out the kitchen window at the workshop where my father was.

On Saturday morning, I sat on the edge of my bed, my suitcase packed and ready on the floor beside me. I heard the back screen door slam and my father's heavy footsteps coming closer. Fear gripped my stomach as his broad shoulders filled up my doorway—an image of pure authority. I didn't move. He'd never hit me before, but there was always a first time.

"You'll need this," he said, taking two giant steps forward, his muscular arm outstretched, his face expressionless. I could see the neatly folded bills in his fist. I started to reach for the money and then stopped, afraid he would snatch it away from me at the last minute. He sensed my hesitancy. "Here," he said, shoving the bills into my hand. The muscles in his square jaw twitched. I felt a yearning toward him, a momentary impulse to say thank you. But before I could speak, he turned and left.

I sat transfixed, staring down at the money. I didn't move. What could have caused such a radical change in my father's behavior? I carefully tucked the folded bills into my pink plastic coin purse and snapped it shut with a loud click. After a few minutes, a strange sense of calm crept over me. I had crossed a line. I was no longer the person I thought I was.

# CHAPTER TWELVE

## *March 22, 2000*

Despite three strong vodka tonics, I hadn't slept much. Sleep would be a forgotten luxury now that would come in fitful bursts, if it came at all. I felt cheated as I lay staring at the cracked ceiling in Arlene's bedroom, listening to her soft purring. Karen was gone so quickly, with no chance to say good-bye. It was like a giant eraser had come down from heaven and just rubbed her out of our picture.

I found Gidge in Arlene's kitchen, which was a portrait of the 1940s with its ceramic tile counters and wooden cabinets that had been painted so many times, the doors no longer shut. Both the gas stove and refrigerator looked like they could have been prizes on the "Queen for a Day" radio program. The only sign of the present was a placard that hung over the stove with the message; "Martha Stewart doesn't live here!"

"Good Morning, Sunshine," I said, trying to sound cheerful. "How are you feeling today?"

"I didn't get much sleep with Jo trying to get on me all night," Gidge replied, without turning around. Her short, red hair looked like she'd combed it with a Mixmaster. "I'd forgotten how she likes to cuddle, the pervert."

I laughed. Like feuding siblings, none of us could stay mad at each other for long. No one apologizes. It just goes away.

"If I made some breakfast, do you think those bitches would eat it?" Gidge asked, plugging in her Mr. Coffee machine.

"Sure. You know us, always hungry," I replied, trying to remember the last time I ate. I sat down at the little round table that was crammed into the only open corner. "You want some help?"

"No, thanks, I've got this down pat." She had gathered all of the ingredients for one of her famous omelets. I sat quietly, watching her. Gidge didn't cook often, but when she did, the results were worth the wait. I could always rely on one of her omelets settling my liquor-soaked tummy.

"You know, even though I never liked the guy, I always thought that Karen would end up marrying Greg some day," Gidge said. I knew Gidge had no use for Greg. From the beginning, she was convinced that he was only interested in Karen for her money.

"And I'll bet he would have married her in a heartbeat, too." Although I wasn't completely sure about Greg's motives, I knew with most of the men in her life, Karen either dumbed down or hid pieces of herself, pretending to be someone she wasn't to make the necessary connection. But with Greg, she seemed to be on equal footing, able to communicate one human being to another.

"But you know Karen; he was too young, he had no money, had no future, et cetera," I said.

I pushed open the plaid café curtains to look outside. A crack had opened in the gray clouds, and a single ray of sunlight streamed through creating a spotlight on the wet lawn, and for a moment, I thought it might be Karen, smiling down on us.

"Her second husband had more money than God, and what good did that do?" Gidge said.

I couldn't argue. It wasn't as though Karen was a cold-blooded gold-digger. Charles Wentworth's hard cash just seemed to sidle up and whisper in her ear, promising to make her happy; or failing that, to cover her in fur. She chose not to resist. Marital bliss for me, on the other hand, had little to do with anything money could buy. My notion of the good life, which I'd picked up from my early years of incessant movie-going, was simple. Like any proper, pure-hearted young lady of the fifties, I believed that what truly mattered was love, true and unconditional love. Needless to say, now that I was older and wiser with an ex-husband who could afford to cover only a sliver of what it had cost to raise our two children, I could better understand Karen's decision to marry a man with deep pockets.

"I don't think Karen liked men very much," I said, surprised that I had spoken the words out loud.

"I think she hated them, if you ask me," Gidge said. I was even more surprised by her response.

"Why do you say that?" I asked, wondering if she knew something.

"Her sabotage of every relationship she ever had, for one thing."

The coffeepot made a loud gurgling sound and spouted a large final puff of steam, signifying its work was done.

"You want a cup?" Gidge asked, turning towards me.

"Black, thanks."

My mind coasted back, resurrecting a night in the late seventies when Karen was in the process of dissolving her second marriage, this time from Charles. Ricky had left me two years earlier. Divorce had forged a deeper friendship between us.

After seeing the movie, An Unmarried Woman, we were sitting in my kitchen discussing how we could identify with Jill Clayburgh's character, and what an asshole her husband was for cheating on her.

"I remember the first moment I knew I hated men," Karen said over her teacup.

I must have looked like I'd just been tossed a hand-grenade. What did she mean? Karen was forever whipping herself into a tortured froth over some man. Now, she claimed to hate them?

"Sarah always went out on Friday nights," Karen said. "If she didn't have a date, she'd go alone or with some girlfriend from the factory." I was used to hearing Karen refer to her mother by her first name. It was her way of disconnecting from their relationship.

Karen set down her cup. "When I was around ten, she started letting me stay home alone instead of going next door to stay with old Mrs. Standeven. God, that woman smelled funny. Like spoiled fruit. And she used to spit on you when she talked. Yuck!"

I let out a laugh, torn between both wanting and not wanting to hear the rest of this story.

"Anyway," Karen went on, "I used to sleep with all my stuffed animals on the bed. My dad sent one every year for my birthday." This was the first time I'd heard her mention her father since we were teenagers.

Karen's pale brows knitted together thoughtfully. She wrapped her arms around her torso, hands on opposite elbows, as if to cover herself up. "The worst time was late one night. I was asleep but voices, Sarah's and a man's, woke me. In that little two-bedroom house on Beach Street, I could hear them clearly even though they were whispering. She was telling the man to be quiet 'cause she had a daughter asleep in the next room, and that he shouldn't have followed her home."

I felt my stomach begin to tense.

"First, I tried to cover my ears with my pillow," Karen said. "When that didn't work, I pulled all my animals up around my head and squeezed them hard against my ears. But I could still hear them. She was giggling and saying things like 'stop' and 'don't' in that little-girl voice she used when her dates came to pick her up. Her 'men friends' as she liked to call them, smelling of cigarettes and that horrible Sen-Sen breath freshener. Pulling me onto their laps, chucking me under my chin." A look of disgust crossed Karen's face. "Liars, they were all liars, being nice to me just to get next to my mother. Lying just like my father did sitting on my bed that morning before he left, refusing to take me with him, pretending to be sorry."

I wanted to reach over and gently take hold of Karen, wrap my arms around her shoulders until I felt her weight give in to me. But I was afraid to move.

"I started praying for them to stop. Dear God, please let that man go home. Please God, I promise I'll be good. What a joke." Karen shook her head. "For a minute, I thought it might have worked because I didn't hear them anymore. I lay very still, thinking maybe there really was something to this praying stuff." Karen let out a puff of air. "But I was wrong. In a few seconds, their voices got louder. 'Come on,' I heard him say in a demanding voice. There were scuffling noises. 'Please don't,' she said. Her voice sounded funny, like she was afraid. More scuffling and then something hit the wall, and I heard her cry out in pain. I jumped out of bed and ran out there, so scared I was shaking. It was dark, but I could see that he had her pinned against the wall and was grabbing at her, pulling at the buttons on her blouse. 'Waddaya mean, no' he snarled, his face close to hers. 'Leave her alone!' I yelled, grabbing him around the leg with both arms and falling to the floor. He was panting, and Sarah was crying. I held tight onto his leg and started hitting him on the back of the thigh as hard as I could with my fist."

As I sat listening to Karen, I felt like I was eavesdropping on her private thoughts, like she didn't mean to be saying these things out loud.

"After what seemed like forever, he let go of her and pulled away from me. 'The hell with it,' he said, waving his arm like he was disgusted. He turned and stumbled out the front door, muttering under his breath, words I'd never heard before." Karen swallowed hard. "Sarah stayed flat against the wall, and I stayed curled up on the floor in front of her, afraid to even blink. What if he changed his mind and came back? A car door slammed, and I jumped. Then I heard the sound of a car engine."

Karen collapsed back in her chair. "When he was gone, Sarah bent over me, and asked if I was all right. I remember looking up to see her face streaked with mascara, her lipstick smeared onto her cheek in a red gash." A long pause. "As if any child would be all right after something like that."

Karen reached up and quickly brushed a tear from under her eye.

The face across the table from me was that of a child's. Such innocence. Such pain. I could hardly look at her. Suddenly, I felt guilty for all the times I'd complained about my feuding parents. Their shortcomings seemed so inconsequential now.

After a moment, Karen shrugged her shoulders.

"So, that's the day I began to hate men. And that's the truth!" She stuck her tongue out and made a raspberry sound like Lily Tomlin did when she played the role of Edith Ann, the five-year-old little girl with the big bow in her hair who sat in a giant rocking chair.

We both let out a nervous laugh.

Right then, I realized how wrong I was to have envied Karen all those years. What I mistook for confidence was merely a front, her sense of humor a defense mechanism to hide the damage. I believed she was the saddest woman I had ever known.

# CHAPTER THIRTEEN

*March 22, 2000*

B y the time we finished breakfast and got organized, it was midmorning. After Rosie went for her run, she said she felt better and wasn't going to cry anymore. Arlene agreed not to smoke in the car, and Gidge promised not to drink in the car. For a short time, we seemed back to normal; as normal as we could be without Karen.

It turned out to be a beautiful morning, sunny and crisp, the first such morning in weeks.

"Let's get the show on the road," Jo called over her shoulder as she pulled her designer roller bag down the front path, looking like an important executive with her cell phone securely hitched on her belt. That was something I wasn't going to miss, being tied to the phone twenty-four, seven.

As we packed the van, I caught a glimpse of the bumper sticker on Gidge's car; "Horn Broken…Watch for Finger." Karen had seen it in a joke shop and bought it for her.

Rosie bounded down the steps with an athletic stride carrying the stack of photo albums in her arms and a gigantic backpack on her back, looking like a human camel. She walked briskly to the car, suddenly stopping and whirling around, knocking Gidge in the face with her hump.

"Watch it!" Gidge exclaimed, giving the backpack and Rosie a not-so-gentle push.

"Sorry," Rosie muttered. "I forgot my water."

After our initial get-together at the Peterson's vacation house, regular visits to Lake Tahoe became a ritual for "the girls." Throughout high school and young adulthood, we practiced a number of skills at the lake: water skiing, cussing, making and drinking Margaritas, imitating Diana Ross and the Supremes. As grown women, wives, and mothers, our trips afforded us breaks from our jobs and our family responsibilities, time to re-energize and enjoy one another's company.

As usual, I drove, and Arlene, with a tendency to get carsick, rode shotgun. A life-long habit, the rest of the passengers drew toothpicks for seats in the car. Gidge got the shortest pick and was relegated to the back, while JoAnn and Rosie sat behind Arlene and me. I had been known to make this trip non-stop in three-and-a-half hours. After so many years of commuting, I'd learned bad driving habits like speeding, tailgating and cutting people off. But today, I was in no hurry.

Gidge hunkered down in the seat, jammed her pillow between her head and the window, and shut her eyes. It felt so strange heading for Tahoe shot through with sadness rather than excited with anticipation. About this time, Gidge would have been passing the tequila bottle around, and I would be freaking out, checking the rear view for flashing blue lights. We would all be talking over each other, interrupting and yet hearing every word.

Rosie was the first to speak. "It was nice of Sam to let us use his van."

I tightened my hands around the steering wheel. I'd made up my mind not to think about Sam, and I was annoyed that Rosie kept bringing him up. I took a deep breath and in my calmest voice, I said, "Yes, it was."

We'd been on the road for about fifteen minutes when Gidge said; "You know I read in the paper the other day that almost four million women are abused by their husbands every year." I looked in the rearview mirror. Her eyes were still closed.

Gidge's mind was a mystery to me. I never knew what she was going to say. I don't think she knew either. Whatever popped into her brain, popped out of her mouth. It could be unnerving. Today, I welcomed the intrusion.

"Did they say anything about how many men get abused by their wives?" Rose asked. I knew where she was going with her comment.

"No," Gidge said, perking up in her seat as if this were a topic of interest.

"What about the time you hit Harry over the head with your vanity chair, and you thought you'd killed him?" I called back to Gidge.

Arlene snorted. "She called me and asked what she should do."

"Shit! The son of a bitch went down like a stone. He was out cold!"

"I remember you asked me what I thought would happen if you didn't call the ambulance," Arlene said.

"Well, I was so mad at the fucker, I really wanted him to die." Harry and Gidge had brought out the worst in each other.

Gidge snuggled back down into her makeshift bed. Just when I thought she must have gone back to sleep, she said, "You know I think Harry was the only husband I truly loved."

The group exploded in protest, along with much head shaking and eye rolling.

"It's true!" Gidge said, defensively. "Remember the time when he was still married to his first wife and he came up to Tahoe for my birthday?"

"Yes, Gidge," Arlene said in a patronizing tone. She looked over at me and pantomimed sticking her finger down her throat. We'd heard this story many times before.

"He told his wife he was going fishing with the guys, so on the way home he had to stop at three different supermarkets 'til he found a whole fish? God, those were the days," she said, dreamily.

"Frankly, I don't understand what a woman sees in a man she knows is a liar and a sneak," Rosie said.

"I was in love," Gidge squawked defensively.

Rosie lip-farted.

"Yeah, but then you married him, and it was all over," JoAnn said. Jo had a way of stating the truth that made it hard to deny.

"I always loved my husbands more before I married them," Gidge explained.

Gidge held the record for ex-husbands with four, Karen had three, and Jo, Arlene and I each had one. Rosie was the only one of us who was still married to her first husband, which was probably why she could be so pious. She didn't know what it was like to be left.

As the miles ticked away, silence returned, as if each of us knew that no amount of casual banter could alter the reason we were on this journey. Listening to the hum of the engine, I forced myself to observe the passing countryside, and willed the muscles in my back to loosen and relax into the upholstery. The scenery was bleak, flat featureless grassland, interrupted by an occasional dirt road; nothing like I remembered seeing on that first sun-drenched morning when Karen, Arlene, and I had piled into Karen's mother's old Buick Roadmaster and headed to Gidge's sixteenth birthday party.

Despite having her license for only a month, Karen was the best driver I'd ever seen, better even than my father who prided himself on his parallel parking skills. She could back down a street in a straight line, execute a perfect three-point turn, and she possessed an uncanny sense of depth perception that allowed her to know the exact moment when she could pass safely.

As I sat in the back seat, watching the velvety foothills pass by the car window, I couldn't stop thinking about my father and his surprising reaction to my blatant defiance. All my life, I had been dominated by him. He decided my every move. And I obeyed faithfully, not wearing make-up, staying away from boys, and getting good grades in the hope that if I did what he said, my parents would stop fighting. It didn't work.

But this, his backing down. He'd never done this before. What could my mother have possibly said to cause him to act this way?

I rolled down the window. The warm summer air that blew in my face brought with it a special aura of change and opportunity, a newfound sense of freedom.

"Casey Arnold asked me to his senior prom," Karen announced, interrupting my pleasant thoughts. I could hear the delight in her voice.

"How fabulous," I exclaimed, leaning forward in my seat. I wasn't surprised. Karen's crush on Casey had developed quickly after he started showing interest in Diane Kirschner, the head cheerleader. Now, whenever she saw him, instead of playing it cool, she flirted shamelessly.

"Who wants to go to a dumb old dance?" Arlene grumbled, checking her lipstick in her compact mirror. Arlene was way past school activities. She preferred keeping her dates to herself.

"I love this one," Karen said, ignoring Arlene as she turned the volume up on the radio. I recognized the song as Three Coins in the Fountain. Resting my chin on the back of the front seat, I closed my eyes and pictured myself in a strapless pink prom dress with layers and layers of tulle, wearing the white orchid corsage he'd given me on my wrist, dancing with Casey Arnold. Everyone is watching as he spins me around. The image fades.

"I'm going to have the band play that one at my wedding reception," Karen said after the song had finished. She often fantasized about what her wedding would be like. The groomsmen would wear powder blue tuxes, and the bridesmaids' dresses would be in the same shade, made of crepe de chine. Karen believed in matching, so the dresses would match the cocktail napkins, the icing on the cake and the ribbons on the party favors. The ceremony would be held at the First Presbyterian Church where she had gone to Sunday school, with a reception immediately following at the new Elk's Lodge. I didn't care where I got married or what color the bridal party wore. I just wanted to marry someone who didn't believe in fighting and would love me forever.

As Hwy 80 began to climb, the craggy mountains stood out so vividly against the clear blue sky that they didn't seem real. We pulled into a rest stop high in the Sierras to eat. Arlene's mother had packed us a picnic basket filled with bologna sandwiches, Hostess cupcakes and a thermos of cherry

Kool-Aid. Karen laid a blanket on the ground and cracked jokes about the cannibalism of the Donner party, dangling a piece of bologna above her red-stained tongue. Despite her playful attempt to ruin my appetite, lunch never tasted so good.

The Peterson's log cabin was almost hidden in the cluster of towering pine trees. Although obviously old, the outside of the house was clean and well cared for. Moments after we pulled into the driveway, Gidge's mother, a highball glass in her hand, pushed open the screen door. Her auburn hair was pulled back into a careless ponytail which, along with pedal pushers and ballerina flats, gave her a youthful and relaxed look.

"Welcome. The other girls are out on the pier," Mrs. Peterson said with a smile, before taking a long pull from her drink.

As we walked inside, the smell of wood smoke filled my nose. The tiny kitchen had barely enough room to "swing a cat," as my Aunt Vi used to say. One wall had open shelves with no cupboard doors. I recognized the stacks of sturdy dishes as the same style that appeared in my mother's Blue Chip stamp catalog. Photos in birch frames lined the opposite wall behind the stove, documenting the construction of the cabin. In one photo, a much younger bundled-up Gidge stood next to a man in a raccoon coat outside the skeletal beginnings of the cottage, her arms crossed defensively, and her face in a pout.

The knotty pine living room resembled a used furniture store with its mish-mash of over-stuffed chairs and couches with balding arms. I didn't see a radio, but a stack of tattered magazines; The Saturday Evening Post, Time and Look, to name a few, sat on the rickety coffee table. Heavy plaid drapes at the windows had seen better days. A large oval rug of braided rags covered most of the floor. Braiding rugs was Mrs. Peterson's hobby, and she had placed one in every room of their house back home. Gidge thought they looked dumb.

"You girls will be sleeping here," Mrs. Peterson told us, gesturing to the floor in front of the fireplace with her glass. We dropped our things and followed her out the back door.

Standing on the back porch, I looked out at the movie-worthy view spread before me. The lake was a sheet, interrupted only by an occasional sailboat or water skier. Behind it, the peaks of the mountains were covered with snow, looking like giant sundaes topped with whipped cream. The sun, high in the cloudless sky, made it unusually warm for May.

"Virginia Ann, your guests are here," Mrs. Peterson called out. I was stunned to hear Gidge referred to by her Christian name. It didn't suit her.

A long wooden pier jutted out seventy-five feet into the lake. Near the end, a variety of chaise lounges and metal lawn chairs were clustered together.

"Hey, out here, you guys," Gidge yelled, standing up and waving. Two other girls turned to look.

Arlene and Karen ran out to join the others, while I took my time, hanging back behind them, feeling shy. What would I talk about? How could I make the others like me? I was probably the least interesting girl I knew, a dork who spent weekends at the movies behind the candy counter, while other girls made out with their boyfriends in the balcony. Next year, I would be a junior, and I hadn't even been on a date!

As I watched Karen and Arlene greet the others, I had the sensation of being invisible. I could see them. But they couldn't see me. I'd gotten good at disappearing when life got too hard, retreating into myself for protection.

Just then, a breeze kicked up and the scent of pine reminded me where I was. Closing my eyes, I inhaled deeply. I was outside my life now, a visitor in a new land, like Dorothy in the Land of Oz. I knew that this was the time to shed my shuttered outlook, allow myself to experience the pleasure and possibility.

When I opened my eyes, I saw Karen gesture to me, as if to say, "Come join me and your new friends." I straightened my shoulders and descended the steps.

As I got closer, I recognized JoAnn Silva and Rose Reyes, both close friends of Gidge's. Jo's coal-black hair was cut short so she wouldn't have to waste time styling it every day after baseball practice. Rose's mane of thick, dark, naturally curly hair was harnessed high on her head with a thick rubber band. Short wisps blew in the breeze around her face. Both of them looked tan already. I never got two shades deeper than fish-belly white, despite getting burnt to a crisp. Peel and burn were the most I could hope for each summer, given my pasty Irish ancestry. So far, I had found nothing good about being Irish, except maybe having blue eyes and dark hair, which people seemed to find attractive.

The girls were sitting side-by-side facing the lake, aluminum tumblers and movie magazines scattered around them. Gidge's bright yellow, one-piece bathing suit accentuated her copper-colored hair. Jo and Rosie wore similar styles, also in vibrant colors. Suddenly, I hated the pink and white gingham-checked suit, and the bathing cap with the pink rubber petals that my mother had bought. They seemed so infantile now. But the sun was warm, and after a while, Karen, Arlene, and I ran back into the house and slipped into our suits.

Jo introduced us to baby oil laced with Iodine, and we spent all afternoon basting ourselves and flipping like burgers every fifteen minutes, as she instructed. I felt so grown up with the foam rubber falsies I had stuffed into my bathing suit. But as I looked around at the others, I knew in my heart that I was more like Margaret O'Brien in a sea of Esther Williams look-alikes.

Late in the day, Mr. Peterson appeared on the back steps wearing plaid Bermuda shorts, a Hawaiian print shirt and a black beret. A quirky World War II veteran, he routinely roused his wife and three daughters in the middle of the night for frantic whistle-blowing safety drills. Instead of fading into the background like most fathers, he deliberately called attention to himself, which infuriated Gidge. She insisted he was brain damaged from the war.

Mr. Peterson waved and gave us a goofy smile as he walked across the small patch of lawn to the barbecue. He picked up a wire brush and began cleaning the grill. His bird-like legs were as white as two quart bottles of milk.

"Look at the poor old son of a bitch," Gidge said, embarrassed by her father's off-kilter dress and behavior. "He thinks he's Peppy Le Pew," she said, referring to the French skunk in cartoons. I felt a strange sense of envy as I watched Mr. Peterson, whistling as he worked. What I wouldn't give to have such a free spirit for a father.

That night after stuffing us with barbecued burgers and birthday cake, the Petersons announced they were going down to the casino for a while.

"Goodnight, little ladies," Mr. Peterson said, clicking his heels and snapping off a neat salute. Gidge cringed. He turned and offered his wife his arm.

Exhausted and sunburnt, we put on our baby dolls, spread out our sleeping bags in front of the fireplace and settled in.

"Put some of this on your shoulders, Liz" Karen said, offering me an open jar of Noxzema. I scooped out a finger-full; pleased she'd remembered my earlier suggestion.

Gidge made a fire, and JoAnn produced a pack of Pall Malls.

"Bring me that ashtray on the mantle, Gidge," Jo said sitting down cross-legged on her sleeping bag next to Rosie. Her warm olive skin glowed in the light from the fire. Karen sat between Arlene and me. Gidge placed the large amber glass ashtray on the floor in the middle of all of us before plopping down next to Jo. Jo opened the pack and offered it around the circle.

"No, thanks," I said, hugging my coltish legs to my chest. I had sneaked one of Aunt Vi's Chesterfields once and gotten sick. Everyone else lit up, including Rosie, but not before she made the sign of the cross.

"Did I tell you guys the latest trick I played on the colonel?" Gidge said. It was weird hearing Gidge refer to her father as "the colonel," like he was some kind of stranger. She French-inhaled her cigarette and blew out the smoke in one perfect stream. "A few weeks ago, I got this idea to put some Nair in his roll-on deodorant. You know, just to see what would happen?" She cracked her gum for effect.

I gasped and covered my mouth with my hand, imagining the potential result.

"Anyway, one morning while we were all in the kitchen, he says to my mother, 'Dee, I think you need to make a doctor's appointment for me.' And she says, 'Why, Dear?' And he says, 'Well, for some reason, the hair under my arms has been coming out in clumps.'" A cocky smile on her face that announced, I-really-got-him-this-time, Gidge said, "The poor son of a bitch thought he had the mange!"

Everyone burst out laughing, except Karen who seemed pre-occupied rummaging through her shocking pink train case.

"Did you tell him what you'd done?" Jo asked.

"No, why would I tell him?" Gidge gave Jo a look. "I just replaced his deodorant with a new bottle. He never knew what caused it. That's the beauty of the whole thing!"

"I locked my s-s-sisters outside in their underwear once," Jo said proudly, unfazed by her stutter.

"Honest?" I asked in disbelief. Jo nodded, obviously pleased with herself. She didn't strike me as the type to be mean-spirited. A wisp of a girl, she looked like she could be blown over by a stiff wind.

"My oldest sister washed my mouth out with soap once," Rosie said.

"What for?" Arlene asked expectantly.

"For using the Lord's name in vain," Rosie said with a shameful look.

"Oh," Arlene said, her tone dismissing Rosie's misbehavior as trivial.

"Wait 'til you hear what Leopard Lady pulled," Gidge said squint-eyed, her cigarette wagging in her lips.

My eyes bulged in amazement. "Who's that?" I asked. I thought I knew everyone in Gidge's family.

"My grandmother. I call her Leopard Lady cause she wears nothing but animal prints. She thinks she's Norma Desmond, fr'crissakes." Gidge rolled her eyes.

"Who's Nora Desmond?" Rosie asked, leaning toward me.

"It's Norma," I said. "She's an old time movie star."

"Anyway, she pissed on the rug in her bedroom and blamed it on the dog," Gidge said. Rosie choked on her cigarette smoke.

"That was quick thinking," Arlene observed with a nod of admiration. She leaned over to tap the ashes off her cigarette.

"Yeah, she's got an answer for everything, that woman." Gidge shook her head. "My mother keeps talking about putting her in a home, but the colonel won't go for it."

I stole a quick look at Karen to see if the conversation had regained her attention. Behind her, standing in the darkened doorway to the kitchen, I caught sight of Gidge's father. My chest knotted up in a fist. How long had he been there?

My face must have registered shock because Karen asked, "What's wrong, Liz?" Following my glance, she sucked in her breath. One by one, Jo, Rosie, Arlene, and finally Gidge turned to look. The room was so quiet you could have heard a cigarette ash drop.

"Forgot my wallet," Mr. Peterson announced. He smiled and walked purposely toward the bedroom, his dress shoes making cracking sounds on the plank floor.

My eyes snapped to Gidge, who had suddenly found the braided rug in front of her very interesting.

Having reached the doorway to the bedroom, Mr. Peterson turned and said. "Virginia Ann, may I speak to you in private, please?" Gidge sighed, got up and with eyes downcast, skulked over to her father. He gestured for her to step inside and quietly shut the door.

Rosie quickly stubbed out her cigarette and waved at the smoke in the air. "What do you think he'll do?" she stage-whispered. "Do you think he'll send us home?"

"No, no," Arlene said, waving her hand as if batting away the question. "He knows we smoke."

"But what if he heard Gidge talking about her grandmother?" Rosie asked. Arlene thought for a second. "Jo, crawl over there, and see if you can hear anything."

"You crawl over there," Jo said.

Arlene made a face.

I rested my chin on my knees and imagined what my own father would say if he caught me in a similar situation, not that I'd ever let that happen. I knew better than to make fun of anyone in my family.

No more than two minutes had passed when Mr. Peterson opened the bedroom door and stepped out.

"Sorry to have interrupted," he said. Again, he smiled. I smiled back for all of us. He walked across the room and out the front door.

There was no sign of Gidge.

"Should we go in and get her?" Rosie asked in a low voice.

"She'll come out when she's ready," Arlene said. "Hand me that Modern Screen, Jo. Is that Tab Hunter on the cover?"

We began a debate over who was more handsome, Tab Hunter or John Saxon, raising our voices so they would carry to the bedroom. Before long, Gidge appeared looking embarrassed. I was relieved that she didn't look like she'd been crying. I didn't know if I could handle Gidge crying.

She sat down slowly and knocked out another smoke from the pack. The conversation tapered off.

"Are you okay, Gidge?" I asked.

"Fine," Gidge said, sounding as if she were trying to convince herself more than us.

The rest of the group was silent, watching Gidge expectantly. Her hand trembled as she lit her cigarette. An owl hooted somewhere outside.

"How much did he hear?" Arlene asked.

"All of it," Gidge replied. She forced smoke out of one corner of her mouth.

"What did he say," Rosie asked quietly.

"He said he was disappointed in me," Gidge said. Her frankness was surprising; both touching and surprising. Then, as if she realized she'd exposed too much of herself, she quickly said, "He also said he thought I'd be happy to know that his armpit hair was growing back."

We might have laughed at that, and things would have been all right. But then Karen said, "Do you have any idea how lucky you are to have a father, Gidge?" I felt a pinch in my heart. We all knew that Karen's father had left when she was five, but she never spoke about it.

Gidge gave a half-hearted shrug.

"Why did your father leave?" Rosie asked.

"Rosie," Jo admonished.

"That's okay," Karen said. "My mother said he left for another woman, but I don't believe that. I think she told me that so I'd hate him as much as she does." I had the feeling Karen was grateful for Rosie's question, as if it gave her an opportunity to unburden herself. "I was forbidden to even mention him. After he'd been gone a while, I started to forget what he looked like. My mother had a picture of him hidden in the bottom of her cedar chest and when she was at work, or out with her friends, I'd sneak into her room and look at it. When I was little, I used to pretend he was only down the street picking up a newspaper and he'd be back to watch Howdy Doody with me." Karen let out a little laugh. "I've never told another soul that," she said.

Suddenly shy, Karen dropped her eyes and smoothed the sleeping bag under her.

"I'll have another cigarette," Jo said, nudging Gidge who hadn't budged since Karen began her speech. Gidge passed her the pack.

I glanced back at Karen, but her face was lowered and there was nothing left of the wistful expression she had earlier. Everything was back to normal, I decided.

I looked around the circle at my new friends and felt a deep, unexpected stab of affection. "Let's promise not to keep secrets from each other," I said. "From now on, we'll tell each other everything."

"Great idea," Jo said.

"I agree," Arlene said.

Karen smiled. I could see genuine pleasure in her face.

"One for all and all for one," Gidge shouted, sticking her arm out in front of her, palm down. Rosie covered Gidge's hand with hers, next Jo, then Karen, then Arlene and me last. Gidge quickly put her other hand on top of the pile and before long, we were all slapping each other's hands, one over the other and laughing.

# CHAPTER FOURTEEN

*March 22, 2000*

Traffic was light, and we were making good time. The dread of reaching our destination grew with each mile.

"Shall we stop at the Landmark for lunch?" I called.

"Huh, what?" Gidge responded in a daze, sitting up and rubbing her eyes.

"I need to go potty," Rose said, taking the last swig of water from her bottle.

"Yeah, I could drain my clam," Gidge said.

The Landmark was owned and operated by Sparky Casterson, and had been in the same place on Highway 80 for as long as I could remember. A typical log-cabin style bar and grill, it was known for serving large portions of hearty home-cooked food. A sign next to the front door read, "Guys—No Shirt, No Service. Girls—No Shirt, No Charge."

The pine walls and bar were stained with thick-layered varnish that looked wet to the touch. The meager lunch crowd reminded me that it was a weekday. Two men in baseball caps sat at the bar drinking Budweiser from bottles and playing liar's dice, while two others in business suits listlessly munched on hamburgers as they watched a basketball game on the television above their heads. At a table by the window, a lone couple hovered over their coffees in intense conversation.

Arlene sat down and lit up. Rose and Gidge made a beeline for the restroom.

"I knew Sparky would never cave to that stupid no-smoking law," Arlene said, gesturing toward the black-plastic ashtray on the table. She took a long drag on her cigarette, holding it in a way that had once made smoking look seductive.

"Being a chain smoker himself didn't hurt," Jo said. "God, that smells good," she said, leaning forward to sniff the smoke. "I really miss smoking, you know. Can you believe we all used to smoke?"

"That was before anybody knew how bad it was for you," I replied. I had quit when Kristen brought home a packet of information from the American Lung Association when she was in the sixth grade. She begged me to give it up, and the guilt was too much for me.

I scooted my chair closer to the table and glanced over at the couple by the window. I noticed the woman had slipped off her shoe and was inching her foot up her companion's pants leg. She said something that made him smile. I couldn't help thinking how much they reminded me of Sam and me when we first met. We, too, used to sit in bars and cafes, drinking and talking, basking in the glow of new love.

Drawing a deep breath, I pulled myself back into the conversation.

"That's why I finally quit," Jo was saying. "I was on my break at work one day, smoking outside next to the smelly dumpster, and all of a sudden I looked around me and thought, what the hell am I doing? Here I am standing by a friggin' dumpster in a back alley, just because I want to smoke."

"Yeah, I quit too," Arlene said, taking another deep drag.

Rose and Gidge returned and sat down just as our waitress approached. Dressed in a black taffeta A-line mini-skirt and white peasant blouse, she could have stepped out of a time tunnel. Her bleached hair looked like the stuff you'd find in a packing crate, and it was backcombed into a 1960s bouffant style that could have been ruined by a ceiling fan. "Lois" was embedded in her white-on-black name badge.

"Are you ladies ready to order?" she asked, her pen poised professionally over her order pad.

"Could you give us a few minutes?" Jo asked politely.

"Sure, no problem," Lois said, sliding her pen and pad into the pocket of her skirt. She turned and walked toward the kitchen, her black leather tennis shoes out of place.

"God! Do you believe that outfit?" Gidge couldn't wait to say. "I haven't seen anything like that in years. Do you think they still sell those skirts, or is that an original?"

"I'll bet it's an original," said Rose, looking after the woman. "And what about that hair?"

"Like Dolly Parton says, the higher the hair, the closer to God," Arlene said, perusing the plastic menu. Exactly the type of remark Karen would have made, I thought with a pang.

"She really should update that style," Rose said.

"What, and displace a whole family of bats?" Gidge said with a snigger.

Gidge's knife-sharp humor, so funny at first, was grating on me. Beginning to feel anxious and fidgety, I excused myself and left for the bathroom.

For years, the Landmark Bar & Restaurant had been known for its Women's Restroom. Every inch of the walls, stalls and even the eight-foot ceiling was covered with writing. Lipstick and ink of every color had been used to either print or scribble words of wisdom, dating back to God knows when.

As I stepped inside, I was greeted by the words, "If you're too old for diaper rash, it must be something else." Behind the door, written in black felt pen, "Sex is like a snowstorm. You never know how many inches you'll get or how long it will last." Under different circumstances, these witticisms would have made me laugh out loud. Now, they just seemed like an endless swarm of meaningless words, not the least bit funny.

I splashed cold water on my face and inhaled deeply. "Come on, Liz," I said out loud to my reflection in the mirror. "Get a grip." My face looked pale and drawn.

As I blotted my face with a scratchy paper towel, I gazed up to the small window that was high on the wall. The sky had turned dark and threatening. If only the clouds would split open and lightning would strike me dead.

An image of my pitiful self only days earlier slipped into my thoughts, giving me a start. It's just as well no one can see how people behave when they are alone, in private. If my gardener or a neighbor had looked through my window, he would have seen a middle-aged woman with unwashed hair, surrounded by cartons of half-eaten Chinese take-out, attired in a Clorox-stained robe and white sweat sox, sitting huddled on the couch staring at the television, clasping onto a remote control, as if she had spent months in that position.

Days of merciless insomnia caught up with me in a rush. My arms felt like they were attached to anvils and my legs could barely support my weight. I was so tired, I thought about flopping down on the old wooden plank floor and slipping off into a coma. It looked freshly mopped and with the heat coming from the old radiator, the room was quite cozy. I couldn't imagine going on to Lake Tahoe. I couldn't even imagine going back out into the restaurant. The clean little restroom seemed like a fine place to set up camp.

After a minute more of such thoughts, I turned and walked into the first stall. As I sat down, I saw it. There, at eye level right in front of me, scratched into the wooden door was a heart about the size of an orange. Inside were the initials, K.C. + E.R and the words, "Lovers Forever." Seeing it now brought a sweet nostalgic pain to my eyes, as I thought back to that night in the early seventies.

Charles had just finished building the house at Tahoe, and Karen invited Arlene and me to join her for the weekend. We rode in Karen's car and, as usual, we stopped for a break at the Landmark.

The place was dark, and the bar was packed. As soon as she sat down, Arlene struck up a conversation with the guy in a faded flannel shirt and tight jeans on the stool next to her. Karen and I were sipping our drinks and talking when our friend Sparky, the bartender, came over and said, "Those two guys down at the end of the bar would like to buy you two ladies a drink." He gestured with his head.

"Tell them no thanks, we'll take the money instead," Karen said. This was one of her best retorts, a lot better than telling them to "buzz off," and it had the same result. Sparky stood stunned, his murky-blue eyes wide and his mouth agape.

"I thought I'd heard it all," he finally said with a laugh. He turned and walked back to deliver the message.

My attention turned to Arlene and her new admirer. She was laughing loudly and gesturing with her cigarette. At one point I heard him say, "Honey, if you were a pair of jeans, I'd wear you out," to which Arlene replied, "It takes a long time to wear me out," as she leaned over and gave him a playful nudge with her shoulder.

Arlene loved flirting. She loved the coy eye contact, the awkward moments teeming with tension, the power of possessing something men wanted and couldn't have. If that meant everybody thought she was a slut, so be it.

"Arlene better get a grip on her carnal fantasies or we could have some trouble here," I whispered to Karen. I worried that someday Arlene was going to tease the wrong guy.

"Well ladies, I relayed your message to your admirers over there, and they weren't too pleased. In fact," Sparky leaned over the bar with his hand cupped around his mouth for privacy, "what they said was that your friend here looks like a real pistol, but what a shame it was that two such beautiful women as yourselves must be lesbians."

Karen pulled a face. "Lesbians!" she exclaimed with mock indignation, placing her hands on her narrow hips. "Just because we prefer to talk to each other instead of them?"

"Hey, don't shoot the messenger," Sparky replied, grinning and raising his hands above his shoulders.

"Lesbians, my ass!" Karen said, getting more upset.

"Hey, let it go, Karen. What do we care what those jerks think?" I said. "Let's get Arlene and get out of here."

"Wait a minute, Liz," Karen said. Smirk in place, she picked a quarter up from the change lying on the bar and walked to the jukebox.

"Follow my lead," Karen whispered when she returned. As Tony Bennett's classic rendition of I Left My Heart in San Francisco began to play, Karen took my hand and led me out onto the tiny dance floor. She assumed the male position and pulled me close. Wrapping my arm tightly around her neck, I laid my head on her shoulder, trying to act serious as I closed my eyes, and we began to sway slowly to the music.

After a minute, I cracked open an eyelid to see our two male admirers sitting awestruck and silent, early cavemen watching the never-before-seen rotation of the first wheel. Slowly, first one, and then the other got up off his bar-stool, walked around the perimeter of the dance floor, eyes downcast, pulled as if by gravity out the front door without looking back. Karen and I stopped dancing and erupted in laughter, wrapping ourselves together in pure pleasure at our power.

We skipped back to the bar, to a grinning Sparky.

"You girls," he said, shaking his gray-haired head.

"That should give 'em something to talk about back at the feed store," Karen said, looking suitably pleased with herself.

In the bathroom, Arlene was re-applying her lipstick in front of the mirror. Stricken with embarrassment, she had fled the scene when we started to dance.

"Oh God! I can't believe you guys slow danced," Arlene said, her speech slightly slurred. I looked at her in disbelief. How many times had I been mortified by her behavior? Never mind.

"Hey, Liz, hand me your pen," Karen called from inside the stall.

"Why?" I asked, rummaging through my purse.

"Just give it to me."

I found a ballpoint pen and passed it to her under the door.

"Hurry up, Karen," Arlene said, wiping lipstick from the corners of her mouth.

"Hey, you weren't in any hurry a few minutes ago when you were hanging all over Homer out there," Karen yelled.

"His name is Donald and I wasn't hanging all over him." Arlene smoothed her tight sweater over her ample hips.

The toilet flushed and Karen stepped out.

"Look at the back of the door," Karen said, handing me the pen and smiling.

Decades later, here I was staring at that silly piece of graffiti—K.C.+E.R. I reached out and ran my fingers tenderly over the letters.

# CHAPTER FIFTEEN

## *March 22, 2000*

One hundred years ago, Lake Tahoe was only accessible to people willing to take two trains and a steamboat to a shoreline resort. Thank goodness all of that changed in 1936, when a road around the lake opened this vacation paradise to anyone with a car.

We made it to the house by late afternoon. In 1957, the barely-paved street boasted only a handful of modest cabins, replaced now by palatial estates. "Houses on steroids," Gidge preferred to call them. I could still remember the way the old place looked back then; no formal driveway, just a small clearing in the pines big enough for two cars; no fancy brick pillars with brass lanterns that went on automatically at dusk, just a homemade wooden signpost that read, "The

Petersons," which you couldn't see after dark. The cottage looked like a place waiting for someone to save it, and that someone was Karen.

She called me in a panic the week before she was to marry Charles.

"Oh, my God, did you hear?" she said in a voice close to tears.

"What? What's wrong?" I asked, wondering if something had happened to Charles.

"The Petersons have put their cabin up for sale."

"God, you scared me. I thought you were going to tell me someone died," I replied. Karen could be such a drama queen.

Gidge's family hadn't spent much time at Tahoe since Mr. Peterson's mother had been put in a rest home, and Gidge's youngest sister had married and moved away. Property values for lakefront property had soared. It made sense that they would want to sell.

"How could they think of selling that place?" Karen said, choking back tears. Out of all of us, Karen loved spending time at the lake best. She rented the cabin from Gidge's parents for a month each summer. It was one of the few constants she could rely on in her otherwise uncertain life.

I took a moment to run the situation through my head. "If it means so much to you, why don't you ask Charles to buy it for you as a wedding present. He can afford it." I couldn't believe how brilliant my idea was. A long pause followed.

"I'll call you back."

Within a week, the final papers where signed. Charles began the renovation immediately. He bulldozed the bungalow and built a 3,000 square foot, two-story chalet. With the ban on new pier construction, he repaired the original one. Ten years later, when they divorced, Karen was awarded the property as part of the settlement.

Mr. Dowd, the caretaker, had cleared the driveway, and there were three-foot clean drifts of snow piled against the surrounding iron fence. The enormous house looked grave and silent against the darkening sky. Karen's Jeep was parked in its usual spot near the front door. Everything about the place tingled with familiarity.

"Maybe somebody should go in first and check out the house?" Jo said.

"What for?" Rosie asked, grabbing her backpack.

"I don't know. It's been empty for a few days. Somebody could have broken in." Jo was a fanatic about security. She lived in a gated community and still locked her front door when she went out to get the mail.

"I'll go with you, Jo," I said as I stepped out of the car. The air still carried the bite of winter. I hunched my shoulders inside my coat.

Although the house was equipped with the latest in security systems, Karen always left her front door key in the large urn planter on the porch.

Jo unlocked the door. With the light from outside, I quickly punched in the security code to turn off the alarm,

Karen's birthdate. She couldn't be bothered to remember anything more elaborate, and since so few people knew her real age, it was a pretty safe choice.

The rest of the group took their time unloading the car. Now that we were here, Karen's absence was much too real.

The house was dark and cold as we stepped inside. I flipped on the light. A chill went through me as I caught a glimpse of Karen's toothpaste-white parka with its permanent creases at the elbows from holding her ski poles or a hot après-ski brandy. It was hanging from one of the pegs over the bench, where residents and visitors alike could sit and remove wet ski boots or muddy shoes.

Jo poked her head into the laundry room.

"Everything seems okay in here," she said. I peered over her shoulder. Inside, between the heavy-duty washer and dryer and built-in ironing board, was the convenience feature Karen loved best; the laundry chute. I remembered the day my son, Kevin, got stuck in it. He was about twelve, when on a dare from Karen's daughter, Julie; he attempted to slide headfirst down the chute. It took the Fire Department over an hour to pull him out. I was so angry; I wanted to leave him there.

As we walked past the master bedroom, I was relieved to see the double doors closed. I wasn't ready to see Karen's personal things yet.

We continued down the long hallway to the kitchen. Jo opened the blinds over the sink. Only a sliver of sun was visible behind the clouds.

"Looks like everything's in order," Jo announced, sounding like a security guard. I scanned the kitchen where we had prepared so many meals together, laughing and criticizing each other for using too much salt or not enough garlic. To please Karen, Charles had installed every luxury, and the kitchen overflowed with the latest appliances and gadgets of the day, half of which she didn't know how to operate. I smiled at the built-in blender/food processor unit.

"Remember the summer Nathan played bartender and mixed up that batch of strawberry Daiquiris?" I said with a smile.

"Yeah, what a mess," Jo said. Rosie's five-year-old son hadn't secured the lid and pink foam exploded all over the walls, the counter and him. Rosie claimed his hair was sticky for a week.

"I'll go turn up the heat," Jo said.

I slipped out of my coat and walked around the long breakfast bar that divided the kitchen from the formal dining area. The house was intimidating in its silence, and I found myself tiptoeing for no reason. I felt like an unwelcome intruder.

As I looked toward the living room, my breath caught in my throat. In the dim light, I could see the large glass coffee table had been pulled in front of the floor-to-ceiling fireplace. On it sat an empty wine bottle and two crystal wine goblets, one half full. At the end of the table, four candles had burnt down to the last of their wicks. Cushions on the floor couch-like had been placed behind the table.

"I'm going for a quick run," I heard Rosie shout. "Anyone want to come?"

"Oh, yeah, right!" Gidge called after her. "The only reason I would take up jogging is so I could hear heavy breathing again."

I was drawn closer to the cozy enclave. The fireplace was sandwiched between a pair of floor-length windows overlooking the lake. Karen often stood at one of these windows, her shoulder against the casing, sipping her morning coffee, and staring out across the water.

Slowly, my eyes traveled around the living room. Karen had a knack for interior decorating. She tried working in a design studio once but became quickly disenchanted when she found that some clients had their own ideas. She was known for being easily inspired, and just as easily bored.

Recently, Karen had become an advocate of the minimalist look, removing knick-knacks and artwork from the natural wood walls so nothing detracted from the view. The only thing she hadn't touched was the tacky 4 x 6 poster clock that we had given her as a joke housewarming gift. It remained in its original place of honor over the couch, looking wonderfully out-of-place. The poster was a black and white photo of John Wayne dressed in full western attire, holding a Winchester rifle in his right hand, the stock braced against his hip and the barrel pointing to a small brass clock face in the upper right corner.

John Wayne had been Karen's movie idol since I'd known her. She would often mimic his distinctive walk while delivering some of her favorite lines from his movies. "A man ought-a-do what he thinks is best."

—⁂—

As I waited at home by the window, dressed in Levi's with rolled up cuffs and my dad's white dress shirt, I couldn't believe my good fortune. One weekend together at Lake Tahoe, and I was part of their clique. It was as though some guardian angel of the lonely had waved a magic wand and poof—friends!

For days after my return, I walked on a rosy cloud through which nothing but my new friends could be seen, heard, or felt. They were my first thought in the morning and my last at night. I wasn't naïve enough to believe the feeling was mutual. But nevertheless, I was happy.

My mother and Aunt Vi had gone out for the evening, and my father was at the kitchen table, riveted to the sports page.

I yanked nervously on my bangs, which my mother's hairdresser had cut too short that afternoon. A horn honked.

"I'm going," I yelled as I grabbed my purse and ran outside, letting the screen door bang shut behind me. No response. None expected.

My father had pretty much left me alone after Tahoe, seemingly grateful to turn the running of my life over to me. He never mentioned a word about my rebellion; in fact, he acted like the whole thing never happened. We did our best to ignore each other. Sometimes, when our eyes would meet across the dinner table, his would skitter away, as if he were afraid if he caught my eye, he would have to explain why he had changed. I wondered if I would ever know.

Jo was driving her boyfriend Jess' car: a 1956 turquoise and white Chevy Bel Air two-door hardtop. The weekend before, the two of them had driven down to Tijuana to have the white leather upholstery "tucked and rolled." I don't know which Jo loved more, Jess or his car.

I slid into the backseat, next to Karen. "What took you so long?" I asked, anxious to let the fun begin.

"Karen had to change her clothes about a hundred times," Gidge complained, cracking her gum. I glanced over and saw that Karen could have been my twin in her jeans and white shirt. A smug sense of satisfaction came over me.

"Here's a dime, call someone who gives a shit," Karen said, hitting Gidge on the shoulder. I smiled. Karen was so witty, firing off one-liners like exploding popcorn.

Jo stepped on the gas, and the glass-packed pipes reverberated under us.

"What time does the show start?" Arlene asked, shoving her sweater into the waist of her toreador pants.

"It doesn't s-s-start 'til it gets dark. We've got plenty of time," Jo said, steering the car expertly with the palm of one hand. I could have cared less about the movie. Just being together was enough.

Again, I pulled hard on my bangs, trying to stretch them. Karen looked over and gave me a reassuring smile.

It was a warm evening, and my posse of friends and I were about to take advantage of dollar night at the Monument Theater, named for the Tomb of the Unknown Soldier, which stood illuminated across the street. Like the smell of cut grass, a trip to the drive-in was a welcome sign of summer.

We pulled up to the cashier's booth.

"Hi, Gidge," the boy selling tickets said, all nerves and pimples.

"Hi, Dennis," Gidge muttered. Jo handed him a dollar bill and stepped hard on the gas pedal.

"Jesus, Jo, you're gonna give me whiplash," Arlene exclaimed, grabbing the back of her neck. Jo made a lukewarm effort to apologize.

"Dennis has such a crush on you, Gidge," Rosie teased.

"He's retarded," Gidge answered, dismissing the notion with a wave of her hand. Dennis Twigg sat across from Gidge in Biology, where he spent most of his time staring at her longingly. Secretly, I thought she enjoyed the attention. Not many boys were brave enough to come near her.

Jo grimaced when the car's undercarriage scraped over a gravel-covered mound as we negotiated our way to the back, near the concession stand. She parked and lifted the speaker from its holder on the battered stanchion and hung it on the window. When she turned up the volume, nothing but static could be heard.

"Shit!" she declared, slamming the metal box with the palm of her hand. Like magic, the static stopped. The music coming from the little radio sounded like it was being broadcast from another planet.

"Isn't that Nick Morelli's car?" Rosie asked, pointing to a black Ford in the row in front of us.

"Yeah, it is," Arlene said, leaning forward to see more clearly.

"If he's with Wanda Hall, I'll bet we'll s-s-see that car rockin' before the night's over," Jo said.

I covered my mouth with my hand to stifle a squeal.

"She's such a tramp," Karen said, refreshing her lipstick.

Always quick to ruin someone's reputation, we were jealous, catty and unfair. It was such fun.

"He's cute. I'd do it with him," Arlene said, flicking her long, dark hair behind her shoulders. My eyelids flew open in surprise. I was still too sexually inexperienced to imagine "doing it" with a boy. The feelings I had about sex were more about love; the kind I'd seen in the movies.

"Arlene!" Rosie scolded, with a pained expression on her face.

"I mean it," Arlene said. "I'd let him slip me the old salami." I turned and looked out of the side window to hide my embarrassment. Arlene had "dated" just about every cute guy in school. Gidge threatened to rub her feet for luck.

"I heard he got detention for a month for cussing in Metal Shop," I said, trying to change the subject. No one seemed to hear. Oh well.

"I love his hair," Arlene said longingly.

"Eeeew, it's full of grease," Rosie said, wrinkling her nose.

A boy walked in front of the car, and Gidge reached over and honked the horn. He jumped about a foot in the air. When he came back down to the ground, he hit the hood of the car with his hand in retaliation.

"Hey, watch it, or I'll sic my boyfriend on ya," Gidge yelled over our laughter. Oh, she was something.

"What boyfriend?" Jo asked, looking at Gidge.

Gidge rolled her eyes. Jo could get away with saying out loud what the rest of us were thinking.

"Okay, I'll sic your boyfriend on him," Gidge said, snapping her gum. "Arlene, did you bring any cigarettes?"

"Why don't you ever buy any?" Arlene replied, rummaging through her purse.

"Because you're the only one who never gets asked for an I.D." Arlene's fully developed figure, coupled with her air of confidence, signaled adulthood.

I asked Karen for her compact and looked at my reflection unhappily.

"I hate my bangs," I announced, acknowledging my obvious disfigurement to show that I knew my faults.

"Why, what's wrong with them?" Karen asked.

"Look at them. They're about a half an inch long." Karen reached over and grabbed my chin, turning my face toward her.

"I think they look great," she said. "They're perfectly even."

If I were a puppy, I'd have been on my back, wriggling frantically from the tummy rub of Karen's compliment.

"What's the movie, anyway?" Arlene asked, not really interested.

"S-s-some western with John Wayne, I think," Jo answered, tapping her fingers on the steering wheel. Her nails were bitten down to the quick.

Karen perked up, John Wayne at the ready: "I buy ya books, I send ya ta school, and still ya don't learn nuthin." She did a pretty good impression for a girl.

"You know, I almost got his autograph once," I said, turning toward Karen.

"No, really?" Karen said, her wide-set eyes sparkling.

"Yeah, my mother took me to Hollywood for my twelfth birthday. We spent three nights in a motel."

I'd never stayed in a motel before, and I had loved everything about it: the clean, fluffy white towels that magically appeared each day while we were out, the sanitized strip of white paper across the toilet, the big double bed where we slept together. But what I loved most was having my mother all to myself. I didn't have to worry about hearing my father bark at her whenever she did something that annoyed him, like when she forgot to buy coffee, or when she didn't iron his workpants the right way, or if she sang show tunes while clearing the table.

"Jesus, Catherine, if I hear Oak-La-Homa one more time, I swear," and he would get up from the table, shaking his head.

For those few glorious days, it was just the two of us. We sat close together on the tour bus, our bare arms touching, tracing our route on the map of the movie star's homes. We ordered the same thing for lunch, a toasted tuna sandwich and a Coke. Everything smelled and tasted and felt more real than anything ever had, or has since.

"My mother and I just missed seeing John Wayne at the Brown Derby, " I said. I had Karen's undivided attention. The feeling of power was exhilarating.

"What's the Brown Derby?" Rosie asked.

"It's a famous restaurant in Hollywood," I answered, irked that she had interrupted my story. Rosie took no interest in Hollywood.

"Go on," Karen said, looking at me expectantly.

"Well, we went there for lunch, and our waiter told us we'd just missed John Wayne. So, my mother asked if there were any other celebrities there, and he said that Art Linkletter was in the booth next to us. My mother loves him, so she sent me over to get his autograph, hoping I might get discovered." I grinned and hunched up my shoulders.

"How exciting," Karen said, fidgeting in her seat. "Did you see anyone else?" I could tell by her expression that she envied me. I rushed on.

"Not really. But we did go to Grauman's Chinese Theater. I put my hands in Judy Garland's handprints, and my mother snapped my picture."

"Wow," Karen said, dreamily.

Arlene passed around the pack of cigarettes, and as usual, everyone but me lit up.

I didn't share all my memories of that trip. How everything lived up to my expectations although I was tongue-tied most of the time. On the train home, my mother and I rehashed every detail like two schoolgirls. She couldn't wait to get the film developed so we could re-live each moment of our adventure with Aunt Vi. When she thought I had fallen asleep curled up next to her on the musty seat, I studied her face as she gazed out the window. Her lips curved up in a half smile, and she had a dreamy look in her eyes. She'd never looked more beautiful, and I'd never loved her more than I did at that moment.

"Maybe you and I could take a trip to Hollywood after graduation," Karen said unexpectedly. Her silver charm bracelet tinkled as she tapped the ashes off of her cigarette.

"Uh, sure, yeah," I stammered.

"It's a deal then," Karen said, crooking her little finger in my direction. I hooked my finger through hers and pulled.

By the time the sun finally dropped from the sky, and the ads for the concession stand flashed on the gigantic screen, I had forgotten about my butchered bangs. I scrunched down in the seat and leaned my head back on the soft white upholstery. The smell of cigarettes mixed with new leather was intoxicating. A halo of contentment surrounded me as I pictured my best friend Karen and me driving along Hwy 1 on our way to Hollywood in a brand new convertible with the top down. The sun is warm on our bare arms, and the radio is playing loudly. I've just said something funny, and Karen throws her head back and laughs.

# CHAPTER SIXTEEN

*March 22, 2000*

The deep, plush carpeting felt spongy under my feet as I walked across the room to the coffee table. Sadly, despite our pledge, Karen and I never took that trip to Hollywood. We both got married right out of high school instead.

I leaned over and picked up the empty bottle to read the label: "Foppiano Cabernet Sauvignon, Sonoma, California," Karen's favorite red wine. Carefully, I replaced the bottle exactly where it had been, as if not to disturb a crime scene.

Standing there, staring at the last hard evidence that my friend ever really existed, my mind was once again spinning. How could someone be so alive one minute and dead the next? This woman had managed to survive a loveless childhood and three failed marriages, and then a little piece of ice or gravel comes along and wipes her off the face of the earth.

I thought of Greg. How devastated he must feel. Or did he? Maybe he was relieved to have her gone. Maybe he was fed up with her dropping in and out of his life whenever she was between husbands, expecting him to be available as if he had no life of his own. Maybe he even swerved on purpose. My eyes narrowed at the thought. No, that's crazy. But, still…

I knew I had to speak to him in person, so I could see his face, so I could find out what really happened.

"Who wants to go to the grocery store with me?" Arlene asked, jangling some keys.

"I'll go," Gidge answered.

Hey guys, come look at what I found, I wanted to shout, but I couldn't find my voice. Instead, I remained riveted to the scene in front of me. It was as though I expected something to move; or maybe if I stared long and hard enough, Karen and Greg would magically appear.

I heard the front door open, and Rosie sprinted down the hall. I turned and in the light from the kitchen, I could see that her cheeks were flushed from the cold.

"That felt good," she exclaimed, wiping her nose on the back of her gloved hand. "There's nothing like a quick run to work out the kinks from sitting in the car for a long time."

I turned back to the sight before me.

A moment later, I felt an arm around my waist—Rosie's.

"Oh, God," she whispered. I covered her hand with mine.

"Can't you just see Karen and Greg here?" I asked, visualizing them sitting close, Karen making a joke, and Greg laughing. They were both such fun and full of fizz, like Sam and I were when we first met.

Rosie and I stood together quietly.

Arlene and Jo joined us, and each of us put her arm around the other. No one said a word. We stood alone in our own thoughts.

Rosie began to sniffle.

"Okay, that's it!" Gidge exclaimed, marching past us. "Somebody grab the rest of this shit and let's put things back where they belong." If it were only that simple.

Gidge bent over and picked up the two wineglasses, holding them at arm's length as if they were infected with some contagious disease. As she turned to leave, I caught a glimpse of the lipstick print on the rim of the half-empty glass. I recognized Karen's color; Estee Lauder's Bare Honey. She had purchased a new tube on our last shopping trip.

I had a weird impulse to instruct Gidge not to wash the glass, to set it aside so we could preserve it, put it in a special hermetically sealed case.

"When are we going to go over our plans?" JoAnn asked, jarring me back to reality. She was arranging the photo album collection on the dining room table like an elaborate centerpiece. Rosie took off toward the bathroom.

"Let's get the supplies in and have dinner first," Arlene suggested. She dropped the empty wine bottle into the trash compactor with a clank. "Where does everyone wanna sleep?"

At the mention of the word "sleep" my chest felt sunken with fatigue. My neck and shoulders were stiff, and I could feel the heartbeats behind my eyes. I sank onto the nearest chair, zapped of every last ounce of energy.

"I don't care where I sleep," I said with great effort. I leaned my head back and closed my eyes. Suddenly, I missed Sam, the way he liked to spoon me in bed, his warm breath on my neck.

Gidge and Arlene left to do the grocery shopping, Rosie agreed to fix dinner, and Jo and I volunteered for clean-up duty. This was the way we worked best; as a team.

In happier times, our meal would have been full of laughter and animated conversation, each of us shouting to be heard. But tonight, we were so quiet you could hear a caper drop. The meal was the longest we had ever had together. We needed to drag it out, knowing that when we finished, we'd have to address the reason we were all here.

By the time Jo and I finished the dishes and made coffee, it was after ten. As I filled Rose's cup, Arlene got up from the table and came back with a writing pad and pen. I realized that I hadn't seen her smoke since we arrived. Although Karen had "Thank You for Not Smoking" signs all over the house, she always made an exception for Arlene.

"Okay, I've made a list of things we need to do," she said, looking down at her shorthand notes. "First, as all of us know, Karen always said she wanted to be cremated and have her ashes scattered in Emerald Bay."

Surveying the table, I saw the grim faces. Jo was gnawing at her fingernail, and Rosie was reaching for more tissues.

—m—

"The morgue is expecting some direction on what to do with the body by tomorrow," Arlene said. Rose let out a whimper, and Jo leaned over to put her arm around her.

"I need a drink," Gidge announced, shooting up out of her chair. "Anyone else want one?"

"I'll have a little Grand Marnier for my coffee," Jo said.

"Me too, please," Rose said, between sniffles. She never drank.

"Okay, let's move on," Arlene continued, sounding peevish. "I'd just like to go down the list, and then we can decide who will do what." She paused and circled us with her eyes like a substitute teacher trying to get her class' attention. "Number one, find a crematorium and make arrangements for the transfer of the body."

"The body? The body! Jesus Christ, Arlene. It's Karen!" Gidge said. She dropped the silver tray of liquors on the table with a bang. "It sounds so cold!"

"Well, excuse me, Gidge, but when did you get to be so sensitive?" Arlene protested.

Rose was bawling. "Don't fight you guys, please don't fight," she said into her crumpled tissue. Jo pulled her close.

"Gidge, get a hold of yourself," Jo said, fixing Gidge with a look. She cleared her throat and said, in a softer voice, "I know you're upset. We all are. But this is not the time to lose it."

Rosie gave Jo an appreciative look. Then she blew her nose.

"Oh, Rose, fr'crissakes, turn off the waterworks, will ya?" Gidge snapped as she sat down hard.

Arlene signaled everyone to refrain from uttering one further syllable. She went on. "Let me finish my list, and you can add anything I may have forgotten. Number one, arrange for the cremation." Arlene shot darts at Gidge with her eyes. Gidge stared back.

Satisfied that Gidge had said her piece, Arlene continued. "Number two, arrange for the memorial service. Number three, contact family and friends, and four, prepare a eulogy." Arlene looked up from her notes. "Now, those are the major things. Is there anything else?"

"What about the obit-obit-obitu-shit! You know, the funeral notice in the paper?" Jo asked in exasperation. I hadn't heard her stutter in years. Her face turned crimson.

"Whoever does the cremation will take care of that," Arlene said, waving her hand in the air.

"Even if we want it in several papers?" Rosie asked, dabbing at her eyes.

"They'll put it wherever you want it," Arlene said. "When my mother died, I had the notice put in the local paper and in the paper in Texas where she and my dad were stationed the longest."

"What about after the memorial service?" Rosie said. "Shouldn't we have something here at the house?"

"Well, who do we think will come to the service, besides Squeak and us?" Gidge asked. She poured herself a rather large shot of Napoleon Brandy. Arlene watched her cautiously over the tops of her reading glasses.

"That's hard to say," Rosie answered. "But I guess there will be some neighbors from up here and maybe some of the staff at Karen's health club or members of her Ski Club? And of course our families."

A flutter of warmth came over me at the prospect of seeing my two children, which was immediately quelled by the probability of Sam's absence.

"What's wrong, Liz?" Arlene asked, studying me carefully.

"I don't think Sam will be coming to the funeral," I said.

"What do you mean?" Rosie asked. I sighed over her question.

Jo reached over and placed her hand on my arm. "You can tell us," she said. "No secrets, remember?" Her quiet smile was reassuring.

"Yeah, no secrets," Gidge called from the end of the table.

"Sam and I...we...he's moving to New York."

Rosie's eyebrows shot up in astonishment. "New York? When?"

"The end of next month."

"Are you going with him?" Rosie asked.

"No."

"Why not," Arlene asked, removing her glasses and leaning her forearms on the table.

"Why not?" I said. My voice rose half an octave with anger, frustration and fear. "Because I can't just pick up and move across the country, leave everything I've worked for, sell the house, abandon Kristen and Kevin. I've got to find another job. I've got bills to pay, and I promised Kevin I'd loan him the money for a down payment. I can't be expected to start a whole new life at my age."

Jo fell back in her chair. "I don't believe it," she said. "You two have lasted longer than most marriages."

"Maybe you just don't love Sam enough," Gidge blurted out, as if nothing more could be expressed until that obvious truth was proclaimed.

I didn't answer, having concluded that this question, like most of Gidge's questions, was rhetorical.

Gidge's eyes bounced from me to Jo. "Why are you giving me the stink eye?" she said.

"What's with you tonight?" Jo said.

"I'm just saying," Gidge said, tossing her hands in the air.

Arlene turned back to me. "Don't listen to her. Have you really thought about this, Liz? I mean, made your list of the pros and cons and all?"

All these questions, mixed with my exhaustion, caused my head to pound. "Look, I appreciate all of your concern, but I really don't want to discuss this any further. Not now."

It was Rosie who came to my rescue. "We understand," she said, as if speaking for the group. She gave me a little smile and I thanked her with my eyes.

"Now, let's get back to business," she said, pouring some more Grand Marnier into her coffee. She was going to be sorry in the morning. "Who else do we expect at the service?"

"I wonder if any ex-husbands will show up?" Gidge said.

"Whose, ours or Karen's?" Jo asked.

"Maybe both," Gidge replied.

Rosie's expression grew alarmed. "Oh, God, do you think so?" she asked.

"I know Jess won't come," Jo said, referring to her ex. "He still blames Karen for our divorce." Karen's offer of a place to live was the push that Jo needed to leave her abusive husband. Jess never forgave her.

"I think Harry will be here," Gidge added nonchalantly before taking a sip of her brandy.

"Did you call him?" Rosie asked accusingly.

"Yes, actually I did, Rose," Gidge said with her nose in the air. "You know how Harry always loved Karen." Why wouldn't he? Karen let Harry and Gidge spend many of their illicit weekends here, while Harry was still married to his first wife.

"I know Fred will be here," Arlene said, doodling on her notepad. All heads turned in her direction, eyes wide in disbelief. As far as I knew, Arlene hadn't spoken to Fred since their divorce had become final.

"Fred has known Karen almost as long as he's known Arlene," I said. "It's only natural that he would want to come."

I didn't know why I came to Arlene's defense. I guess I was just hoping she was right. Fred was one of my favorite people, and until she mentioned him I didn't realize how much I missed seeing him.

Cruising campus in his suped-up Chevy, trolling for girls, Fred Heflin intrigued Arlene. Freshly discharged from the Navy, he offered a worldliness beyond the boys she was used to dating. Rumors chopped lightly around him, that he had a wife back home in Indiana, and that he'd spent time in the brig. Neither one was true. At first, he frightened me. He seemed moody and self-absorbed. But soon his humor and goodness became obvious. He made a point of befriending each of us girls, soliciting us as advocates in his quest to marry Arlene. And his dogged persistence paid off. I can see him yet, this rough, tough, ex-military man abandoning his uniform of jeans and a white T-shirt for a dark suit, adjusting his tie before tying the big knot, blinking back tears as he marries Arlene under a rose-covered arbor in her parents' backyard.

"What about Ricky?" Arlene said. I flinched. The thought hadn't occurred to me. "I...I'm sure he wouldn't, not after all these years."

"You never know," Arlene said, lifting her glass.

"It sounds like this could get real interesting," Gidge said, leaning back in her chair, smirking. "We could stage our own version of Family Feud."

"Don't forget Greg," Jo said. The mention of Greg's name got everyone's attention.

"Why would he show up?" Gidge said with an edge in her voice.

"Well, I—"

"You know, I keep thinking about something Karen said not long ago," I said. "She told me that Greg had scraped together enough money to put a down payment on the restaurant last year. Something about the way she said it made me wonder if she'd put up most of it."

Gidge let out a brief snort of contempt. "I wouldn't be surprised."

"I hadn't really given it much thought until now," I said. "I wonder if he's in her will."

A hush fell over the table. I halfway wanted to be talked out of my suspicion. Rosie refused to look at me. Arlene drew a section of her lower lip between her teeth and slowly released it. Gidge sat with folded arms, her face fixed in the special look that meant she had made up her mind about something and would not be swayed.

"You're not suggesting—" Jo said, her eyes narrowing.

"I'm not suggesting anything," I said. "Just thinking out loud."

Another moment passed before Arlene said, "Well, considering all the possible attendees, I guess we probably should have something here at the house afterward." She jotted something on her pad.

We were back on track, mistrust put aside, doubt held at bay. For the time being.

"Okay then, we need to decide what to do about food if we're having people over here," Rose said.

"I don't think we should spend a lot of time cooking," Jo said, as she checked her Rolex. "Why don't I hire a caterer?" No longer imprisoned by her husband or her stutter, Jo had become a successful real estate broker. She had everything catered—wrote it off as business entertainment.

"That's really not necessary, Jo," Rosie said. "I want to cook. It will be my gift to Karen."

A tight bank of tiredness wrapped itself around my eyes and sinuses.

"I have a suggestion," I said, anxious to call it a night. "Arlene, why don't you and I handle the crematorium arrangements? Gidge and Jo can find a place for the memorial service and write the eulogy, and Rosie can handle the get-together here at the house. How does that sound?" Experience told me I'd have no resistance.

"So long as I don't have to go near a morgue, I'm good," Gidge said, sounding surprisingly amiable. The brandy might have had something to do with it.

"Fine," Jo said, extending her hand in Gidge's direction. Gidge shook it.

"Let's talk about timelines," Arlene said, sounding relieved to have assignments delegated and accepted. Rosie convinced Jo that she didn't mind cooking. Gidge and Jo decided on Saturday for the service and made plans for gathering information for the eulogy. Arlene started a list of people we would each call. And I made a silent promise to myself that tomorrow I would see Greg.

# CHAPTER SEVENTEEN

## *March 22, 2000*

The sheets were crisp and cold as I snuggled down under the covers in Julie's old bedroom. I thought of Gidge's remark about my not loving Sam enough. Her accusation should have cut me to the quick. But it hadn't. Maybe there was a kernel of truth in her words. Maybe it took more love than I was able to give, to restart my life with Sam. I considered the possibility.

The pines creaked outside the window. I pulled the layers of blankets up under my chin, and recalled the look on Arlene's face when she'd mentioned Fred's name. She tried so hard to act indifferent to the prospect of seeing her ex-husband, but I heard the nervous quiver in her voice.

As I turned off the lamp, I couldn't help feeling excited about their seeing each other. I had a special place in my heart for the two of them as a couple. If it weren't for their marital problems, I would never have met Sam.

It was the summer of 1980, not quite three years after Ricky and I had split up. Disillusioned by love, I'd thrown myself into my work and raising my children.

As I pulled into the driveway on a Friday night at the end of an especially grueling week with everything going wrong from losing my office keys to missing an important deadline at work, all I wanted was a nice hot bubble bath and a quiet weekend at home.

"Auntie Arlene left you a message, Mommy," ten-year-old Kristen announced, jumping up and down with excitement, her pigtails dancing in the air. "She said she'd be here tomorrow."

Arlene and Fred had been living in Reno for two years. So far, the move hadn't turned out as well as they had expected. Fred's plumbing and heating business was yet to make a profit, and their teenage son, Timmy, had been in trouble at school.

"Thanks, honey," I replied, smiling and squeezing her knobby little shoulders.

I knew what to expect. Another load of Arlene's pent-up frustration was about to be unleashed, after which she would be ready to party.

She hit the house like a hurricane the next afternoon. "That son of a bitch," I heard her yell, as she barged through my front door. Kristen ran to meet her. "Sorry, KK, but your Auntie Arlene is really pissed off. Where's your mother?"

She started in the minute she saw me. "He won't do anything to try and salvage what little we have left." She dropped her purse on the floor, and dismissively tossed the mink jacket onto the couch that Fred had bought to appease her when they first moved to Reno. "If I know him, he'll wait until they repossess the damn house before he admits we're bankrupt!"

"Hey, how the hell are you, anyway?" I said, smiling from across the room, my hands on my hips.

Arlene made a face. "Oh sorry, Liz," she said. "I've been getting more angry with each mile down the mountain." She crossed the room in three giant steps and gave me a big hug. Kristen was right behind her.

"I need a drink," she said into my ear. "KK, why don't you pour Auntie a nice glass of your mother's white wine, huh?" Arlene bent over and pinched Kristen's cheek.

"Okay," Kristen replied, running to the refrigerator to oblige.

"Come sit down," I urged, gesturing toward the couch. "You're home now, you can bitch all you want."

For the next couple of hours, I listened intently as Arlene ranted and raved about how Fred was letting his business go down the drain. I let her vent, and as I expected, with the help of a few more glasses of wine, she was ready to forget her troubles and get happy.

After dinner, we retreated to my bedroom to prepare for our night out. Somehow Arlene coerced seventeen-year-old Kevin into babysitting his little sister. He would have never done it for me.

"Do you have anything sexy I can wear?" Arlene asked, poking around my closet in nothing but her underwear and ass-kicking black boots.

"I don't know." I plopped down on the bed. This could take some time. Arlene was two inches taller and two sizes bigger than I, but she could wear some of my blouses and most of my sweaters. Over the next hour, she tried on at least ten different tops before settling on a cream, long-sleeved sweater with a V-neck that showed some cleavage.

"There," she exclaimed, apparently satisfied with what she saw in the mirror. Genetically, Arlene wasn't blessed with beautiful features; her nose was too long, and her eyes were too close together. But the air of confidence she exuded more than made up for her non-beauty queen looks.

"What are you going to wear, Liz?" she asked, affixing the last of her Lee Press-on Nails.

"What I have on, I guess." I looked down at the khaki pants and white oxford shirt that comprised my weekend uniform. Who cares what I wear. I'm just the designated driver on this trip, anyway. "It's 8:30. We'd better get going." Maybe if we got there early, we could leave early.

"Where are we going?" Arlene asked eagerly as she ran a pick through her over-permed hair. Her gold hoop earrings shimmered in the light.

"A girl at the office told me about a new club in Alamo. She said it seemed to appeal to people of all ages, which means maybe those of us pushing forty won't feel like somebody's mother there." I slipped into my comfortable loafers and smeared some gloss over my lips.

"You make it sound so enticing," Arlene replied sarcastically. She pressed down hard one last time on each of her fake nails.

I could hear the music pounding as we pulled into the parking lot. Arlene had been chain-smoking all the way. She was "as nervous as a cat in a room full of rocking chairs," as my Aunt Vi used to say. I hated when she got like this.

"This must really be the "in" place. It looks packed!" She leapt out of the car. I had to run to keep up with her.

As we approached the entrance to the club, I could see the seething mob inside; a solid mass of humanity, shoulder-to-shoulder, packed into every available inch of space. The thought of rollicking with a bunch of sweaty desperate losers, speculating about this person or that, making small talk, rubbing their bodies against mine made me want to open my veins with a crab fork.

I would have given anything if Arlene had changed her mind right then, but knowing her, that wasn't likely. I let out a resigned sigh.

"Welcome to Scats," the huge bouncer said, baring his big white incisors in more of a sneer than a smile. His black T-shirt was so tight I could see his nipples through it. He grabbed for my hand. I pulled back.

"I'm just gonna stamp your hand," he said in a tone that asked, "Haven't you ever been to a club before?"

I looked down in disgust at the smear of red ink. "What's this for?" I wanted to know.

"In case you want to go out and come back in," he said with a wink, like we had some secret code of understanding.

Once inside, Arlene got even more excited. She dug her fake fingernails into my arm as she scanned the room.

"Wow, this place is full of guys!" Sure enough, as far as the eye could see, there were men of every shape and size. "Let's get a drink," she said. Using me as a battering ram, we made our way through the crowd.

At the bar, she elbowed her way in and proceeded to get the bartender's attention by leaning over and squeezing her upper arms together, causing her cleavage to expand upward—a move she'd learned from Karen. He was there in a heartbeat. As I stood behind her, trying not to get trampled, I could feel the rise in room temperature caused by the sheer number of people around us. Arlene handed me a vodka tonic and we were on our way again, pushing toward the far end of the bar where there was room to breathe. She was leading the way when she stopped abruptly, causing me to slam my drink into her back. I watched helplessly as the liquid surged forward over the rim of my glass and onto the back of the sweater I had just picked up from the cleaners the day before. Arlene didn't seem to notice. Oh, this is going to be a fun evening.

"Liz, look! Twelve o'clock," she said over her left shoulder. I stepped up beside her. I should have known – a sighting.

It was like a great white hunter spotting a helpless animal in his gun-sight.

"Quick, look, look!" she demanded, poking me with her elbow. Giving in, I stood on my tiptoes in an attempt to see over the crowd in front of us. There he was, looking right at me, one of the most gorgeous men I'd ever seen. His arms were crossed in front of him, and he was holding a beer bottle in his hand in a masculine but classy sort of way; the way James Bond might if he were doing a Budweiser commercial.

I lowered myself back down to the floor.

"Did you see him?" she wanted to know.

"He's married," I replied in a nasty tone. I took a sip from my half-empty glass.

Arlene turned to face me. "Do you know him?" she asked. Her left eyebrow went up in an arch.

"No, No," I said. "I can tell by looking."

"Oh, don't be silly," Arlene replied, giving my arm a playful slap. Her bright red fake nails looked like bloody daggers. "Besides, I don't want to marry him. I just want to have a little fun." Grabbing my wrist, she began pulling me along behind her toward the gorgeous stranger.

"Hi, there, I'm Arlene and this is my friend Liz. Come here often?" Oh God, how embarrassing. I averted my eyes and shifted from one foot to the other.

"Hello I'm Sam," I heard him say in a deep voice that had the timbre of a radio announcer. "My first time."

I tried to make myself invisible. If Arlene had targeted this guy, she wasn't getting any competition from me.

Besides, I was through dousing myself with notions of romantic love with its thrilling highs and crippling lows. In truth, I was one bad date away from being bitter.

Arlene said something I couldn't hear, and he replied. I felt a hand on my elbow.

"Would you like to dance?" a disembodied voice asked from behind me. Turning around, I came face-to-face with a short, fifty-something man with thinning gray hair and skin to match.

"No, thank you," I replied with an apologetic smile. I was used to being flirted with by AARP members. The man smiled, bowed and began to walk away backwards, like a peasant who had just met royalty. I was touched.

Arlene was now deeply engrossed in conversation with Mr. Gorgeous, hanging on his every word. Feeling like a third wheel, I tapped her on the shoulder and whispered in her ear that I was going to the ladies' room. Head down, I plowed through the crowd toward the restroom sign, trying not to breathe in the cigarette smoke that hung heavy in the stale air.

As I washed my hands, I thought about all the other nights I'd found myself in this kind of situation with Arlene. Karen used to say, "It's like she has a can of tuna fish under each arm!" Since high school, despite her unremarkable looks, Arlene had been able to cast a spell over just about any man she wanted by simply looking at him with dark eyes that held the promise of something more. Occasionally, when we girls went to the drive-in movies, Arlene would slip off to neck with one of her many boyfriends. When she came back, her lipstick would be smeared and her clothes all askew and wrinkled. One time her blouse was even buttoned wrong, but she didn't seem to notice, or if she did, she didn't care. I thought I had grown to accept her just the way she was and yet now, after our decades-long friendship, her blatant flirtatiousness still aggravated me.

I stared into the water-stained mirror and saw a reflection that had all the seductive allure of road kill. My eyes began to sting with tears. What was it about Arlene that bothered me so much? Was I envious of her allure, high on her hormones, spring-loaded for sex? Or did I morally disapprove because she was married? A bit of both.

But more than that, Arlene had a certainty about her that I was all too aware of lacking myself. She knew who she was, and made no excuses for her behavior. Even when I had turned the page from girl to woman, that sureness escaped me. I questioned my every move, afraid to deviate or wander off the path that was expected of me. And look where taking the safest course had gotten me. Resolutely single, and alone.

I let out a dismissive grunt. Pushing away pinpricks of regret, I applied some fresh lip-gloss and gathered myself together.

When I returned to where I'd left them, Mr. Gorgeous was gone, and Arlene had latched on to another victim who was dressed all in black: black jeans, a black silk shirt, and a black leather vest. He resembled a poor-man's Johnny Cash.

His hair was shoulder-length, slicked back with gel, and he smelled unpleasantly of Musk cologne.

"Hey, Liz," Arlene said excitedly. "Look who I found?" Like I was supposed to know this guy? "It's Jerry from Harrah's," she clarified, hanging onto his arm with both of hers. "He's one of my favorite Black Jack dealers, aren't ya, Jerry?" She rubbed her boobs on his arm.

"If you say so," Jerry replied, almost salivating. "This little lady really knows how to play the game." His beady little eyes were riveted to Arlene's cleavage. "She can sit at a table longer than anyone I know." Wow, there's a real talent.

"Can I buy you ladies a drink?" Jerry asked, stuffing his hand into his left front pocket. His jeans were so tight, it was a real effort.

Arlene replied eagerly. "I'm drinking Rum and Coke and, Liz will have a vodka tonic." Jerry winked and turned toward the bar.

"I can't believe it," she said, grabbing my arm. "I flirt with this guy every time I'm in there. What are the odds I'd meet him down here?" She flipped the hair off the back of her neck, like an annoying teenager. "He's visiting his sister in Dublin," she explained, as if I cared. All I could think of was poor Fred at home in Reno, working his butt off trying to make ends meet.

"Is he married?" I asked, curling my lip.

"How the hell do I know?" Arlene snapped. "Like I said, I'm just here for a little fun." She didn't need to glare at me.

I occupied myself by scanning the crowd. The dance floor was jammed, and every cocktail table was full. I caught myself looking for Mr. Gorgeous. Maybe he'd left. What did I care? He was obviously married. All the good ones were.

Jerry returned with our drinks. Luckily, I couldn't taste much liquor in mine. I had a feeling it was going to be a long night. When the disc jockey played Rod Stewart's, "Hot Legs," Jerry asked Arlene to dance. My body began to involuntarily sway to the music, and before I knew it, my friend the gray ghost was back.

"Would you like to dance?" he asked once again.

"Oh, no thanks. Maybe later." I lifted my drink in a kind of salute. He smiled knowingly and left, this time turning his back on me. I guess my status must have dropped after a second refusal.

"Hello again." That voice. Mr. Gorgeous was back. "May I have this dance?" I felt like a wallflower at a school dance. Me? You want to dance with me?

Without waiting for an answer, he reached out, took the glass from my hand and sat it on a nearby table, covering it with a napkin. As he walked in front of me, I took the opportunity to check out his shoes. "You can tell a lot about a man by his shoes," Aunt Vi used to say. His were two-toned, slip-ons made of very soft brown leather. A good sign.

Clumsily bumping into other people, we were forced to dance close, unable to talk much over the roar of the music and the crowd, one song after another, both of us sweating profusely, my forehead stuck to his cheek. All too soon, the lights that signaled closing time came on. I was surprised at my disappointment.

"Oh God," I winced, squinting against the harsh light, still standing in his arms on the dance floor. "I must look awful." I shaded my eyes with my hand.

"You look beautiful," Mr. Gorgeous answered. Feeling a blush coming on, I quickly turned my head and began searching the crowd for Arlene.

"There she is," I said nervously, aware of the warmth radiating from his body. Arlene had come out of the ladies' room and was walking toward the bar where Jerry stood waiting.

"Hey, Liz," Arlene said excitedly, as I stepped up beside her. I could tell by her eyes that she was sloshed. "Look!" she exclaimed, holding up her index finger. "I lost one of my nails!" She puckered her mouth in a Shirley-Temple-like pout.

"We'll buy you some more tomorrow," I said, smiling at Sam, apologetically. I was embarrassed for him to see my friend this way, as if somehow her condition was my fault. I had always been quick to take responsibility for the short-comings of others.

Jerry piped up and mumbled something about the four of us going out for breakfast.

"Thanks, Jerry, but I've got to get my friend here home," I said, wrapping my arm around Arlene and steering her toward the front door. Sam hung back to distract Jerry.

"Where we going?" Arlene asked, walking like Tipsy McStagger.

"You ladies have a good time?" the beefy bouncer asked. Arlene stopped and teetered.

"Sure did, honey," she cooed as she reached up and pinched his cheek hard. He winced. I gave him a feeble smile before hurrying Arlene down the steps toward the parking lot. I didn't want any trouble. In her current condition, Arlene could be trouble.

"Wasn't that a coinkkeydink, Liz?" Arlene slurred, as we reached the car. "I mean meeting Jerry down here?"

"Yeah, a real coincidence," I said, pacifying her as I opened the passenger door and stuffed her inside. She was out the minute her butt hit the seat.

Mr. Gorgeous appeared beside the car.

"You didn't think I was going to let you get away without getting your number, did you?" he asked, a little out of breath.

"I'm really not dating at the moment," I said. I slammed the passenger door shut. Arlene rocked in her seat.

"How about you give me your number, and I promise not to call for at least a month?" I stifled a smile, and shifted my gaze to the ground, afraid to look at him, afraid that his sweet smile and slow-dance eyes would crack the hard shell that had become my emotional armor. "Would that be long enough?" He stuck a pen and a scrap of paper under my nose. What the hell.

"Sure," I said. I jotted down my number.

"Are you sure you're okay to drive?"

"Yes, I'm fine, thanks." I shuffled my feet. "Well, goodnight then," I said.

The traffic was light as I accelerated onto the freeway. I punched at the radio buttons until I found some soothing music and began re-running the events of the evening; the way he held me when we danced, not too tight but tight enough to let me know he was interested, the feel of his warm hand, the smell of his lemony aftershave.

"I'm alive," I whispered, in a tone not unlike Frankenstein's monster. I felt a sense of elation, a kind of giddiness. "An attractive man asked for my phone number. Not Arlene's. Mine." I tilted the rearview mirror so I could see my face, expecting to see someone different. But there was only me. I glowed in secret triumph.

The next morning, I was sitting at the breakfast bar in my robe having my second cup of coffee, when Arlene stumbled around the corner. She looked like she'd been pulled through a hedge backwards.

"I found my fingernail!" she announced proudly, holding the piece of red plastic up in front of her face. As she walked toward me, I could see she had rubbed her mascara into a pair of raccoon rings around her eyes.

"Where was it?"

"Stuck to my pubic hair."

—m—

Lying on the edge of sleep, steeped in the memory of that night, I was overwhelmed with feelings for Sam. On impulse, I snatched up the cordless phone next to the bed and dialed.

"Hello," Sam said, sounding a bit cross.

"Did I wake you?" I asked.

"No, no. I'm working on a report for a meeting tomorrow..." He stopped short, as if he just remembered that our once easy relationship had become strained and complicated.

I knew he was waiting for me to say something.

"I was just wondering if you'd come to Karen's service," I said. A pause. "We're going to try for Saturday." Another pause, long enough to drown in. I wanted to say more. I wanted to say that I missed him terribly, that I didn't think I could get through this without him, that I didn't want him to go to stupid old New York.

"I have an appointment with a realtor in New York this weekend," Sam said in a level, unapologetic voice.

"Oh," I said. I could feel him slipping from my grasp. "I understand." I heard the resentment in my voice. I was sure Sam heard it, too.

"No, I don't think you do," Sam said. There was no malice in his tone. In fact, there was a tenderness in his words. I covered my eyes with my arm, and let out a breath. Why had everything turned to shit?

"I'm sorry," Sam said.

"No problem," I said, once again donning my emotional flak jacket. "Have a safe trip." I punched the "talk" button on the phone to disconnect.

"Screw you," I said out loud, punching my pillow to a pulp.

# CHAPTER EIGHTEEN

## March 23, 2000

It was still dark, when I awoke from a fitful night's sleep. Illuminated by moonlight, the bedroom developed like a Polaroid, getting sharper as it came slowly into focus. I was disoriented, then remembered. The terrible loss hit me again.

I tried to picture Karen's face. But the image wouldn't come. I tried harder to see her, blinking back my panic. How could I have forgotten the curve of her smooth cheek, that perfectly arched brow? But still nothing. Except for my unspeakable sadness.

It's hard to predict the way, or the moment, when two human beings will connect with each other. The process is often a gradual one. The incident that cemented the camaraderie between Karen and me occurred after Gidge's birthday party, days before school was out.

Casey Arnold didn't ask Karen for a second date after the prom, so she set her sights on Mike Leary, one of the star baseball players. When word got out that he and his long-term steady, Sheila Halvorsen, had broken up, Karen developed a renewed interest in baseball, cheering at every game and hanging out near the boys' locker room afterward. When Mike finally asked her out, she was happier than if she had been crowned Homecoming Queen, which she was the following year.

The Saturday they were to go to the movies, Karen asked me to come over and help her pick out what to wear. Normally, Arlene would have joined us, but that day she was babysitting for a neighbor. I'd have Karen all to myself.

We spent the afternoon listening to records and going through her closet. Just before dinner, as we lay on Karen's bed leafing through Photoplay magazine, the phone rang. Karen jumped up and ran into the hallway that separated her room from her mother's, where the phone sat on a spindly mahogany table.

"Oh, hi, Mike," I heard her say. The conversation was short, and when she hung up the color had drained from her face. Mike had cancelled their date.

"He says he has to work," Karen said, tossing her head in disbelief. Mike delivered prescriptions for old Mr. Shipman, the pharmacist at the drug store.

"Then he'll have more money for next time," I said, trying to sound supportive. Karen flopped down on the bed next to me.

"If there is a next time," she said. Her voice was flat and dejected, as if no one in the world knew or cared how she felt. I wanted to put my hand on her face, skin so sheer that you could see the blue veins pulsing at her temples. Or touch her arm, covered with pale fine hair like the blow-ball of a dandelion. But I didn't feel like I knew her well enough.

"Why don't you and I go to the movies?" I said. "I don't have to work tonight and Funny Face is playing." I waited. I couldn't read her expression. "Audrey Hepburn is in it," I added, hoping that might make a difference. "Come on, it'll be fun."

Seated in the top row of the balcony, well away from the other moviegoers, Karen and I were engrossed in the film when all of sudden, she jerked my arm, causing me to spill my popcorn all over my lap.

"Look who just walked in," she hissed. Brushing kernels onto the floor, I squinted in the dark. A couple was climbing the stairs, holding hands.

"It's Mike," Karen said.

"No," I whispered.

Karen leaned forward in her seat to get a better look. "And he's with Sheila."

"What an asshole!" I exclaimed. "What a dickhead, jerk-off, asshole!" My hand rushed to cover my mouth. It was too late. Somebody shushed me. I slid down in my seat.

Karen looked back at me in surprise. Her cheeks puffed out, and she burst out laughing. When she caught her breath, she said, "Liz, I've never heard you talk like that before. You've been spending too much time with Gidge."

"Well, he deserves it," I said. If I were a guy, I would have marched right down there and punched him out.

"You're right. He deserves it. Let's get out of here." Heads held high, we stomped down the stairs, through the lobby and out of the double doors of the theater.

Around the corner at Mr. B's Fountain, we had just ordered two Cokes when Karen said, "How dare he stand me up and then take out his old girlfriend. Who does he think he is, anyway?"

"Who does he think he is?" I echoed. I didn't even know the guy, and I hated his guts.

Karen rubbed her hands together. "I read about this prank once where you fill a paper bag with dog poop and put it on someone's front porch, and then you light it and ring the doorbell." I stared at Karen in shock. Talk about spending too much time with Gidge. This one had her fingerprints all over it.

"Then what happens?" I asked, my eyes wide in anticipation.

"You'll see." She leaned toward me and grinned wickedly. A co-conspirator grin. A we-are-in-this-together-now grin.

We agreed to rendezvous at my house after school the following Monday. My father was at work and my mother ran her errands on Mondays, so we had the place to ourselves.

Armed with a rusty sand pail and shovel I found in my garage, we wandered the neighborhood in search of the perfect pile of dog crap. Based on research of the specimens we found, we selected the Wallace's cocker spaniel, Dexter, as our accomplice. He belonged to the old couple next door and was allowed to roam freely, pooping his way around the neighborhood. After nailing down the details of our plan, we were ready to go.

Just before dusk, Karen and I set off on our walk across town, me carrying the brown paper bag at arm's length trying not to inhale, and Karen clutching a big box of kitchen matches.

The town of Parkerville may have been less than thirty miles from San Francisco, but peace and stillness reigned over all. Our journey took us down streets of clapboard houses with white picket fences and tidy yards. Birds twittered and flitted in the trees and bushes. In the vacant lot on the corner where the neighborhood boys played baseball, two men, their voices carrying in the quiet, watched over a small fire that burned away a pile of dry brush.

As I walked alongside Karen, I felt as though there were two of me. One was yesterday's Elizabeth Reilly, the timid daughter of battling parents, living in a state of dread, afraid to speak out. The other was today's Liz, a confident fun-loving girl who enjoyed adventure.

We turned the corner of Maple Avenue and spotted Mike's 1950 Chevy coupe parked proudly in the circular driveway, near the front steps. As the last rays of sunlight filtered through the two big Chinese Elm trees in Mike's front yard, we stormed the front porch like a couple of infantrymen from a World War II movie. In rapid succession, I dropped the bag, Karen lit it, and I rang the doorbell. Then we shot across the street and crouched low behind a three-foot hedge, craning our necks around the end of the thick greenery to get a clear view. Hanging on to each other for balance, we watched as the sack of shit blazed on the front porch. Slowly, the front door opened, and a hand pushed the screen door back. Karen squeezed my arm so hard it brought tears to my eyes. Still dressed in his uniform, Mr. Leary, the town's fire chief, jumped forward with both feet and came down full force on the flaming bag. Behind him, I could see Mike, just inside the doorway. Shit flew everywhere, all over Chief Leary and down the front of Mike's white T-shirt.

"Goddamned, son of a bitch!" Chief Leary yelled at the top of his lungs. Karen and I laughed so hard, we both peed our pants.

At that moment, time separated into before-Karen and after-Karen; and nothing could ever be the same.

# CHAPTER NINETEEN

## *March 23, 2000*

Impatient for company, I dressed quickly and tiptoed out of the bedroom and into the loft. Tufts of Gidge's red hair were sticking out from under the mound of covers on the twin bed nearest the railing. She was whistling through her nose in an unflattering fashion, proof that she was still sound asleep.

As I reached the bottom of the stairs, I was surprised to see the light on in the kitchen.

"Hey, Rosie, you're up early," I said, grateful for someone to talk to.

"I couldn't sleep. I'm going out for a run," she replied, propping her foot up on the barstool and tying her shoe. She showed no signs of a hangover from the brandy.

"Thanks for making the coffee," I said, noticing the pot on the counter.

Rosie looked like she was ready for the Olympics in her navy and white running suit, her gravity-defying, frizzy curls now sprinkled with gray, pulled back in a ponytail low on her neck. You'd think after all her years in the sun, she'd look like the American Cancer Society's poster child for skin cancer. But her olive-colored skin was as supple and unblemished as ever. No one would guess her to be much over forty, let alone the grandmother of a sixteen-year-old.

"So, when's your next marathon, Rose?" I asked, pouring myself a cup of coffee.

"Oh, I don't have anything planned now until summer. I'm doing a 10K charity thing next month for Breast Cancer, but no big races for a while."

Listening to Rosie made me want to turn in my comfy loafers for a pair of Rollerblades. But my prickly resistance to any form of exercise that made you sweat held me back. Outside of lovemaking, the closest I ever came to sweating was wrestling a sheet of paper out of my laser printer.

"You're a marvel, you know?" I gave Rosie's ponytail a playful tug as I passed behind her, like I used to when we were in high school. Never much good at accepting compliments, color swarmed to Rose's face.

I admired Rosie's open-armed approach to life. Unlike me, she wasn't afraid to try new things. On her fiftieth birthday, she celebrated by parachuting out of an airplane. I celebrated mine with a day at the spa.

"I tried to get Karen to run with me," Rosie said, bending from side to side with her hands on her hips. "Even told her we could go later in the morning 'cause I knew how she hated to get up early." Rosie enjoyed being fit. Karen exercised in hopes of recapturing the sheen of youth. "But she wasn't interested. She preferred aerobics and classes at the gym." Rosie pulled her forehead to her knees. The St. Christopher's medal she wore around her neck swung over her head.

"Oh God, remember when she got all of us to go to Linda Evans for the free visit when they first opened?" I asked, starting to smile at the memory.

"Was that the time Gidge let out that giant fart on the treadmill?" Rosie asked, her shoulders raised in pre-giggle anticipation.

"Yes! I can still hear Gidge. 'Nobody listens until you fart.'"

"Karen was so mad," Rosie said, laughing. "She told Gidge that thanks to her, she could never go back there." I loved Rosie's laugh, high-pitched and contagious, like a child being tickled. It felt so good to laugh. Karen used to say that it was like jogging on the inside.

Rosie shook her head. "I'm sure going to miss her," she said with a sigh, pulling on her mittens. I nodded, knowing that if I spoke I would surely fall apart.

"Well, I'm off. See you in a while." She bounded down the hall and out the front door like a superhero on call.

I walked over and sat down at the dining room table. In the face of death, we were good at creating a diversion by telling old stories, keeping our memories alive, keeping Karen alive.

My thoughts turned to the medal Rosie wore around her neck. Raised by deeply religious parents, Rosie had sloughed off the trappings of her Catholic background—weekly confessions and daily guilt—while retaining some semblance of what might be described as Christian kindness. Unlike most of us, she had no gripes about her life, and you'd be hard pressed to find anyone who didn't like or admire her.

A toilet flushed upstairs. Jo appeared wearing a long black-watch plaid flannel nightshirt and thick white socks, her cell phone in hand.

"Good morning," I called from the darkened dining room.

"Shit, you scared me," she replied, slapping her free hand to her chest. "What are you doing sitting there in the dark?" she asked, walking over to the coffeepot. She laid the phone down on the counter and picked up a cup.

"I couldn't sleep."

"I know what you mean. I doubt any of us will have a normal night's sleep for a while." She poured herself some coffee. Like me, Jo was nothing without her morning coffee.

"I know Karen's probably got some Halcion around here," she said. Karen was the queen of prescription drugs. She could always be relied upon to supply whatever we needed to treat everything from depression to a bladder infection.

Jo sat down next to me. "That stuff gives me a hangover," I said.

"I only use it for emergencies. This certainly qualifies."

We sat there, quietly sipping our coffee. I studied Jo's small, delicate face, elegantly etched cheekbones, slightly severe mouth. It occurred to me that hers was a face like Rosie's, which looked best unadorned.

"It must have been quite a shock, being laid off like that," Jo said out of the blue.

I looked her in the eye. "You have no idea."

"What's your plan?" she asked over the top of her cup.

I harrumphed and looked down at my stockinged feet. "Work is all I know how to do. I'm not much good at anything else." I wiggled my toes.

"That's not true." I turned back to look at her. "You're good at being a friend," she said with great conviction. I blinked. "Are you forgetting that you and Karen saved my life?"

As a teenager, Jo's boyfriend Jess Alvarez was a soft-spoken boy with a gentle manner who was enthralled by cars and preferred them to people. But after they were married, he grew into a dominating man who drew sustenance and strength out of controlling his wife. Each year he became more possessive, insisting on knowing where she was every minute.

In the late eighties, once again single, Karen was working as a waitress at an upscale restaurant, not for the money which she didn't need, but because she still believed that happiness came in pairs, and she thought it might be a good place to meet her next husband. She got Jo a part-time job as a hostess for a few hours each weekend, which was all Jess would allow.

Arlene and I decided to surprise them by showing up for lunch one Saturday. Jo had a real shiner, one that couldn't be hidden even by the heavy pancake make-up she had carefully applied. This wasn't the first time I'd seen marks somewhere on her body. An occasional bruise appeared here and there, and once I commented on a nasty scratch on her neck that she claimed she got from her neighbor's cat.

"Hey, Jo, what happened to your eye?" I asked, standing in front of the hostess station.

"Oh, it's nothing," she answered. She turned away quickly to show us to a table in Karen's section.

Once Arlene and I were alone, I hissed, "That son of a bitch! You know he hit her."

"I know, but it's happened before and she hasn't done anything about it." Arlene's response touched off memories of my Aunt Vi's brief marriage to an abusive man who used her as a punching bag. I remembered my mother sitting next to my aunt's hospital bed, holding her hand and crying, and me at age eight standing in the corner, watching. I wanted her to do something, say something, tell Aunt Vi that she could come and live with us. I wanted her to rescue her sister. But she just sat there, sniveling like a baby, and I hated her.

"All the more reason we should do something about it." I felt my face heat up. "If he keeps beatin' on her, we could lose her altogether." I turned away from Arlene in disgust.

Karen came over to take our order, sporting a star-wattage smile. "What a nice surprise," she said.

"What's with Jo's eye?" I asked.

"Scoot over," Karen said, her expression quickly changing to a frown. She looked to assess Jo's whereabouts before sliding into the booth.

"I think we ought to confront her," I said in a loud whisper.

"I agree," Karen said. "I think if we do it together, she might listen." I looked over at Arlene, who shrugged her shoulders. I made a disapproving clicking sound with my tongue.

"Jo and I usually have a bite together when the restaurant closes after lunch." Karen said. "Can you guys stay?"

"Of course," I answered, not waiting for Arlene.

An hour later, Karen took the lead. "I've been meaning to ask what happened to your eye, Jo?" she asked with a voice full of warmth. The four of us were jammed into a dark, secluded booth for two. The only light came from the thin crack under the front door and the flickering candle on the table.

Jo lowered her head. No one spoke. It was only when Jo sniffed that I realized she was crying.

"Remember, no secrets," I said. We waited. It didn't take long.

"Okay, he hit me," she said in a little voice that sounded nothing like her.

"Why?" Karen asked softly, putting her hand gently on Jo's arm.

"Oh, I pissed him off, I guess," she said into her lap. "It's hard to make things stop once they're out of control. It's as much my fault as it is his."

"Don't say that, Jo," I said. My throat felt dry and stiff.

"You get used to it," Jo said. She sounded like some pathetic victim on a television talk show. But this was my friend; the feisty teenager who had once locked her sisters outside in their underwear.

"What did you say to him before he hit you, Jo?" Karen asked.

A single tear slid down the side of Jo's nose before she answered. "I asked him if I could go to the lake for your birthday next month."

Karen cocked her head. "You asked him if you could go to the lake and he hit you?"

"No, not right away." Jo blotted her face with the back of her hand.

"When?" I asked, trying to keep the emotion out of my voice. Even in the dim light, the bruise under her eye was clearly visible. It looked painful.

"He asked how come I'd rather spend time with you guys than him. 'It's always the girls; the girls this, and the girls that,' he said."

"And what did you say?" I asked.

"I said because they're not mean to me like you are, you motherfucker." Karen's hand flew to her mouth. Arlene, who had been sipping her wine, choked and sputtered.

"You called him a motherfucker?" I said. I so wanted to believe that the old Jo was back; the one who could stand up for herself.

"And it felt so good!" Jo said. She smiled and winced with pain. There was a long moment of shocked silence, and then Arlene erupted in laughter. She laughed so long that Jo started laughing, too. Karen and I joined in. We laughed together for a long time. So long that my ribs began to hurt.

"Seriously Jo, you need to get out of there," Karen said, when she had gathered herself together. "You can move in with me."

"Oh, I don't know, Karen." Jo's face was once again serious.

"Look, you've been talking about getting your real estate license. You can stay with me and study for it." Karen was determined to make this happen. "You don't even have to pay rent."

"Sounds like a great offer," Arlene said, wiping wine off her chin.

I asked Jo point-blank if she loved Jess.

"I...I don't know anymore," she admitted.

"Then it's settled," Karen said.

The next day while Jess was at work, with Rosie and Gidge's help, we moved Jo and her personal belongings into Karen's house. First, there was a flurry of late-night phone calls from Jess pleading with Jo to come back; things would be different, he would change. When Jo refused, he showed up in person, beating on Karen's front door.

"Go away. She doesn't want to talk to you," Karen yelled through the door. She paced in a tight circle, her head down, hands on her hips. I'd dropped by on my way home from work and was sitting next to Jo on the couch, my arm wrapped tightly around her narrow shoulders. He banged harder; so hard that I was sure the door would come off of its hinges.

"Maybe I should talk to him," Jo said, her voice straining as she tried to keep it even and light.

"No way," I said shaking her gently. The pounding stopped. Jo and I sat statue-still, neither of us breathing. Maybe he'd left? Several moments passed.

"Goddamn it. Let me in!" Jess yelled. He sounded drunk. There was a loud crash, as if he had thrown something heavy at the door. Jo and I both flinched.

"That's it," Karen said, throwing her hands in the air. "I'm calling the police."

"Tomorrow we go for that restraining order we talked about," I said, picturing how poor Aunt Vi looked that day in the hospital. I couldn't let that happen to my friend.

The poster clock ticked softly, as Jo and I sat together remembering. "Karen told me it was you who instigated the intervention, that it was your idea to speak up." Jo turned to me with grateful eyes. I smiled wanly, not knowing how to take credit for simply doing the right thing. "If you guys hadn't moved me out, I would have stayed with Jess and one day, he probably would have killed me," Jo said matter-of-factly.

"Oh no, Jo, I can't believe that you would have stayed in that abusive relationship." I wanted to be reassured.

"Don't be too sure," she replied, pulling her knees up under her nightgown. "Oh, I know it was abusive, but financially it was easier than being out on my own." A painful admission that could only be made by a woman who had done a lot of self-reflection and moved on. Jo ran her finger around the rim of her cup. "Anyway, I don't think I ever properly thanked you."

"You're welcome," I said.

Knowing that I had helped Jo was comforting; that together, Karen and I had made a difference in her life. An image of Karen popped into my head, a megawatt smile spreading across her face.

# CHAPTER TWENTY

## *March 23, 2000*

"A person sure can't get much sleep around here with all this noise," Gidge said, padding past us in bare feet and flopping down on the couch. "What time is it anyway?"

I glanced at the poster clock. "5:30."

"We used to come home at 5:30, not get up at this time." Gidge yawned and lifted her short legs up onto the coffee table. "What are you guys talking about?"

"Husbands," Jo replied, moving to the living room to sit next to Gidge.

"Now there's a pathetic topic."

"Hey, you never told us what it was like seeing Johnny at Joey's wedding after all these years," I said, coming closer. "How did he look?"

"You wouldn't believe how handsome he still is, the son of a bitch."

"No," Jo said, curling her legs up under her in anticipation of some high-octane women talk.

"Yeah. His hair is a beautiful silver gray and he hasn't gained an ounce."

Gidge scratched the top of her head, causing her hair to stand straight up like the top of a pineapple.

"God, that divorce was one of the worst," I said, shaking my head. "I almost got a hernia pushing you through the window into his apartment."

"I can't believe she talked me into driving, while she bombed his brand new Corvette with eggs," Jo said.

"You? I can't believe I stood there and watched her cut off one sleeve of every shirt, jacket, and sweater he owned. And then, she cut off the right leg of every pair of pants. All those beautiful, expensive clothes." I clucked my tongue.

Gidge let out a snort. "I was good, wasn't I?"

"She took forever," I said, ignoring her comment. "I kept saying, 'Come on, Gidge, we've gotta get out of here,' but she was like a woman possessed, gathering all the remnants in a plastic garbage bag, and then carefully rehanging each mutilated garment."

Sneering, Gidge said, "The prospect of the look on Johnny's face when he pulled out his best suit spurred me on."

Jo rolled her eyes.

"It was the only real pleasure I got out of the whole ugly mess," Gidge said defensively.

"What about the generous amount of child support and alimony you got?" Jo asked. Her voice rose with indignation. "All I got was a bunch of bills when I left Jess."

"Oh, quit bitching," Gidge said, slapping Jo's leg. "You've got more money than you know what to do with now."

"Humph," Jo replied, backing off reluctantly. She resented life made easier by ex-husbands.

"You know what was interesting?" Gidge asked, rubbing sleep from her eyes. "When I saw him at the wedding, I felt nothing." I wondered if I would feel nothing if Ricky walked into the room. I doubted it.

"Really?" Jo asked, arching one permanently tattooed eyebrow. "That's hard to believe."

"I think I went through so many emotions during that divorce, I just used them all up."

"I never understood why you and Harry couldn't make it work," Jo said. Harry Krupman doted on Gidge, referring to her as his "little firecracker." She called him "her Kroutman." They teased each other incessantly, each giving as good as they got until the teasing got nasty. Hence the stitches in Harry's head.

"I just got too old for that shit," Gidge said with a sigh.

"You should award medals for bravery to the men you marry," I said. "Cutting up their clothes and hitting them over the head." I swatted her on the leg.

"At least I didn't give up on marriage," Gidge said, giving me a sideways glance.

I considered spouting some snappy retort, but I decided to let it go.

The front door opened.

"It must be Wonder Woman," Gidge said, gesturing with her chin and smirking, as if to say by spending her life jogging, Rosie was only pretending she wasn't going to die someday like the rest of us.

Rosie sprinted into the room.

"Phew. It's really cold outside," she said, unzipping her parka. Her cheeks were the color of apples. "Why is everyone up?"

"I'm not," Gidge said, falling over into Jo's lap and closing her eyes.

"You guys are really loud, you know," Arlene called down from the loft.

"Sorry," I yelled up. "Come join us." Jo went to get the coffee pot, and refilled our cups.

"What's going on?" Arlene asked, slumping into a chair.

"Oh, we were just reminiscing about husbands," I answered.

"Speaking of husbands, I wonder if Dale will come to the service?" Arlene said, referring to Karen's last husband, a red-meat-chomping man who wore hand-tooled alligator cowboy boots to make him taller. "I know he still lives somewhere around here."

"Asshole," Gidge said without opening her eyes.

"You think every man's an asshole," Arlene sniped. She pulled her robe closer around her body. "I thought he was a really nice guy. He was so good to her, buying her that huge diamond ring and taking her on the Orient Express. And then, she had the nerve to criticize his lovemaking after their divorce."

Arlene pretended to resent Karen's disrespect for her ex-husband. But she knew better than any of us that Karen used humor not as a weapon, but as a parachute.

"She used to say having sex with him was like going to a taffy pull," I said.

Jo let out a laugh. "Karen could be so devilishly cruel," she said.

Gidge pushed herself up onto her elbow. "Look, what Karen needed was a man who was smart and witty, someone who would treat her as an equal instead of a trophy. And Dale wasn't it." She fell back into Jo's lap. "That man was so dumb, he needed instructions to put on a hat."

"Gidge, that's mean," Rosie scolded.

We fell silent for a while. I picked up my coffee cup and looked out the window at the lake. Dawn was beginning to lighten the water. Through the gaps in the trees, I could see gentle waves sucking at the rocks. Gidge's description of the type of man Karen needed reminded me of Sam. Smart. Witty. Someone who treated me as an equal. He wanted us to go to New York as partners, he'd said. Throughout our relationship, we'd always been partners. We'd complain to and console each other, share our hopes and dreams. Many a Sunday morning, I'd lie with my ear on his chest, and listen to him talk. I'd lift my face to look at him and he'd smile. Then he'd duck his head to kiss me on the mouth.

It's curious how myopic I had become over the years about our relationship. We'd been together so long, I had deluded myself into thinking it would last forever. Just like my job. Just like Karen.

"I think Karen was just trying to deal with her feelings of abandonment," Rosie said, breaking our silence. Heads turned. Just when you thought Rosie was the Pollyanna of Parkerville, she'd say something so right on you'd think she was the Dalai Lama.

"Maybe you're right, Rose," Jo said. "When we were living together, I talked her into trying my therapist, but when the questions got too deep, she stopped going."

"Maybe she wasn't ready to work on herself?" I said, recognizing a lot of myself in my comment. "It's so much easier to blame others."

"Especially in Karen's case, with her father leaving her at such a young age," Jo said.

"Ah, yes, daddies," Arlene said with a sigh. I knew she was thinking about her own sorry father, an alcoholic who spent his days sitting in the dark, staring into a bottomless glass.

My thoughts snapped back to the stark white hospital waiting room, where my mother and I sat together, while my father lay dying down the hall. One week after my fiftieth birthday, he'd had a stroke that left him paralyzed and in a coma. The doctor said it was only a matter of time.

In shifts, Aunt Vi and I exhausted every trivial topic of conversation we could think of, trying to distract her from thinking about him. Wrung out from the waiting, I felt as stale as a week-old donut.

"I threatened to divorce him, you know," my mother said, her eyes fixed on the television set that hung from a metal bracket in the ceiling, her words empty of any emotion. Aunt Vi looked up from her magazine.

"What?" I asked, stunned to attention. My throat was dry from too much coffee, and the word came out like a screech.

"That time when you wanted to go to Tahoe with your friends."

I shook my head in confusion. "What are you talking about, Ma?" Lately, there were times when she didn't make much sense.

"In high school," she said. The images on the television screen were reflected in her bifocals. "He knew I meant business." I searched her still-pretty face, now lined with worry. "I told him he may have crushed my spirit, but I wasn't going to let him crush yours," she said flatly.

I took her frail hand in mine. I held it for a long time, not speaking. We both looked at the television, as if for help.

"I'm going to go check on him," my mother finally said, lifting her body with great effort. She shuffled out of the room, her once straight shoulders now rounded with age.

"It's true," Aunt Vi said from across the room. Like a robot, my head turned to look at her. In the gritty light she looked much older than she did in the shadows of her apartment, her cheeks traced with a web of wrinkles. "She gave him an ultimatum and your father backed down."

"Well, we've got a lot to do if we're going to have this service in two days," Arlene said getting up from her chair. "Where's the phone book?"

"I wonder if Karen has a copy of her will around here some place?" I said, rising to follow Arlene. "I'd love to see if Greg is mentioned in it."

# CHAPTER TWENTY-ONE

*March 23, 2000*

G idge and Jo selected the "Little Chapel of the Pasture," a small non-denominational church just outside of Tahoe City for the service, which luckily was available on such short notice. When Arlene called the Coroner's Office to tell them of the arrangements, they requested that someone come down to claim Karen's personal effects. They also recommended a crematorium and suggested she contact them immediately to arrange for the transfer of the body. The Body. That word. Every time I heard it, I shuddered.

Arlene called the crematorium and promised to hand deliver a check to ensure the "cremains" would be ready in time for the service.

"They're going to try to sell you an urn," Rose informed us. We were once again gathered around the dining room table. "When my mother-in-law died, they guilted Jay's dad into spending over $500 on a brass urn."

"We're going to scatter her ashes on the lake. What the hell do we need an urn for?" Gidge wanted to know.

"Karen would have a fit if we spent $500 on a stupid urn," Jo said, sounding annoyed.

I raised a finger. "Why don't we ask them to use the Treasures of Truth chest?" I asked, referring to the brass box where Karen kept special photographs and letters, mementoes of her past. Originally filled with candy hearts, the decorative container was a Valentine's Day gift from her father when she was a child.

"Karen would like that," Rosie agreed. "But you'd better take it down there and ask to be sure it's big enough. There are a lot of ashes, and they're very heavy."

Arlene sat up straight. "Really?"

"Yeah, it's amazing how heavy they are," Rose answered. "I was horrified. There are pieces of bone and teeth."

Arlene and I pulled into the morgue parking lot, and I killed the engine. Fear clutched at my stomach. The neighborhood was bleak, mostly low industrial buildings. I sat and stared at the sterile-looking building we were about to enter with its light green corrugated metal siding and single door with a small, square window in it. On the window, I could see cheap decal letters that read, "City Morgue."

"God, is this it?" I asked, expecting something more official looking.

"This is the address they gave me," Arlene said, checking the scrap of paper in her hand.

"But there aren't any cars here. Maybe they all went to lunch. Maybe we should come back later." The urge to run was almost overpowering.

"Now, Liz, you know we have an appointment. There must be an employee parking lot in the back or something," Arlene said in a motherly tone.

"Here, I brought a little something to give us courage." She reached over the back of the seat and lifted up a tote bag. Placing it carefully on her lap, she unzipped the top and produced a tall thermos and two Styrofoam cups.

"What's this?" I asked.

"I thought we could use some hot brandy." Arlene filled a cup with steaming liquid and handed it to me. The aroma brought back fond memories of our old skiing days. I blew into the cup and took a sip. It burned all the way down, just like I remembered.

"Do you think Greg had something to do with Karen's death?" I asked. I could tell by the look on Arlene's face that she wasn't prepared for my question. "It's just that this whole accident thing doesn't add up," I said.

"You've been under a lot of stress lately, Liz," Arlene said. I didn't deny this. "Don't start playing detective. Leave that to the police."

"I will," I said. Except I wasn't willing to wait for the outcome of the police investigation, which could take weeks. I'd called Greg and arranged to meet him.

We sat quietly, sipping our drinks. I glanced over at Arlene's comfy, cushioned lap; soft, welcoming thighs inviting me to lay my head down, close my eyes and go to sleep. Ah, sweet blissful dream-free sleep. I'd forgotten what it felt like.

I drained my cup too quickly and offered it up for more.

"What time is it?" I asked, wishing time would stop.

Arlene checked her watch. "We're late," she snapped. "Let's just go in and get this over with." She snatched the empty cup from my hand and dropped it back in the bag with hers. As she picked up the thermos, I reached for her wrist.

"Arlene," I gulped.

"What?"

"I just want you to know that I love you," I blurted out. I may not have had the courage to tell Karen, but I sure wasn't going to let another opportunity pass me by.

"Oh, that's just the booze talking," she assured me. "Come on, let's do this so we can get out of here."

I stepped out of the sanctuary of the car, feeling as though we were headed toward certain doom. My pulse quickened as I imagined Karen's body lying lifeless inside.

The sky was clear except for a few high windswept clouds that looked like someone had run a comb through them. The way the sun was reflecting off the asphalt, it gave the illusion of thousands of stars scattered on the ground; a sight much too lovely for a place like this.

Behind the front door was a small waiting area. The moment I stepped inside, I wanted to leave. At one end of the room was a counter with a sliding glass panel above it. Arlene took charge by walking directly to the counter and rapping on the glass. I scurried over to one of the metal folding chairs. The seat was so cold it made my butt cheeks clamp together.

Suddenly, everything seemed infused with death. Think of something else, something funny. That's what Karen would do.

I glanced over at the dog-eared magazines on the table next to my chair. What kind of magazines would be appropriate for a place like this? "Do-it-Yourself Autopsies" or maybe "The Latest Trends in Body Bags." Tickled at the thought, I felt ready to laugh. Arlene dropped into the chair next to me.

"What did she say?" I asked, hiding my smile behind my hand. A familiar tingling sensation played at my lips, the first signs of inebriation.

"Someone will be right with us."

"Good," I replied, shifting in my seat. I could feel my face getting hot, as if all the blood from my body was gathering in my head. How much brandy could one of those little cups hold, anyway? Two shots maybe? Three? Four?

"Phew! It's really hot in here, isn't it?" I said, unzipping my parka and fanning myself with the sides.

"No, it's actually freezing in here," Arlene said, looking at me suspiciously. "Are your lips going numb?" She'd known me too long.

"No, I'm fine, thank you very much," I said, sputtering and turning away. Please God! Don't let me have a laughing fit.

Just then, the glass slid back to reveal a Latin-looking woman in a white uniform. "Dr. Demiter will see you now. His office is down the hall, first door on your right." Her voice was cold and insensitive. Maybe that was the only way she could stand having such a horrible job. What kind of person could work in a morgue?

She shut the glass with a clang.

Arlene got up and walked across the room. "Come on, Liz," she said, holding the inside door open.

"Isn't she going to show us the way?" I said in a stage whisper. "What if we make a wrong turn and go into where the bodies are?" Slowly, I stood up.

"Elizabeth Ann, Goddamn it!" Arlene hissed. I took baby steps across the green asphalt tile floor. Arlene reached out, grabbed my upper arm, and yanked me into the hallway. "Pull yourself together," she warned.

Almost immediately, I was aware of an odor, the faint whiff of a chemical I had smelled before. My nostrils pinched. I was five years old again, in Dr. Sattler's office, about to have my tonsils out. The nurse was holding something over my face that smelled sickeningly sweet, and the doctor was asking me to count backwards from 100. 99, 98, 95, 70…

I came to lying on a scratchy couch with Arlene and a strange man leaning over me. Their faces were huge and misshapen like those pictures taken with a "fish-eye" lens. They were talking to me, asking me something, but I couldn't make out what it was.

As my head cleared, I heard Arlene say, "She's white as a ghost!" I could tell by the tone of her voice that she was worried.

The man, who was standing very close to her said, "She'll be fine." He stuck something under my nose.

"Holy shit!" I yelled, bolting upright. They both jumped backwards. "What the hell is that?" I was immediately embarrassed.

"It's ammonium carbonate, dear. Smelling salts," the man said with a smile that showed corn-kernel-yellow teeth. Karen would have joked that this guy could really benefit from a Vanna White Tooth Whitening Kit. "I'll get her some water," he said, smiling at Arlene. He turned and left.

"Liz, are you okay?" Arlene asked, sitting down next to me, and putting her arm around my shoulders.

"What happened? Did I faint?" I asked, rubbing my forehead with my fingertips. "It must have been that brandy and then that smell. God, did you smell that horrible smell?" I searched Arlene's face.

"What smell?" She raised a quizzical eyebrow at me. "I didn't smell anything."

The man reappeared holding a paper cup.

"Here, my dear, drink this, and you'll feel better." I took a tentative sip. It was water; nice cold water, and it tasted good. "There, that's better. The color has come back to your face." He lifted my chin and looked into my eyes. Apparently satisfied with what he saw, he turned and walked to a chair behind a desk. I noticed his navy blue slacks were worn in the seat and his dress shirt had a frayed collar.

"Now then, Ms. Shoren, if you'll just take a seat here." Arlene followed his instruction. "As I mentioned to you on the phone, I have all of the deceased's personal effects here along with the necessary copies of the death certificate that you will need." He patted a plastic bag on top of his desk next to a nameplate that read Dr. Maurice Demiter, County Coroner.

"Do either of you ladies have any questions for me?" he asked, not taking his eyes off Arlene.

"I can't think of anything right now, Dr. Demiter," Arlene said in a low sultry voice.

"Maury, please call me Maury," he oozed, leaning forward and reaching both arms across the desk. What the hell is he doing? Is he going to kiss her? I sat on the couch, slack-jawed, watching.

"Here's my card. Please, if you should think of anything, anything at all you'd like to ask, call me at this number, day or night. My service can always reach me."

Christ! The coroner is hitting on Arlene. I wondered if Karen could see them. An involuntary snort came out of my nose. Neither the good doctor nor Arlene seemed to notice.

"Now, Ms. Shoren, I'll need your signature right here, please." He pushed a clipboard across the desk, and pointed a pen in her direction. Arlene signed and got up from her chair.

"Well, we must be going," she said, extending her hand toward her new fan. "Thank you so much for everything." Her voice had an unnatural breathiness. I watched them shake hands for what seemed like a full minute.

"It was nice meeting you, Ms. Shoren," he said. This time he emphasized "Ms." He must have asked her if she was married. "Oh, and you, too, Ms. Aaaaa," he added as an afterthought, looking over at me while still holding Arlene's hand in both of his.

"Hayden, Ms. Hayden," I acknowledged, giving him a sour look. Arlene picked up the bag and glided toward the door, where she did a kind of half pivot before opening it. Standing there with her pelvis thrust forward, she looked like a model with hemorrhoids.

"Shall we go, Elizabeth?" she cooed, smiling and holding the door open. When I made no move to get up, her eyes ballooned in size, and she made an almost imperceptible gesture with her head that signaled we were supposed to leave.

Carefully placing my empty cup on the table, I grabbed the arm of the sofa and hoisted myself up. For a moment, I felt dizzy. The doctor remained standing behind his desk, grinning in Arlene's direction. Probably afraid I would see what had popped up below his belt.

Still a little woozy, I made my way past Arlene and into the hallway.

"Goodbye," Arlene swooned, closing the door.

Once outside, the fresh air cleared my head quickly. The sun was shining so brightly, it made my eyes ache. Painfully aware of the plastic bag full of Karen's things lying on the back seat, I pulled out onto the main road. I could smell the faint aroma of chemicals emanating from it.

As we drove in silence, I replayed the scene in the coroner's office in my head. So what if he'd started it? Arlene didn't have to respond. That stupid expression she got on her face, looking out from under hooded eyes. Had she forgotten that our friend's body was lying dead, just across the hall? Did she even care?

Anger began to swell in my stomach. Did Arlene have any moral guidelines? Was anybody out of bounds?

Glancing in her direction, I felt a flash of raw indefensible hatred toward her. I slammed on the brakes, jerked the wheel and swerved off the road into a clearing causing Arlene to lurch forward and grab for the dash to keep from being thrown off the seat.

"Jesus Christ!" she shouted, as the van bounced from side to side over some deep ruts before coming to a stop just short of a guardrail. I threw the gearshift into Park.

"Are you on some kind of medication I should know about?" I yelled, resisting the urge to lunge at her, to wrap my hands around her turkey-like neck and throttle her. "Because if I didn't know better, I'd think you didn't give a shit about losing Karen." My rage found its target. I uncoiled like a cobra. "What was that back there?" I asked, jabbing at the air behind me with my thumb.

"I don't know what you're talking about," Arlene replied, feigning innocence.

"You forget, sister. I've seen you at work for years. Whenever there's a man in the room, you zoom in like a fly to shit!" My head felt like it was about to explode.

Arlene's face began to contort into something out of a horror movie. "Shut up!" she yelled at the top of her lungs. "Shut up! Shut up!" A large blue vein popped out on her forehead.

"No, I won't shut up," I screamed back. I wanted her to break down, to completely fall apart. "You haven't shed one lousy tear for Karen." I wanted her to hurt like I did. "You're more interested in seducing the coroner." There. I'd said it. And I was glad.

Arlene's dark eyes narrowed into slits. "How dare you," she growled. "You don't know anything about my feelings for Karen." Red-faced and enraged, the words shot out of her mouth like carefully aimed arrows. "You don't know how much I loved her, what she meant to me." She leaned in close to me; so close that I could see the pores in her not-so-smooth skin. "Do you have any idea what it's like to have your last memory of someone be a stupid fight?" I recoiled at her words. "In an instant, to say something that will give you heartache for the rest of your life? And you can't do a damn thing to change it!" She paused. "Just because I'm not a whimpering basket case like Rosie, or a Little Miss Weakling who faints at the drop of a hat like you, doesn't mean I don't have any feelings!" Her eyes burned into mine. "How dare you judge me," she snarled. For a minute, I thought she was going to hit me.

"I have every right to judge you," I barked back at her. "My best friend is lying dead back there." I wasn't going to let her talk herself out of this one. "We need to talk about this right now," I demanded, stabbing my finger downward.

I sat poised like a Rottweiler sizing up the mailman. After what seemed like eons, Arlene's shoulders dropped in a sign of defeat, and she let out a long sigh.

"I can't," she said softly, turning to look out the side window.

"You will," I said grabbing her arm. She snatched it away, and wouldn't look at me. I waited. I would wait for as long as it took.

"I made a mistake by telling her," Arlene said, still turned away from me.

"Telling her what?"

"We were on the phone, and she was doing her fantasizing about how wonderful Casey was and how she should have stayed married to him. For years, I've listened to what a devoted father he was, and what a great lover he was. I was just sick of hearing it." Arlene shook her head once, hard. "So I told her." My stomach jumped, afraid of what was coming. "I mean what difference could it make after almost forty years?"

Arlene looked me in the eye. And I knew.

"You slept with Casey?" I asked, hoping I was wrong. Arlene turned away at my words.

She let out a puff of air. "I don't know what the big deal was. It was after they'd separated," she said. "Besides, sex is just two people jerking off together."

Shock closed my throat. How could she make sex sound so meaningless?

I slumped back against the car door.

# CHAPTER TWENTY-TWO

*March 23, 2000*

Anger and frustration rode with me all the way back to the house. Neither of us spoke. To think, just moments earlier I'd told Arlene I loved her. Now, I could barely control the urge to reach across, open the door, and push her out.

I tightened my grip on the steering wheel. Arlene was a woman who always followed her instincts, high and low. But this was beneath even her.

The pungent aroma of Rosie's minestrone greeted us as we walked into the hall. I inhaled deeply to cleanse my nasal passages of the medicinal odor of the morgue, and center myself. I brushed past Arlene, and opened Karen's bedroom door just enough to slip the plastic bag of her personal belongings through, and drop it on the floor. The others were seated at the dining table, about to eat lunch.

"How did it go?" Jo asked, ladling soup into a bowl for each of us.

"Our friend here fainted," Arlene answered, not daring to look at me. Rosie dropped her spoon at the news.

"I just got a little overwhelmed, that's all," I said. I wanted to say it was nothing compared to how I felt when Arlene disclosed that she'd slept with Casey. I poured myself a splash of wine and gulped it down. Arlene took the chair farthest away from me. Good thing.

We had just begun our meal, when the phone rang. The sound went through me like an electric shock, causing me to jump in my chair. Karen's voice came from the recorder.

"Hey, pilgrim. I'm out roundin' up rustlers right now, but if'n ya leave your handle, any message and how I kin reach ya, I reckon I'll give ya a holler when I get back to the ranch." It was so eerie to hear Karen's voice after she was dead. Goose pimples popped out on my arms.

"Hi Karen, it's Shelby from the gym. I just wanted to call to say we missed you at Pilates, and I hope you'll be there next week. See you then."

I could see a look of yearning in Rosie's eyes. I sensed she wanted to hear it again.

We sat huddled at the table, helpless and struck dumb. Karen's beautiful ghost seemed to be floating above us.

"I'll turn off the recorder," Jo said, rising up from her chair.

I glanced down the table at Arlene. She looked utterly detached, her face set in a stony look. It had been a long time since I'd had such a powerful sensation of disliking her.

I couldn't breathe. I had to get out of there.

I grabbed my jacket, rushed out the front door, down the steps, across the driveway and onto the frontage road, which followed the lake's edge. The sky was cloudless, and the air was so clean it stung the insides of my nose. Snow still sat on the highest branches of the pine trees, although most of it had melted on the ground.

Mimicking Rosie's style, I raised my forearms, my hands in fists, chugging back and forth in front of me, eyes straight ahead, legs and arms pumping rhythmically, my breath coming out in front of me in little puffs.

All of a sudden, I felt the need to run, run hard, away from Karen's voice, away from Arlene's devastating admission, away from Sam, away from all of it. As I fell into the rhythm of running, my heart rate quickened. I tried to focus on nothing but what I was doing. Right, left, right. I was going at a good clip, when I stepped on something that caused my ankle to twist. Ouch! Why is it that Rosie can run hundreds of miles without a single injury, and I go out for ten minutes and get crippled? I bent over to rub my ankle, and when I straightened up, in front of me stood the familiar stand of pine trees that marked the edge of Dave Brenner's old property—the Peterson's neighbor. Cautiously, I took a step on my injured ankle and felt a slight twinge. I hobbled across the street.

The trees had grown considerably and now formed a dense green canopy over the house. The outside had been winterized and looked well taken care of. There were no cars around.

Tucked at the base of the pine-studded slope, a snowball's throw from the house, stood the wooden shed where Dave had stored his boating gear. I limped past the shed and clambered up the boulders strewn along the shore, favoring my sore ankle. I glanced down into the lake, which was as clear as bathtub water. Overhead, the sky was a brilliant aqua-blue, setting off the sharp white edges of the distant mountains, much as it had been that day years ago.

—◈—

"This is Dave, the Dumb Dentist," Gidge said, shading her eyes with her hand.

It was the second day of Gidge's sixteenth birthday weekend and my heart was so light, I thought it might fly right out of my chest. I couldn't stop smiling. My newfound friends and I had just put on our bathing suits and come outside.

"That's his blue and white Chris Craft over there." Gidge signaled with her head toward a boat moored nearby.

Dave was a clean-cut guy who could have been anywhere between twenty and thirty. His sandy-colored hair curled up around his ears, giving him a boyish look, and freckles were spattered across his nose and cheeks, as if someone had flicked a brush full of brown paint in his direction.

"How about taking us water skiing?" Gidge asked, grinning in anticipation. I felt my cheeks redden. She had more nerve than a broken tooth, as Aunt Vi used to say. But Dave didn't seem to mind. He smiled back as if he had expected the request, and when he did, his chapped lips looked like they'd seen the business end of a cheese grater.

Dave asked Karen if she skied, and when she gave him a sun-bright smile and said yes, he scuttled off toward the boat, the soles of his rubber flip-flops making flapping sounds against his heels.

It was obvious from the beginning of our boat ride that Dave was smitten with Karen. He couldn't take his eyes off her. She looked breathtakingly beautiful in her navy and white nautical bathing suit, her sun-blond hair whipping around her face and catching in her Revlon Powder Pink lipstick. Dave almost drooled as he watched her cleavage bounce up and down each time the boat hit a wave.

"What's that place over there?" Karen asked from her perch on the bow of the boat, where she posed like a calendar girl with one knee over the other.

"That's Emerald Bay," Dave replied, nodding toward a bay sheltered from the sun by lush pines. A small island lay centered in the mirror-still surface.

"Look at the color of that water," Karen exclaimed as we passed by. I could see how the place got its name. The teardrop-shaped bay looked like a green pendant dangling from the lake's blue body.

"The prettiest place on the lake," Dave said, slowing the boat to a stop. "Okay, who wants to go first?" he asked, surveying us with his squinty eyes. A moviegoer rather than an athlete, fear trickled through me at the thought of being chosen. I'd never been water skiing.

"Not me," Arlene announced, taking an experienced swig of a beer from the bottle she'd lifted from the Petersons' refrigerator.

"I'll go," Karen announced, climbing down from the bow with Dave's help. She skied like a pro, jumping back and forth across the wake. Jo went next, popping up out of the water like a cork at the first pull of the boat. And then, it was my turn.

"Come on, Liz," Karen urged, slathering another layer of iodine-spiked baby oil on her long legs.

"Okay," I said. The last thing I wanted was to disappoint Karen.

Dave strapped the Mae West life vest tightly around me while explaining the technique of water skiing. My heart was pounding so loud, I was sure he could hear it. "Let the boat pull you up, bend your knees, if you fall remember to let go of the rope." So many things to remember.

On my first try, I managed to pull myself up to a squatting position, but I couldn't hold the skis straight, and I fell backwards giving myself what Gidge laughingly called "a Lake Tahoe douche." Dave was patient, and after the fourth try I was up. Everyone onboard cheered. The wind burned my cheeks and made my eyes water, as Dave opened the throttle. My arms were stretched tight like rubber bands out in front of me. The mixture of terror and excitement felt like ginger ale fizzing in my brain. Watching the tips of my skis part the water like the bow of a ship sent shivers through my rigid body. Just as I began to feel a sense of accomplishment, I lost my balance and plunged headfirst into the water. When I surfaced, I was greeted by two pink rubber pieces of foam, floating in front of me. It took me a minute to recognize my falsies.

—◊◊◊—

I stood on top of the rock, closed my eyes and breathed in the years of my youth. Reeling out like an old movie in the back of my mind, I pictured those young teenagers we once were: clear-eyed, full of energy, and ready to take on the world. Lately, I found the more I was faced with the future, the more I ached for the past—not the NASDAQ nineties, but the past of a childhood I couldn't wait to escape at the time. A part of me longed to be a kid again. Life was so much simpler when going "eeny-meeny-miney-mo" made decisions, and mistakes were corrected by simply shouting "overs." The rest of your life lay in front of you, rolled out like a red carpet. And you and your friends would live forever.

# CHAPTER TWENTY-THREE

*March 23, 2000*

The air had warmed by the time I started back to the house. I moved slowly as I unzipped my jacket and lifted the hair off my neck. I thought about how long Arlene and I had been friends, so long that our private jokes had been reduced to one word. We had complained, consoled, and talked our way through many a crisis. In the days that followed her son Timmy's death, I'd sat with her on her sofa gently rocking her back and forth as she shuddered and sobbed. And when Ricky left, she'd done the same for me. But when it came to men, it took a lot of forgiving to stay friends with Arlene.

I shook myself to throw off the resentment I felt.

As I approached the house, I caught sight of a silver SUV pulling into the driveway. Someone stopping by to pay his respects, no doubt. A man with a shock of white hair stepped out of the car, dressed in a black leather blazer, faded jeans, and gunmetal boots. The minute I recognized Ricky, I felt my breath catch in my throat.

He looked my way. I waved hesitantly. He waved back.

"Hey there," he said, walking up to meet me on the road. "Long time, no see." Fifteen years to be exact, at Kristen's graduation from nursing school. "How are you holding up?"

I lowered my eyes and shook my head, unwilling to trust my ability to speak just yet.

"I was sorry to hear about Karen. Kristen called me." I hugged myself. "Really makes you realize how short life is." I looked up at him. There were deep squint lines around those crystal blue eyes that used to stare at me with such lust.

His glance wavered away, and he looked down at his feet. I examined him as carefully as I could without being obvious. "I thought I'd come to the service, if it's all right with you," he said, shifting from one foot to the other.

"Why wouldn't it be all right?"

"Oh, I don't know." He kicked the heel of one boot on the toe of the other; a habit he had when he was nervous.

"It would be nice if you'd come."

We talked for a few more moments, small talk about how he liked retirement, our children, nothing that veered close to old wounds. Before he turned to leave, his face took on a serious look.

"I made a big mistake, a long time ago," he said. His eyes lingered on mine for a moment. I let what Ricky said slip painlessly into the back of my mind to be examined later, so that the alert, front part of my mind could remain free enough to keep me in command of the situation. That way, I could maintain the right expression and respond appropriately.

"I'll see you Saturday," he said. Then he turned and walked back to his car.

As I watched him drive off, I realized how seeing him again had shone a spotlight on my unresolved feelings; feelings that had been tucked away like a land mine.

A horn honked behind me. I limped to the side of the road and waved my apology. I stood for a long time my hands jammed in my pockets, looking off in the middle distance, hoping some small pivot would set me back on track.

# CHAPTER TWENTY-FOUR

*March 23, 2000*

A s I gingerly stepped up the front steps of the house, I could hear the muted sound of music playing. I recognized the song immediately as the Theme From a Summer Place, by Percy Faith. Karen's favorite.

I stood on the landing, momentarily lost, taking nourishment from the memories of countless sun-block free summer days spent lounging peacefully on the deck, staring up at a cloudless sky, the sound of our playing children mingled with the music in the background.

When I entered the living room, a sight I hadn't seen in years greeted me. Rosie and Jo were slow dancing, their arms wrapped around each other in nostalgic bliss. Gidge was slouched on the sofa, watching. Arlene sat on the floor near the window, her nose close to a magnifying mirror, busy plucking her eyebrows.

I was careful to walk around the perimeter of the room, so as not to disturb the dancers. As I sat down next to Gidge, I was surprised to feel her arm slip around my shoulders. Since the news of Karen's death, we all seemed to feel the need to touch each other more often; a nudge here, a punch on the shoulder there. Even Gidge.

I leaned my head back on her arm, closed my eyes and let the music wash over me. To sit quietly and listen was a welcome respite. When the song ended, I opened my eyes to see Rosie attempting to dip Jo backwards. Jo lost her balance, and the two of them fell in a heap on the carpet. They exploded in laughter.

"I'm going to wet my pants, Rosie," Jo warned. "You better get off me!" Rosie rolled over onto her back, next to Jo. They lay there together, side by side, laughing.

"You're only young once, but thank God you can be immature all of your life," Gidge said to me, pointing to Jo and Rosie with her chin. I smiled.

The sound of the next record dropping onto the turntable caught my attention. The Ray Coniff Singers, another favorite LP of Karen's. I could almost hear her humming along.

"Where've you been?" Rosie asked, raising herself up onto her elbows.

"Outside talking to Ricky," I said matter-of-factly.

Rosie's jaw dropped.

Jo's eyes bulged in surprise. "Ricky Hayden?" she said, sitting upright on the floor.

"No, Ricky Ricardo," I said.

"Okay, give," Gidge commanded, shifting to look at me.

"There's not much to tell. He asked my permission to come to the service. And I told him that would be nice."

"And?" Arlene said, fanning herself with her hand, a familiar gesture that indicated a hot flash.

"And that was about it." I wasn't ready to share Ricky's admission, especially with Arlene. I wanted to hold on to it until later when, in a calmer and wiser moment, I could sort out my feelings.

"So, how does he look?" Gidge wanted to know.

"You'll see on Saturday," I said. I reached into the basket of magazines at the end of the couch, a clue that the subject was closed.

"What are you doin', Arlene?" Jo asked, crawling toward Arlene on all fours.

"Plucking my eyebrows," Arlene answered, not turning away from her task. "The light here is perfect for seeing the gray ones."

"At least you have eyebrows," Jo said. "Thank God for permanent make-up." Jo peered into the mirror over Arlene's shoulder. "I hate looking at myself in the mirror," she said. "It's too depressing."

"My extra time in front of the mirror is spent looking for chin hairs," Gidge declared.

"That reminds me," Rose said. "Remember a few years ago, when we were all up here for a girls' weekend, and we were talking about getting old and having sex?"

"Hell, every conversation we've ever had has been about those two topics," Gidge said.

"Anyway, Karen said that after age forty, a woman should never be on top," Rosie went on.

"That was assuming there was sex after forty," Jo said.

"And when I asked why, Karen told me to lay a mirror flat on the kitchen counter and bend over and look down?" I glanced over to see Gidge making a face like she was going to start screaming with boredom.

"I never told her but I tried it, and she was right! I looked like one of those dogs with all the folds of loose skin. You know, a Shar-Pei." Rosie pushed her cheeks forward to illustrate her point. "I haven't been on top since."

"You know what I hate about getting old?" Arlene said.

"Oh, are we making a list?" Gidge said, rolling her eyes.

"Worrying that I'm going to wet my pants every time I sneeze." Snickers of agreement. "Next, we'll be wearing adult diapers."

"Not me," Gidge grumbled. "They remind me too much of those inch-thick Kotex pads that rubbed you raw?"

Jo cringed. "And the dreaded sanitary belt with the metal clips."

I closed my magazine and tossed it back into the basket. "You know, sometimes I actually miss my period," I said.

"Are you crazy?" Arlene said. "That's the one good thing about menopause."

"You may miss your period, but I miss my pubic hair," Gidge said.

Rosie let out a whoop. Leave it to Gidge to one-up me.

"Speaking of pubic hair." Jo snapped her fingers. "Do you think we should look for Karen's vibrator and get rid of it? You know, before someone else finds it?"

"Oh God, I forgot about Mr. Pinky," I said. "Gidge, you were so bad at that Fuckerware Party." I hit her on the shoulder.

"Hey, I wasn't the only one raising hell," Gidge said.

"I wasn't there," Rosie reminded us. "Remember, Jay wouldn't let me go?" Her face was wreathed in one big self-satisfied grin. Rosie liked using her husband's supposed disapproval as an excuse when she didn't want to do something.

"Yes, Rose, we remember," Gidge said in a patronizing tone, as if she were humoring a child. I caught Gidge's eye and winked.

"I lied to Jess and told him I was going to visit my sister," Jo said. Her expression showed she was pleased with herself.

—⁓—

In the late seventies, women began inviting their friends and neighbors to get-togethers in their homes, where they could buy sex toys. The hostess would earn points based on the total purchases, much like the structure of a Tupperware party; hence the name "Fuckerware" party. Only at these parties, the hostess gift might be a cock ring instead of a Jell-O mold.

Out of curiosity, Arlene decided to host one of these pleasure parties and invited "the girls," along with a few other open-minded friends and neighbors. Secretly, I was feeling more than just a little uneasy about attending. I wasn't looking forward to imagining my friends naked and horizontal, experimenting with bedroom accessories.

We girls went over early to have a few drinks to loosen up. In the kitchen, I was drinking glass after glass of the rum punch Arlene had made. When she smiled at me, I pushed aside a plant that hung in a macramé holder and grabbed her by the elbow. "I don't want to touch anything," I whispered. She nodded knowingly.

We were pretty well oiled by the time the party started, which helped reduce my anxiety. Arlene's small living room was crowded with folding chairs in anticipation of a big crowd. Like birds on a wire, Jo, Arlene, Gidge, Karen, and I all squeezed onto the rattan couch, our hips touching each other.

The demonstrator, Mrs. Beetle, had arrived weighed down with three over-sized Rubbermaid containers. A plain woman in her fifties with the sweet smile of a child, Mrs. Beetle looked like she belonged in the church choir instead of hawking sex toys.

"I'm sure you've all seen or heard of fruit-flavored lubricants," Mrs. Beetle said with confidence, as she rummaged through one of her tubs. "But the ones I'm about to show you also heat up when you rub them on. Here, rub some of this on the back of your hand." She handed a plastic bottle to Karen.

"Rub it on this," Gidge said out of the corner of her mouth, pretending to lift her skirt. Karen slapped her on the leg.

"Pass the bottle around when you've finished testing it," Mrs. Beetle instructed. "The next item is our Ben-wa Balls." She quickly produced a handful of silver shiny balls, the size of jumbo-sized jawbreakers, connected by a chain. They reminded me of the ball bearings Humphrey Bogart rolled around in his hand in the movie, Caine Mutiny. "For centuries, women have used these to strengthen the muscles of the vagina." Mrs. Beetle offered the string of balls to the woman seated on her right, who had been introduced to us as Marilyn Carter, a neighbor of Arlene's. Reluctantly, Marilyn held out her hand, raising her eyebrows.

"Do you have some a little larger for the mature woman?" Gidge asked, scooping clam dip onto a chip.

"Like bowling-ball-size?" Karen asked, tossing her blond hair as she laughed.

Mrs. Beetle ignored the interruption, but I noticed some of the other guests squirming nervously in their seats.

"Okay, now here's a little gadget that we've received rave reviews on, especially from women who have jobs in manufacturing, like on an assembly line." She held up what looked like a plastic soap holder, suspended from a thin elastic belt with a battery pack. "You can strap this on in the morning and have multiple orgasms all day," she said with a straight face.

An unexpected yelp escaped me.

"Now, yer talkin'," Arlene said, popping up from her seat and reaching for the apparatus. She scrutinized it carefully, turning the switch on and off, watching the ring of plastic vibrate violently. When she was satisfied that she understood how it worked, she passed it to Gidge, who stuck the contraption up her skirt, and rolled her eyes in mock ecstasy.

"Gidge," Jo scolded, aware of the disapproving looks on the faces of the other guests.

"Oh, I'm just kidding," Gidge replied, taking the thing from between her legs. "Here," she said, tossing it to Jo, who tossed it to me. Me to Karen, Karen to Arlene, and soon we were playing a grown-up version of the grade-school party game "hot potato."

Mrs. Beetle ignored our childish antics. "Now, let's move on to the star of our product line," she said. With that, she reached into a tub and pulled out a huge black dildo with a crank on the end. My face registered such shock it made Karen laugh.

"Holy Shit!" Gidge exclaimed, expressing my reaction in words. The neighbor, Marilyn Carter, pulled back in horror.

"Meet Mr. Blacky," Mrs. Beetle said, as if she were introducing a real person. By the looks on the faces around the room, I wasn't the only one who had never seen such a thing. A hush fell over the group.

"Do you have anything for a beginner?" Karen asked in a quiet voice. Arlene let out an explosive laugh. I followed first with a rolling chortle, and then we were all laughing—big throaty hahahaha laughs—laughing so hard that tears leaked out of our eyes. Even Arlene's stuffy neighbor, Marilyn, let out a few nervous titters.

"Why, yes, I have just the thing," Mrs. Beetle answered, when she could be heard over the racket. She reached into another tub and brought out a much smaller, flesh-colored vibrator. "This is Mr. Pinky," she said. The vibrator hummed with an intensity that Pavarotti would admire. Karen was sold.

—⁂—

"I'm serious," Jo interjected. "Somebody should go into Karen's bedroom and find that damn thing and get rid of it."

"I vote for you, Jo," Gidge teased.

"Look for Karen's will while you're in there," I suggested.

"I don't know what I'd do without my vibrator," Arlene said, sitting heavily on the couch next to Gidge. "I haven't had sex in so long, I think I probably qualify as a recycled virgin." I doubted that was true.

"I know what you mean," Gidge agreed. "My nookie days are pretty much over, too."

"Hey, listen to this," Jo said, looking up from a page in Cosmopolitan magazine. "According to this article, last year close to 90,000 women got breast enlargements and 60,000 women got reductions."

"That reminds me," Gidge interrupted, "I read somewhere the other day that the latest trend in plastic surgery is reconstructing vaginas."

"What?" Jo shrieked.

"Yeah, women are going in for everything from a twat tightening to prettying up the old labia lips."

"Where do you read this shit?" Arlene asked, curling her lip.

"It was in one of those fashion rags; Bazaar or Vogue or something," Gidge answered indignantly. "Anyway, eventually everything sags. I guess now you can even have your snatch lifted."

"Unbelievable!" Jo marveled as she rifled through the magazine.

"They probably even do pubic hair transplants, " I said. "No more bald beavers." Jo laughed at the bizarre prospect.

Rosie wasn't joining in the folderol. I asked her what was wrong.

"Karen would have loved this conversation," she almost whispered, her eyes wet with tears.

"Jeez, Rosie," Gidge said, throwing up her hands.

I glanced at my watch. 4:30. I'd arranged to meet Greg at the restaurant at five. I didn't want the others to come with me, afraid if he felt ganged up on, he'd be less likely to open up.

"I need a few things from the drugstore," I said, getting up from the couch. My ankle felt better.

"We're going to eat around 6:30," Rosie said, taking a swipe under her nose.

Agreeing to be back in plenty of time, I jumped in the van and headed to Incline Village.

# CHAPTER TWENTY-FIVE

*March 23, 2000*

As I eased Sam's van onto the frontage road, my thoughts bounced back to when Karen first met Greg; actually, when we all first met him. It was 1976, and we had gathered at the lake to celebrate Gidge's thirty-fifth birthday. My cohorts and I had decided to try a new restaurant called the Blue Water Lagoon across the street from the Hyatt Hotel and Casino.

With a cap of snow-white hair and impeccably attired in a smart navy-blue suit, the Maitre d' escorted us to a large round table. We hadn't been seated long before a young blond waitress wearing all black approached us. I suspected her underwear was black, too.

"Excuse me, does anyone here have a gray vulva?" she asked with concern in her voice. The table went silent. After a short pause, Karen turned to Gidge and said, "Have you been sick?" Gidge high-fived Karen. We all laughed. Karen's quick humor was lost on the waitress, and she rushed off to look for the customer whose car was about to be towed.

"I'm starving," I announced after regaining my composure. I opened my menu and leaned my elbows on the table, causing it to wobble. Noting the table's unsteadiness, Arlene signaled to the host illustrating the deficiency by rocking the table back and forth. In a few moments, a dark-haired, blue-eyed busboy appeared wearing a crisp, neatly pressed white dress shirt, black slacks and a black tie. His shoes were polished and every hair was in place. Armed with a piece of cardboard, he lifted the tablecloth and bent over. His butt looked like two basketballs in a sack. Once down on all fours and out of sight, Gidge started. "A little to the left, please. Oh, that's it," she moaned. "Now, a little lower." When the poor kid stood up from his submerged position, his altar-boy-fresh face was bright red.

"Don't pay any attention to her," Karen said, giving him a warm smile. "Hi, I'm Karen Christensen." She extended her hand. Single at the time, Karen used her maiden name. "What's your name?" she inquired, looking deeply into his cobalt-blue eyes.

The young man took her hand and continued to blush. "Greg, Ma'am. Greg Ronelli." He lowered his eyes to reveal beautiful long, black lashes.

"It's Miss, honey, not Ma'am. You should never call a lady Ma'am unless she's your mother."

It was the first of many lessons she would teach him.

The road hugged the shoreline so tightly that the lake appeared close enough to touch. Turning onto the highway, I began the steep climb up the mountain, craning my neck to see out of the window. This particular landscape with its broad sweeping view of the lake, gray plank docks cutting into the blue water, majestic evergreens splitting the sky, never failed to astonish me. Shaped by a lifetime of visits, this stretch of road was so embedded in my memory that I could have driven it blindfolded.

My mind drifted as I pulled out to pass a slow RV. Then, in the heartbeat it takes for the front bumper of a truck to top the hill ahead, everything changed. The truck going well over the speed limit was bearing down on me, his headlights flashing, signaling me to get out of his way. A guardrail protected the shoulder on my left, and the RV blocked my right. I had nowhere to go. No time to brake back behind the slow-moving RV. I stomped on the gas pedal and turned my wheels hard to cut in front of the RV. As I resisted the urge to close my eyes, death flew by in a blur of black metal, its horn blaring and then dying away. Once safely back in the lane, I was afraid to take my eyes off of the road in front of me. At the stoplight at the bottom of the hill, I raised my trembling hand to the rearview mirror and gave a weak wave of apology to the driver of the RV. She honked as she made a left turn at the intersection, a gesture of understanding. Even after the light turned green, I was unable to move. The light turned red again and my mind went strangely calm, as if part of me had lifted right up out of my body and was sitting on the electrical cable overhead, watching from a safe distance. With my eyes closed, I thought of Karen and how her brush with death hadn't ended so favorably. How powerless we are, over and over, thinking we have it all under control.

A horn honked. Startled, I looked up to see that the light was green again. I stepped down on the accelerator. Driving the remaining miles, I focused on the road. A mud-splattered Volvo passed by, its tires hissing on the wet asphalt. Clumps of dirty snow lined the driveways into gas stations and convenience stores. My hands gripped the wheel, as if I could hold onto all that might have been lost: my children, my friends, Sam. But hadn't I lost him already?

I pulled up and stopped in the empty parking lot in front of Greg's restaurant, still shaken. Perhaps I should delay my visit, pick a time when I felt better able to cope. But the service was in a couple of days, and I needed some answers.

New wood siding covered the front of the low one-story building. Next to the door, a large, brightly colored lead glass window depicted the lake, a vibrant blue, with white snow-capped mountains in the background and a lone sailboat sitting on the still water—probably done by one of the many local artists in the area.

The front door was propped open, letting in the fresh air. I knew what I was going to say to Greg. I just needed to get on with it. On the count of three, I got out of the car.

Leaning in the door, I shouted, "Hello? Anybody home?" A rustling at the far end of the restaurant by the bar caught my attention. I took a tentative step inside.

"Hello?" I called again. "Greg, is that you? It's Elizabeth." The room was dark and with the light behind me, I couldn't see a thing. Footsteps were coming toward me, slow at first, and then faster, until he appeared in front of me wearing beige khakis, a black polo shirt and two-day-old stubble. In the years since I'd seen him, he'd lost some of his boy-toy good looks. Now in his mid-forties, his scalp was beginning to show through his once thick dark hair, and his Barbie-like waist had grown a couple of inches.

"Come in," he offered, not quite meeting my eyes. "I've been waiting for you."

As he walked over to a table and pulled out a chair, I noticed his right hand and wrist were bandaged, and he had a butterfly patch over his right eye. I sat down.

"Can I get you something to drink? Tequila, is it?" he asked. There were dark circles under his eyes.

I needed something to steel myself. "A vodka martini, please."

Greg left to get my drink.

I shed my jacket and hung it over the back of the chair. Around me, the tables were innocent of clothes, and there wasn't a sign of the tra-la-la associated with the more up-scale restaurants in the area. The clientele was probably blue collar, a combination of employees from the casino across the street, and some locals. Not a great recipe for success. I hoped Karen hadn't invested in the place. But what did it matter now?

I drummed my fingers on the table and chewed on the bitter unfairness of Karen's death. Something wasn't right. I could feel it. I'd never known Greg to have an accident, not even a minor fender-bender. Why now? Just after he'd become the proud owner of a new restaurant. I wondered if the police made this connection; wealthy girlfriend loans boyfriend money, then accidentally falls off the back of his bike. Yeah, right!

I knew I needed to calm down if I wanted to get the answers I came for. Where was that drink? I leaned back in my chair and slid one leg over the other, a tactic I'd used at work to appear open and objective in difficult situations. By the time Greg arrived with our drinks, I had collected myself.

He sat down across from me.

"Greg, tell me what happened," I said, my voice devoid of inflection.

He looked down. The fingers of his left hand rubbed the bandage on his right hand. I could tell by the look of the makeshift dressing that he'd wrapped his hand himself. Most likely didn't want to risk going to the hospital and being questioned.

He was quiet for some time. It was everything I could do to sit and wait for his answer. I wanted to grab him by the collar and shake it out of him.

He furrowed his eyebrows, as if he were putting careful thought into what he was about to say.

"I know you don't believe me, but I loved her, Liz," he finally said quietly, avoiding my eyes, still rubbing his hand. "I've always loved her." It wasn't what I expected to hear. I thought the deepest thing about this man was his dimples. But his declaration didn't dampen my suspicion.

"Over the years, we joked about getting married." He choked up, stopped, waited, and then went on. "But she was never serious. It was a game we played." He looked up and his faded blue eyes pooled with tears. "But lately, she seemed different. Last week, when she called to say she was coming up, before she hung up she said, 'Greg, would you marry me if I asked you to?' Just like that, out of nowhere." He shook his head in disbelief. "I said, 'You just say the word.'" Once again, he bowed his head and sat quiet and thoughtful. Slowly, he brought his bandaged hand up to his face and wiped his nose on it. "Ah, shit." He picked up his glass and drained it. "I need another drink," he announced, getting up from his chair. "Can I get you another?"

I shook my head no.

He turned and walked back toward the bar, his head dipped and body arched forward as if bracing against the wind.

I replayed the past few minutes in my head, looking for any of the red flags that years of interviewing job applicants had taught me. His tone, his body language, all except his hesitancy to make eye contact indicated he was telling the truth about his feelings for Karen. But men often claimed to have loved women who they then murdered. A coldness sank into my heart.

When he returned with his fresh drink, I leaned forward in my seat and launched forth again.

"Greg, I need to know exactly—"

"I know you do," he interrupted. This time he looked me right in the eye. "We were coming back from dinner in Reno," he began, setting his drink on the table. "Karen had a lot to drink. We had a couple of glasses of wine at the house, and then she was doing Bombers before dinner. I stuck to Perrier." I must have looked like I didn't believe him. "I passed the breathalyzer test," he added, raising his eyebrows. I nodded. "Anyway, she was in one of her party moods," he continued. "You know, having a great time, feeling no pain."

I knew how she looked when she was like that: cheeks flushed, eyes bright.

"She begged me to take the shortcut home over Mount Rose. At first, I said no way. But, it was late and…" He shrugged his shoulders. "Anyway, when we got to the crest of the mountain, she yelled in my ear to go faster. The road had fresh salt on it, so I speeded up a little." He paused to take a long pull of his drink. Taking the cue, I uptilted my glass. "Then she starts yelling, 'Come on, Ronelli, don't be such a wuss! Open this baby up.'"

He let out a snort. "She knows how careful I am on my bike. It drives her nuts." Greg's expression darkened. I sat motionless.

He cleared his throat. "And then, she let go."

At first, I didn't hear what he said; the words were so unexpected.

"What?" I squawked.

He hesitated, just a beat, drawing back a little in his seat. "She just let go."

WHAM! It was like someone had kicked me in the stomach. All my breath was sucked out. A tight metal band around my chest kept my lungs from expanding. In the thick silence that followed, I could feel the heat rising to my face.

"Course, I didn't tell the cops," he said, making wet circles on the table with the bottom of his glass. "I told 'em we hit some black ice."

Sitting there rooted to the chair, everything around me seemed suspended, just out of reach.

"Greg? What are you saying?" I asked, when I could breathe.

"I swear to God, she let go," he replied, staring at me with unflinching eyes. "It wasn't an accident. She didn't slip."

"You said yourself she was drunk. She could have lost her grip?" I said in a pleading tone of voice.

"No, she practically pushed off."

"Why would she do such a thing?" I asked. My hand was trembling so badly, I had to set my glass down to keep from spilling what was left of my drink.

"God, I've asked myself that question a million times, over and over again." He tilted his chair back and looked up at the ceiling.

"How did you hurt yourself?"

"I guess I scratched my head and cut my hand climbing down to her. I don't remember." Greg touched his forehead. "The second I felt her arms unlock from around my waist, I slammed on the brakes and the bike began to skid. I went into some brush on the high side of the road. When I got off the bike, I didn't see her anywhere. I realized she must have rolled down the embankment."

He began picking at the gauze bandage on his wrist. "It was too late, though. When I found her, I could tell by the way she was lying that her neck..." His voice was suffused with hopelessness.

I sank back in my chair. How could I be expected to believe this? How could anyone?

"Why are you telling me this?" I eyed him with sour mistrust. He looked puzzled. "There's got to be a reason." I could feel the pressure inside me ratcheting up. "Why didn't you keep it to yourself?"

"Look, Liz, I have no reason to lie to you." He reached across the table for my hand. I snatched it away.

"Don't you?" Our eyes locked. "Aren't the police conducting an investigation?" I growled, picturing him in a police line-up.

Greg slumped back into his chair and hung his head. The only sound in the room was the gurgling coming from the aquarium behind the bar. I stared at him for a long time, waiting for an answer. None came.

When he finally raised his head, the color of his face looked ashen, even in the semidarkness of the restaurant. He looked like he wanted to say something more.

My chair made a violent scraping sound as I stood.

"I have to go," I said, leaving teeth marks in every word. As I walked past him, Greg's fingers brushed my arm.

My legs felt so unsteady, I didn't think I could make it to the car. The gravel crunched under my feet as I concentrated on putting one foot in front of the other. Was Greg capable of murder? Was his story just a cover-up? Or could it be possible that he was telling the truth?

Once inside the car, I laid my head back against the seat. Why did he have to tell me this? I was just coming to terms with Karen's death, and now this. For the second time in less than a week, I felt the world sputter and crash.

I sat there for a long time, my synapses misfiring. Thoroughly disoriented, disconnected images of Karen danced across my mind. I saw her schussing down the slopes, graceful as a gazelle in her one-piece white ski outfit, her blonde hair blowing out behind her, her beautiful face flushed from the cold. Next, her limp body lying in the dirt all twisted and broken, her hair caked with blood, and her face scrapped and bruised. The vision faded. I shuddered.

I closed my eyes and shook my head, trying to jiggle all the pieces back into place, like one of those little plastic games we had as kids, trying to get the BB pellets into the little round holes.

When I opened my eyes, two gray-haired ladies with stooped shoulders were walking in front of the car. Dressed from head to toe in polyester, each had a handbag over her arm, the way my mother used to carry hers. As I watched, the taller one reached over and put her arm around her friend's shoulders and squeezed. I couldn't take my eyes off them. This was supposed to be Karen and me at their age. Since we were in our forties, we'd talked about spending our twilight years together, old ladies with failing hearts and throbbing joints inhabiting adjourning apartments located in some place warm like Palm Springs (or "God's Waiting Room" as Karen liked to call it) where we would dye our hair blue and play shuffleboard. The lawn would be littered with Ensure cans after a Friday night blowout. Oh, how Karen and I would laugh at the prospect.

I felt tears pressing up into my eyes.

"Shit, shit, shit," I whispered fiercely, slamming my fist on the dash repeatedly. It didn't help.

Helpless, I dropped my forehead onto the cold steering wheel with a thud. I felt an overwhelming sadness, a dumbfounding grief. As I sat huddled in the front seat, tears starting falling into my lap. I sobbed uncontrollably. Each time I thought I had stopped crying, another wave would hit me.

I don't know how long I sat there, but when the last tear had fallen, I looked around to see it was pitch black. The sky was drilled with stars. It took me a minute to remember where I was. I pressed the button for the electric window. It hummed down a couple of inches and a stiff cold breeze hit my face. I reached for the seat belt.

# CHAPTER TWENTY-SIX

*March 23, 2000*

As I pulled slowly onto the road, I wished I could talk to Aunt Vi. Full of salty wisdom, she would know what to say to straighten me out. She always did.

Tear-softened, I summoned an image of Aunt Vi dressed in her fashionable black suit, the one she saved for special occasions, carefully accessorized with a plum-colored cloche and black gloves ending just about her wrists. Although she didn't make much as a long distance operator at the phone company, she managed to pay her rent and find enough left over to dress well.

Escaping from a short marriage to a brutal husband, she never looked back, choosing instead to lead a free and largely unattached life filled with adventure. It was with Aunt Vi that I had tasted my first Peking duck, saw my first foreign film, and drank my first glass of Port wine.

What would Aunt Vi do in this situation? Get hold of your emotions. Check with the police. Examine the facts. Putting myself in Aunt Vi's place helped calm my damaged spirit.

I allowed the red-lit needle of the speedometer to tremble up through fifty.

"You were gone a long time," Rosie said, as I walked into the kitchen. She didn't look up. If she had, I'm sure my red-rimmed eyes and puffy face would have alarmed her.

"We were about to send a posse out lookin' for 'ya," Gidge called from the living room. A roaring fire crackled in the fireplace and someone, probably Rosie, had placed candles around the room, which were burning brightly and filling the house with the scent of evergreen and vanilla.

"Is everybody here?" I asked, grateful for the dim lighting.

"Yes," Rosie replied, intent in chopping something on the cutting board. "We're just about to eat."

Gidge looked up from the magazine she was reading. "What did you buy at the store?" she asked, the way a person will when she already knows the answer.

"Nothing," I answered, slowly making my way toward her. I felt like a walking bruise. "I went to see Greg." A log in the fire popped, spraying sparks. "I wanted to find out exactly what happened, and I needed to hear it from him."

Rosie stopped chopping, and came into the living room, a worried look on her face.

"What did he say?" Gidge asked.

"I'll wait until the others come downstairs." I didn't feel sad anymore. I didn't feel anything really, just hollowed out.

"What's the big mystery, anyway?" Gidge said.

"I said, I'll wait," I snapped. It was Gidge's turn to be silent. Gidge, who was never at a loss for words, suddenly couldn't find her tongue.

After Arlene and Jo joined us at the table, I was very aware of the undivided attention that was being paid to me.

"Please, don't anyone interrupt until I've finished." They were stunned into obedience. "I went to see Greg this afternoon, and asked him to tell me exactly what happened." All eyes were on me. "It seems that they were coming home from dinner in Reno and Karen had had a few drinks. She was in high spirits and told Greg to speed up; she wanted him to go faster. He increased his speed, but she kept yelling for him to go faster."

I couldn't help but feel the slightest stitch of doubt about what I was about to say. Was it right to tell them, even if I wasn't sure I believed Greg? I clasped my hands on the table in front of me and tried to swallow, but my throat was very dry.

"And then, he felt Karen let go." The sound of my voice trailed off into the deafening silence. The faces of my oldest and dearest friends looked like they had been freeze-dried.

"What the hell else is he gonna say?" Gidge snarled. "He's the one who killed her." Her face twisted into an ugly sneer.

"Don't be ridiculous," Arlene replied, waving Gidge off with her hand.

"No. It was an accident," Rosie muttered softly, unconsciously fingering her St. Christopher's medal on its thin chain.

"Bullshit!" Gidge yelled, slamming her fist on the table, causing the dishes and silverware to rattle. "This is fucking bullshit, and I'm not buying it!" She shot up from the table, staggering slightly as if dazed by the shock of what she had just heard, and stomped out of the room. No one made a move to go after her.

Rosie, vacant-eyed and pale, stared at me for a long moment. Jo sat with her eyes downcast, rubbing her forehead with the pads of her fingers.

"I know it sounds crazy," I said.

"Well, as far as I'm concerned, this has nothing to do with us," Arlene remarked, nervously straightening the silverware.

I looked at her in amazement. "What do you mean?" I asked.

"I mean Karen is dead, and it doesn't really matter what Greg thinks happened." She sounded a bit huffy now.

"What the hell are you talking about, Arlene?" I challenged. My head was beginning to throb from the martini I had drunk too fast. "What if Greg is lying? What if Gidge is right? Does that matter?"

"Of course, that matters," Arlene said, pulling herself up straight in her chair. "That would be a police matter. I'm just saying if he's telling the truth, we have nothing to gain by telling anyone else about this. I mean, who really needs to know?"

"Julie," Jo said, barely above a whisper. I looked into her face, and she nodded yes.

"Oh, my God. Suicide." Rose said. She cupped her hand over her mouth, and looked at me with pain in her dark eyes.

The word "suicide" hit me like a slap in the face. Until that moment, I hadn't allowed myself to make the direct connection.

"Can I say something?" Jo asked, raising her hand like a polite student in class. Heads turned her way. She cleared her throat. "I would have given anything not to have been the one who discovered my mother the day she hung herself. For years, I asked God why he chose me instead of my father." Jo's voice was calm and controlled. "If my father had found her, I know he would have sheltered us kids from the truth. He would have told us that she had a heart attack or died of some undetected disease. But I was the one who found her, and I knew that it wasn't an accident. She didn't accidentally tie that rope around her neck. She didn't accidentally slip off the stool. She purposely killed herself." She paused. "And not a day goes by that I don't wonder if there was some sign I missed or something I could have done to stop her."

Jo's eyes locked with Arlene's. Then, to my astonishment, she added, "But Julie is not a child. And if this turns out to be the truth, no matter how painful it might be, we have no right to keep it from her." Jo reached over and put a gentle hand on Arlene's arm.

Arlene had nothing to say. It occurred to me that Arlene might feel guilty, given what had happened between Karen and her. I hoped so.

After dinner, the feeling of unrest intensified. Rosie was hyperactive; Jo depressed; Arlene argumentative; and me anxious. Gidge stayed out of sight. The wind kicked up, too. Tree branches slapped and windows rattled, adding to our edginess.

"I'm going to see if I can find Karen's will," I said, unable to sit still. Arlene exhaled a sigh, which betrayed more impatience than sadness. I shot her a sour look, and set off toward Karen's bedroom.

As I opened the door, I remembered the white plastic bag from the morgue lying on the floor just inside. I closed my eyes, and slid the bag aside with my foot.

Inside the darkened room, moonlight filtered through the pine boughs and scattered patches across the bed and onto the floor. Determined not to let my surroundings distract me from my mission, I shut the door and flipped on the light.

"Just get on with it," I instructed myself firmly, as I walked across the room to Karen's Queen Anne desk, which she'd taken in lieu of a commission during her brief stint as an interior decorator. Except for some bills and miscellaneous papers, my search of the desk came up empty. Next,

I burrowed through her dresser drawers, her closet, and the Treasures of Truth chest, doing my best to keep sentimental thoughts away. As I sorted through Karen's belongings, I was careful to put each thing back in its original place. No sign of a will.

I wasn't ready to give up. Finding out the truth had become my one clear goal. Tomorrow morning, I'd call the Reno police department and check on the status of the investigation.

On my way to bed, Rosie stopped me in the hall. "It must have been an accident," she said in a rush.

"I think so too," I said, patting her hand.

But I didn't believe it.

# CHAPTER TWENTY-SEVEN

*March 23, 2000*

I lay awake staring at the beamed ceiling, as the wind pushed at the windowpanes. Jo's words echoed inside my head. A sign. Was there a sign the last time Karen and I were together? Although it was only a few weeks ago, it seemed like the distant past. So much had happened since.

I searched my memory. Did I miss something? Something in her tone; a sign that she was depressed? Didn't she say something about life being riddled with surprises? A profound feeling of personal failure made me squirm. A good friend would have been able to do something.

My mind floated back to a recent email exchange I had had with Karen. Her message included an attachment entitled, "The Definition of a Friend," with a list of cute examples. I had dashed off a quick reply reminding her that a true good friend is someone who pretends to be a lesbian just to shock a couple of Rednecks in a bar, or a person who loans you her new bathing suit, despite knowing about your leaky-bladder problem. I knew she'd get a kick out of being reminded of our memorable trip to Palm Springs.

Sometime in the mid-80s, when we were both in our early forties, Karen begged me to go away with her for a weekend. Thrice divorced, she had given up on the idea of connubial bliss with men her own age, and turned her efforts toward finding a rich older man; a Sugar Daddy. Palm Springs seemed like the perfect place to look.

The heat hit us as we stepped off the plane onto the tarmac. No one in her right mind visits the desert in July, but here we were with enough luggage for a month's stay. As we sat in the back of the cab, our bare legs sticking to the cracked leather seat, we passed an abundance of small stucco houses with checker-square-like patches of Crayola-green synthetic-looking turf in front. One of the yards was sprinkled with pink plastic flamingos. This place seemed frozen in time, a retrospective of the 50s and 60s. The gas station on the corner of the main drag had a fiberglass roof in a shape that resembled a kidney. The whole thing looked like it could become airborne in a stiff wind.

Suddenly, I expected to hear Frank Sinatra crooning from someone's hi-fi, and I could almost smell the onion dip, cigarettes and Scotch that were the main ingredients of every good party in those days.

As we pulled into the portico entrance of our hotel, two octogenarians shuffled out of the front door; one dressed in a mint green leisure suit and the other in plaid Bermuda shorts, white socks and dress shoes. They were both puffing on giant cigars and had shiny bald heads.

"Okay, which one do you want?" I quipped, nudging Karen with my elbow.

We settled into our room, and before dinner Karen had mapped out our itinerary. She had done considerable research and knew exactly where she wanted to go. Our hotel was selected for its location. Everything was either in walking distance or a short cab ride away. We were on a mission.

The next morning after breakfast, we made our trek to the pool. Karen had forgotten her swimsuit and since I had packed two, I loaned her my new one. She filled it out better than I ever could. Small children could have taken shade under her chest. By now, of course, I was smart enough to know that boobs didn't matter. But still, I felt a twinge of jealousy. Most days I didn't want to be Karen, but there was still that occasional pang.

Karen was adamant about getting to the pool early so we could position ourselves properly; near the bar, facing the entrance so we had a bird's-eye view of all comings and goings.

The minute I dropped my beach bag on a lounge, a pool boy with a stack of fluffy towels seemed to materialize out of nowhere. Deeply tanned with starched white shorts and slicked-back hair, he reeked of Paco Rabanne cologne.

I marveled as he covered my chaise perfectly, wrapping and tucking with the precision of a professional bed maker.

We ordered Bloody Marys and settled in for a morning of drinking, people watching, and Sugar Daddy hunting.

"Check out the hunk pushing the wheelchair," Karen said, looking over the top of her Jackie O sunglasses. She puckered her glossed lips and took a sip of her drink through a straw.

Across the pool, I saw the tall, Greek-god-like man. He was naked, except for a sliver of a swimsuit in vibrant yellow latex, obviously purchased abroad. It looked like he had stuffed a potato down the front. His muscular arms rippled as he strutted behind a wheelchair occupied by a little old man who had more gold chains around his neck than Mr. T.

"You take the one in the wheelchair," I said. "I'll take the hunk." I shielded my eyes with my hand to see better.

"Do you think he's his manservant?" Karen asked with renewed interest.

"Maybe he just works at the hotel," I speculated.

We both watched intently as the attendant propelled his charge forward, acknowledging a few admirers as he passed by, nodding and smiling.

"Look at him preening," Karen said quietly.

Upon reaching the end of the pool, the attendant turned the chair at a 90-degree angle, and began easing it down the built-in ramp. Now, I could see the little man clearly. He couldn't have weighed more than a hundred pounds.

"Can you imagine sleeping with him?" I whispered.

"Who? The old man or the attendant?" Karen asked.

"The old man, you idiot," I replied, slapping her arm.

Just as the water began to cover the old man's legs, someone from behind called out to the attendant, and he turned to see who it was. At that moment, the buoyancy of the water lifted the wheelchair occupant out of his seat, and the weight of his jewelry caused him to plunge face first into the water. Splash!

In a panic, the attendant reached out and grabbed the man by a tuft of his thinning hair, pulling him back into his chair. I turned to see Karen double over to contain her laughter.

"Don't pee in my new bathing suit," I warned, choking on my own guffaws.

"Oh God," Karen said, wiping the tears from under her eyes. "The only way I could be with someone that old is if he were paralyzed from the waist down and just wanted me to read to him."

"He could get Don Juan there to do that." I said.

"I can't imagine having sex with someone that old," Karen said. We shivered in unison. "It would be like trying to shove a marshmallow into a piggy bank."

I sputtered.

"Oh, I don't know," Karen said with a sigh, as she lay back in her chaise. "I don't know what the hell I want. I can't seem to keep a marriage going, but I hate being single."

"You just haven't met the right man," I said, trying to sound reassuring.

"You're so lucky to have found Sam. Why don't you want to marry him?"

"I've already explored the wild frontier of domestic life." I pushed my sunglasses up my nose.

Karen gave me a disapproving look. "I think you're afraid," she said in an accusing tone. I wiped the beads of perspiration off of my upper lip. I could feel her eyes burning into me. "Well?" She wasn't giving up.

"Even if he asked me, which he hasn't, and I did marry him, it would only end in another divorce." Before Karen could respond, I said, "Besides, I like being single. No one to call when you're going to be late, no snoring to keep you awake, no smelly socks to pick up off the floor."

Pleased with my response, I lifted my Bloody Mary and slurped with the full force of a vacuum cleaner, being careful not to poke my eye out with the celery stalk.

"Well, as much as I don't want to get married again, I hate being single," Karen said, turning the topic of conversation back to herself, as was her way. "I keep wondering how I ended up like this." I, too, wondered. We all wondered. "I always thought Casey and I would stay married forever?"

I studied Karen's face in disbelief. Somehow she had blocked out the fact that she was the one to end that marriage.

"It's all my parents fault." Here we go with the absent father, promiscuous mother routine. I felt myself beginning to tense up in anticipation of the hapless victim speech. "It's my mother's fault really," she clarified.

"As if I didn't know that." I rolled my eyes behind my sunglasses.

"She drummed it into me for as long as I can remember. 'You need to find a man to take care of you, Karen,' she would say. 'It's just as easy to love a rich man as a poor one'. God, that's all I heard."

"I'm sure she only wanted what was best for you." Nothing I could say could appease Karen when she got on this subject. She refused to admit that after a certain age, you control who you are.

"Then why did she have the constant parade of men coming through our house?" Karen propped herself up on both elbows and turned toward me. "God, if I hadn't had Arlene's house to escape to, I don't know what I'd have done."

I couldn't take anymore. "Stop," I shouted, holding up my arm like a traffic cop. Karen's head jerked backward. "Remember, she did the best she could," I said, wagging my finger at her.

Karen studied me carefully, as if waiting for me to justify my comment. Then, after a moment, she grudgingly said, "Yeah, I know." She collapsed back on her chaise lounge with a sigh.

"Besides you can't change the past. Yesterday is history, tomorrow is a mystery, and today is a gift. That's why it's called the present!" My smile was impish.

"Puh-leeze," Karen said with a smirk. "Let's order some Nachos, Miss Present," she added, reaching for the plastic menu on the table between us.

"Let's face it, all of our families were pretty dysfunctional," I said, unscrewing the cap on my Bain de Soleil. "We just didn't have the labels back then. My parents doing their impression of sparring partners, Arlene's father drunk and running around the house with a German Luger pointed at his head, and Jo's mother hanging herself. Come on." I smeared an orange glob of goo on my chest.

"We sure were a far cry from the Nelsons," Karen agreed.

"And what about Gidge's family?" I went on. "Her dad marching around the house like General Patton, saluting himself in the mirror." I could see the corners of Karen's mouth begin to turn up. "And we all thought her mother was so perfect with her little shirtwaist dresses and her weekly hair appointments. The woman was a raging alcoholic!"

"Remember how she would always call her drink her 'refreshment'?" Karen said. " 'Gidge, bring Mama her refreshment, please'. That fake Southern drawl that got thicker with each drink."

"But, you know, I never saw her drunk."

"Maybe she was always drunk, and we never saw her sober," Karen said.

"Hmm," I said. "And that crazy grandmother that lived with them." I shook my head.

We all knew dozens of grandmother stories that few would believe, like the time Gidge's father had his lodge cronies over for dinner, and Leopard Lady came out in her robe and flashed them. And the many calls from the neighbors at Tahoe, complaining about her habit of sunbathing in the nude. Gidge used to say she looked like a piece of beef jerky.

"No wonder Gidge turned out to be the Queen of Quirk," Karen said.

"So your mother had a few boyfriends," I said. "Big deal." I drained my glass and let out a hiccup.

—m—

Soon, it became too hot to laze by the pool. Karen's preplanned itinerary was temporarily set aside in favor of an afternoon spent in the air-conditioned shopping mall across the street. We found a little boutique filled with outrageous resort wear that can only be found in places like Las Vegas and Palm Springs. Karen was in rare form, posing in front of the full-length mirror in a hideous tiger-striped jumpsuit, complete with stirrup pants and shoulder pads the size of compact cars, sucking in her stomach and thrusting out her melon-sized boobs. She threatened to buy a garish cover-up from the sale rack that was encrusted with red, white and blue sequins; an obvious leftover from the 4th of July inventory. I loved seeing her like this, her inner child running around unsupervised.

That evening we had dinner reservations at Melvyn's, the swank restaurant and lounge that martini-soaked celebrities and well-heeled residents were known to frequent. If you were looking for a Sugar Daddy, this was surely the place.

Nestled in a grotto of greenery, the restaurant was hidden from the street like a secret. The bar was packed, and a number of anxious patrons hovered in the foyer. An ordinary person might have been intimidated, but not Karen. In the same way the great screen goddesses like Garbo, Dietrich, or Hayworth must have made their entrances, she pulled herself up to her full height and stepped forward, looking sexy enough to warm a corpse. The sea of mere mortals parted to make way for her.

"May I help you?" the suave tuxedoed host at the podium asked. He looked like a cross between George Hamilton and Napoleon, tanned and short.

"Yes, we have a reservation for eight o'clock," Karen answered with a seductive whiff of superiority.

"Ah yes, Miss Christensen, is it?" he asked. How did he know? "Welcome to Melvyn's." Karen extended her arm with the decorum of a duchess who expects her admirers to kiss the back of her hand. Standing on tiptoe, he reached over the podium and did just that. "Your table is ready." He acted as if he knew her, as if she came there all the time. I felt myself puff up, proud to be her dinner companion.

The dining room with its lush leather banquettes and strategically placed potted palms, suggested an air of intimacy not found since the 40s. As we were escorted to our table, I was awed by the museum-quality paintings on the walls. Dining here would be memorable, even if the food was mediocre. But it wasn't. The chef had done amazing things with each dish. We savored our meals, rolling small bites of food around in our mouths and commenting on the flavor and texture. Karen had ordered a bottle of vintage red wine, and we lingered at the table amid the beauty of the room.

"So, it looked like there was a good crowd in the lounge when we came in," I said, sipping my wine, not wanting to leave.

"Uh-huh," Karen replied, her nose in her glass.

"Or maybe you'd rather go back to the hotel and look for Mr. T in the wheelchair?"

"Oh, gawd." Karen rolled her liquid-blue eyes. I let out a chuckle and refilled her glass.

"I just don't want to grow old all alone," she said. There it was, out on the table, exposed like the underbelly of the delicate fish we had just eaten. "I have this recurring dream where I'm sitting alone in a room, all shriveled up, the only sound the gentle sucking of a respirator." Her eyes glistened with a hint of moisture.

"Hey, nobody wants to get old alone," I said, feeling a little melancholy myself. "I don't want to be one of those old ladies who throw birthday parties for their pets."

"You won't. You have Sam," Karen said, letting the words hang in the air between us, as if inviting me to either confirm or dispute her observation.

"Maybe," I said, studying the contents of my glass.

"Why are you so stubborn when it comes to Sam?" Karen asked, unfolding and folding her legs. "He's exactly the sort of man most women would give anything for—straight and true."

"Yeah, right," I said, sounding peevish.

"You know what your problem is?" Karen said, wielding her spoon in the air. "You're rigid."

"I'm not rigid."

"You're an ironing board."

I had always marveled at Karen's ability to start life anew each time she met a new man, full of hope and possibilities, as if the past didn't exist.

"You said it yourself, this afternoon. I'm scared, okay?" I punctuated my comment with a nod.

"Of what?"

It was my turn to roll my eyes. "Of what? That my shoes don't match my purse. What do you mean of what?"

Karen thought for a moment, and then she said, "You're scared of being married, and I'm scared of being single. We're quite a pair."

Our conversation was interrupted by the appearance of our waiter, an elderly gentleman with hunched shoulders. What remained of his gray hair circled the bottom half of his head like a dust ruffle. With a knuckly and unbalanced hand, he laid a leather folder on the table, the fan of lines at the corners of his eyes deepening as he smiled and encouraged us to take our time.

Karen stared at his back as he shuffled away.

"Listen to me," I said leaning forward. Karen turned to look at me. "You're a middle-aged woman who looks young.

You'll find someone." Karen reached across the table and squeezed my hand. The light in her eyes signaled her pleasure in my company. "And if you don't, we can be bag ladies together. You and your cart, and me with mine," I added with a smile. The prospect seemed to cheer her up.

"Maybe I should just stick with Mr. Pinky?" she said.

"At least he doesn't leave a wet spot," I replied.

With the bill settled, waiters hurried to pull back our chairs, their presence signaling that the table must be cleared and prepared for the next duo of well-heeled diners. We half-heartedly stepped into the bar and were greeted by a roomful of people twice our age.

"Let's just sign the mourner's book and leave," Karen quipped from behind her cupped hand. Lifting our chins in disdain, we turned and arm-in-arm, walked out.

—⚏—

I squeezed my eyes shut. Letting my mind wander back to that long-ago dinner with Karen reminded me of Sam. I tried to hope he'd be happy in his new job, his new home, for his sake, but I couldn't quite manage it.

The house was quiet. Everyone else was asleep. I had nothing to listen to but the sound of my own lonely breath.

# CHAPTER TWENTY-EIGHT

## *March 24, 2000*

I snapped awake from a dream in which I was trying to save Karen from drowning in the lake. I squinted at the bedside clock. 5:03 Disturbed by the dream, I pulled my sweats over my pajamas and put on my heavy socks.

I opened the bedroom door quietly, and tiptoed out into the loft. No sign of anyone else being awake.

In the kitchen, I flipped on the light and began to make coffee. One more day to go and the week's ordeal would be over. But the real ordeal, the loss of Karen, would be with me always. And I knew at times I'd catch a whiff of her perfume or see the back of a blonde head bobbing through a crowd, and be overwhelmed by grief.

As the coffee brewed, I wandered over to the sliding glass door. In my pre-coffee haze, the same questions kept haunting me. What if Greg was telling the truth? What if Karen did push off his bike on purpose? That suggests a world different from the one I know. Where any damn thing can happen. Which is exactly what this present circumstance feels like. But Karen would never do such a thing. She was too vain to take her own life.

As I strained to see the lake through the darkness, I caught a glimpse of an object on the end of the pier. Cupping my hands around my eyes, I leaned closer to the glass. Something or someone was out there. I turned and walked across the room and down the hall to turn off the alarm. Either it hadn't been set the night before, or someone had turned it off this morning. I lifted my parka off the peg and headed back toward the sliding glass door, which wasn't locked.

The cold air hit me like a wall of ice as I stepped outside. Closing the door behind me, I pocketed both my hands for warmth. My insulated socks offered little protection from the cold wooden planks of the deck. I squinted toward the end of the pier, but it was still too dark to see clearly. Suddenly, the object moved. My stomach jumped. Who would be out here at this time of the morning? I couldn't yell without waking the world, so there seemed no other choice but to go see for myself.

The wet grass made a squishy sound under my feet, as I crossed the small patch of lawn. Keeping my eyes riveted on the figure in front of me, I stepped onto the pier. The boards sprang under my weight, so that I rose and fell with each step. As I moved closer, I could make out the shape of a person sitting down, wrapped up in a blanket. Just then, I recognized the red Indian blanket Karen kept in the hall closet.

"Hello?" I called in just-above-a-whisper. No reply. I leaned forward and looked into the opening in the blanket, where the person's face was.

"Gidge. What the hell are you doing out here?" I asked, both relieved and confused. Her only response was to pull the blanket closer. I could have counted on one hand the times in Gidge's adult life when she'd been up before the sun rose.

Sighing, I sat down next to her, hugging my knees to my chest. Gradually, the cold permeated my body.

"Gidge, it's fucking freezing out here," I said, peering into the front of the blanket. I could see that her nose was bright red, and there were snail-like tracks glistening on her cheeks.

"Oh, Virginia Ann Peterson!" I said, reaching over and pulling my friend close. She let her head fall onto my shoulder, and we sat huddled together, our breaths coming out in front of us in little clouds. I became numb to the cold as we watched the sky begin to lighten. The water was a dark, muddy gray. It reminded me of wet ashes.

"Do you think Greg is telling the truth?" Gidge finally said in a fragile voice.

"I don't know," I said.

"People are supposed to keep going. No matter what, you can't give up," she said, as her tears welled up, and her voice dissolved.

"I know, sweetheart," I said, giving her a squeeze of consolation. A long time passed before she spoke again.

"Karen wasted her happiness, you know," she said. "Everyone's so fucking scared of being happy!" As I was considering her last statement, she said, "Remember when Karen came with me to divorce court and explained to the judge that just because I cut up Johnny's clothes didn't mean I was crazy?"

"How could I forget? You said she was like a regular female Perry Mason."

"She was. I remember the exact words she said to the judge. 'This woman didn't slice up her estranged husband, your Honor. She was just practicing some therapeutic cutting.'" Gidge shook her head. "If it weren't for her, I would never have been given custody of Joey." She wiped her nose on the blanket.

"I know." It was all I could think of to say.

Once again, we were quiet. The only sound was the lapping of the water against the pier pilings.

"Why would she let go, Liz?" Gidge asked. "It just doesn't make sense."

"I have no idea," I said.

I pictured myself weeks earlier, slumped in front of the TV, grief-stunned and job-panicked, briefly contemplating doing my own Sylvia Plath impression.

"Have you ever had thoughts of self-destruction, Gidge?"

She turned to me and blinked, looking puzzled.

"You know, wanting to off yourself."

"Actually, the summer after my divorce I sat on this very pier and thought about how easy it would be to tie a big rock to my leg and jump in." Gidge sniffed and wriggled inside the blanket. "But thinking about it and doing it are two very different things."

I nodded in heartfelt agreement. Life was disappointing at times, but still. I reached over and gave her a pat on the leg.

"In the end, they all go," Gidge said. "Parents, husbands, kids, even friends. What's the point of caring about anybody?"

Gidge was right. Everybody left you eventually. But that didn't stop us from clutching at life as if we could control it; as if by holding on hard enough to the people we cherish, our careers and even possessions, we might never be faced with loss.

"Why do we even exist?" This startled me, coming from Gidge of all people—a stubborn, cantankerous, feisty woman not given to philosophy.

"Whole religions have sprung up to answer that one, pal," I said, moving to get up. My knee popped.

"Ouch! Come on. Let's go inside where it's warm." I rubbed my frozen butt with both hands, hoping to re-start the blood flow. "We'll have some nice hot coffee, and talk some more." Slowly, she made a move to get up.

"Goddamn, son of a bitch!" she exclaimed, as her foot got tangled in the blanket.

"Here, let me help you, you old twat." I grabbed her arm and pulled the blanket from under her foot. "I don't want to be fishing you out of the lake."

"Why did she have to go with that son of a bitch anyway; him and his fucking motorcycle? Who does he think he is, Easy Rider?" Gidge honked her nose loudly in disgust.

I felt the corners of my mouth lift as I pointed her toward the house, wrapping my arm firmly around her short, but sturdy body.

"I tell you, he better not show his face around here. I'll kick his ass!"

"I know." I kept pushing her toward the house.

"Jesus Christ, it's cold out here," Gidge exclaimed, as if she had just noticed.

"No shit, Sherlock!" I said.

"Remember the bats we had that summer?" Gidge asked, looking up longingly at the huge pine tree next to the house. Her red nose was starting to run.

"Yes."

"Remember the Bat Patrol?" she asked, as we climbed the steps onto the deck.

"All those stupid knee-high nylons filled with moth-balls," I answered.

"And still the bastards buzzed us in bed every night," she said with a sniffle.

Gidge stopped short in front of the door. She looked up at me with tear-filled eyes, and I saw the gentleness in her face.

"We sure had some great times, didn't we, Liz?"

"We sure did. But they're not over yet."

"It won't be the same without Karen," she said bleakly. I had to agree.

# CHAPTER TWENTY-NINE

## *March 24, 2000*

I sent Gidge upstairs to take a hot shower. After turning up the heat, I went to the kitchen to pour myself a hot cup of coffee. As I took the first sip, I heard Gidge's words. "Everyone's so fucking scared of being happy." At that moment, a heaviness in the air pushed against me, the feeling that Aunt Vi stood beside me with arms crossed. I cocked my ear in anticipation.

"Am I afraid of happiness, Aunt Vi?" I held my cup with both hands, and gazed out the kitchen window at a giant pine tree, moisture dripping from its boughs. When was the last time I was happy; I mean throw-your-hat-in-the-air happy? I couldn't remember. I waited for Aunt Vi's answer. None came.

I wandered over to the dining room table and flipped open the photo album marked Volume I. A yellowed Polaroid stuck under the sheath of plastic: Karen and Casey, Arlene and Fred, and Ricky and me, all of us with red dots for eyes. New Year's Eve. We wore pointy hats and held noisemakers. A paper horn was wedged in Ricky's mouth, his cheeks puffed out. Those were the early days, visiting each other's houses bearing tuna-noodle casseroles and bean dip, playing Tripoly at the kitchen table, while our children sat glued to the TV in the other room. Who was it that said, "Often what brings us happiness also wounds us?"

I thought back on Ricky's confession to me the day before. For years, I'd longed to hear him acknowledge he'd made a mistake when he left. I was sure I would take pleasure in his admission, and flaunt what he'd lost in his face. But I was wrong. For the first time, I felt sorry for him.

I sighed, and closed my eyes. When I looked back at the picture, I soaked up the joyful image and let it cheer me over this life that hadn't turned out as I had envisioned.

A car door slammed. Julie must have taken the red-eye. I sat my cup in the sink and went to unlock the front door. She walked in wearing a three-quarter-length suede coat with fur trim and matching pants, looking like the model she was, tall, dark and beautiful. A burst of cold air swept in with her.

When she saw me, she dropped everything: her keys, her shoulder bag and the large canvas satchel she carried.

Julie had never been a crier, but her face crumpled up as she threw herself into my arms.

"Oh, Squeaker," I said, hugging her hard. She was as thin as a rail, except for the two hard implants that were her breasts.

Keeping her close, I led her toward Karen's bedroom. I opened the door and steered her toward one of the stuffed chairs in front of the fireplace, being careful to avoid the white plastic bag from the morgue lying on the floor just inside. She collapsed into the seat. I picked up the remote from the hearth and with the click of a button, the gas logs burst into flame. Sitting down across from her, I took both of her hands in mine. They were like ice.

"I hadn't talked to mom since her visit last month, you know?" Julie said, as though we were in the middle of a conversation. She sniffed and began to scrounge in her coat pocket. "When she told me she was coming down, I told her my agent was having this dinner party and to plan on going." She pulled out what looked like a cocktail napkin and ran it under her nose. "On the night of the party, while we were getting ready, I noticed she was really worked up. She was a nervous wreck. I said, 'Look it's no big deal, Mom. You've met most of these people before'."

I nodded, not wanting to interrupt.

"First she starts telling me what I should wear; 'No, not the red sheath, Squeak, that accentuates your tummy. No, that one makes your butt look big'. I mean, I make my living off this body. Doesn't she think I know what to wear?" Julie took another swipe under her nose. "Anyway, so we finally left for the party almost an hour late and she's got on this dress with her boobs all hanging out."

Karen knew how and when to bring out those big guns. Over the years she'd accumulated a closet full of V-necked sweaters, low-cut dresses and eye-popping underwire bras to wear when she needed them.

"When we get there, she starts drinking Bombers. Usually, she drinks white wine, so I'm totally thrown. I watched her like a hawk." Julie nervously patted her jacket pockets again.

"Do you happen to have a cigarette, Auntie Liz?"

"No, honey, I stopped smoking years ago." I leaned forward attentively, my elbows on my knees. "So then?"

"So then, she starts hanging all over Sid. Sid's my agent," she explained. "She's only met him once, but she's acting like they're best buddies. Poor Sid, he doesn't know what to do. She's got her arm around his shoulder, and she's acting all weird and I'm freaking out. I'm thinking what the hell is the matter with her?" Julie's hands began to tremble, either from the cold or nerves. "So then, somebody comes and tells me there are some people in the other room who want to meet me. She was busy emoting all over Sid, so I left."

I'd seen Karen like that before, desperate and clingy, thrusting her boobs in men's faces, as if that was all she had to offer.

Julie reached up and ran her fingers through her long hair.

"Anyway, after a while, I went back to look for her, and she was gone. I went from room to room, and just when I was beginning to panic, I saw her sitting alone on the couch in the living room, staring into the fire. She had an empty martini glass in her hand. I walked over and sat down beside her and asked if she was having a good time. After a long pause she snarled, 'Where the hell have you been? I've been ready to go for an hour.' I explained that I was right next-door. She didn't say a word. She just kept staring at the fire. I didn't want to start a scene, so I told her I'd go get my purse and we'd go. I was only gone for a minute but when I came back, the front door was standing wide open and she's nowhere to be found." Again, Julie combed her hair with her hand. "So I ran out the front door, but I didn't see her. I looked over where they'd parked my car and she wasn't there. Now, I'm thinking, Shit! Did she start walking? Where the hell is she? So I go over and ask one of the valets if he's seen her and he tells me some pretty blond lady just got in a cab and left. And I said cab, what cab? And he says someone called a cab." Julie's huge brown eyes were aglow with tears. "I couldn't believe it!" she said, tilting her head back and looking at the ceiling. "I leave her for five minutes and she takes off?"

Unable to control her emotions any longer, Julie buried her face in both her hands and broke down. "She flew home that night," Julie said through her sobs. "She wouldn't even let me take her to the airport."

I went to her, sat on the arm of the chair and wrapped my arms around her.

"And now she's dead," she said, her voice muffled behind her hands.

"Oh, Julie. I'm so sorry," I said.

She laid her head on my thigh and cried. I moved her hair away from her face, tucking it behind her ear. It was thick and soft, just like her mother's was at her age, only dark.

I couldn't help thinking how no mother is ever completely a child's idea of what a mother should be. And no child is exactly what a mother expects.

"She was very proud of you," I said. "You know that."

"No," Julie said in a soft voice.

"From the time you were born, you were the light of her life." A twinge of guilt passed through me as I remembered that Karen didn't always put Julie first in her life, not unlike her own mother. The men sometimes took precedence.

"I remember when your mom found out she was pregnant. She kept saying that she didn't care if she had a boy or a girl, just as long as she had a healthy baby. But secretly, we all knew she wanted a little girl." I continued to pet her. "And when you were born, she was so happy. She had been stashing away grocery money to buy frilly little pink and white dresses for you."

Julie lay quietly in my lap, gazing into the fire.

"When I went to visit you both in the hospital, I couldn't believe how excited she was. I remember walking into her room and being shocked to see her sitting on the edge of the bed in her robe and slippers. And before I could even say hello, she said, 'Come on, Liz, you've got to see her. She's the most beautiful thing you've ever seen'. So we trundled off, arm in arm, down the hall to the nursery to look at you through the window. And there you were all wrapped up tight in your little bassinet."

Gently, I tweaked Julie's earlobe. She mustered a small smile.

"Your eyes were wide open, and I swear you were looking right at us." I ran the back of my hand over Julie's smooth cheek.

"Your mother squeezed my arm so tight, I had a bruise for a week." Another small smile. "And then she said, 'Look at her! Isn't she the most precious thing you've ever seen?' And before I could answer, she said, 'I'm not going to screw this up, Liz.' When I looked over at her, I had never seen more love in your mother's face than I did at that very moment."

I sat there holding Julie, feeling a flood of disappointment in my friend. Oh Karen, how could you leave this beautiful child without even saying goodbye? You did screw it up. Big time.

I convinced Julie that she should get some sleep. Exhausted, she undressed and crawled into Karen's bed. I tucked her in and turned to leave, when I spotted something on the floor. A plastic wallet insert had slipped out of the bag of Karen's personal things. I reached down and picked it up. In the front section, I could see a yellowed card with the words "In Case of Emergency" printed on top in black letters. Arlene's name and phone number were written in Karen's big bubbly handwriting. I slid the packet into my pants pocket and quietly closed the door behind me.

# CHAPTER THIRTY

## *March 24, 2000*

Sitting alone at the table, sipping my second cup of coffee, I thought back on our era of early motherhood. How unprepared we were, not much older than children ourselves.

At age nineteen, Karen was the first to have a child. Impending motherhood only enhanced her beauty. She somehow escaped morning sickness, swollen ankles and hemorrhoids. Not one stretch mark marred her pale, round belly.

After Julie was born, we all gathered at Karen's on a regular basis to dote on the baby, a pack of love-crazed godparents. Pregnant myself, I memorized Karen's every move, how she cradled Julie in her arms being careful to support her head, and how she tested the milk on her wrist to be sure it wasn't too hot.

I asked why she chose not to breastfeed. "I've heard it makes your breasts sag," she said with admirable candor.

"My baby would probably starve if I nursed." I laughed.

Caring for an infant seemed to come naturally to Karen, while I was terrified at the prospect of having a baby. I'd once left my favorite baby doll out in the rain for four days, and its face peeled off.

My mother tried to prepare me for what it would mean to have a baby in the house. "You won't get much sleep for the first few months," she said with a knowing smile. Truth be told, once Kevin was born, I didn't want to sleep. I perched next to his bassinet like an owl on a limb to make sure he was still breathing. I loved to examine his tiny fingers, letting them instinctively curl around my forefinger; and his toes, shorter than the end of a Q-Tip. I giggled at the way his mouth made little sucking noises while he slept, and laughed out loud at his big burps.

"Takes after his father," I joked to Ricky, who beamed with delight.

Ricky was a great help, volunteering for the two a.m. feeding, even though he had to be up at six o'clock to go to work. Some mornings, I'd wake to find them both sound asleep in the easy chair; Ricky slumped down and the baby lying contentedly on his chest. I could hardly keep from crying.

Sufficiently caffeinated, I called the Police Department at a little after eight. A woman trilled 'good morning' before placing me on hold. I wanted to hear something that would implicate Greg, something concrete that would justify my gnawing suspicions. I stood looking into the high, silent living room richly bathed in yellow morning light from the windows. When she came back on the line, I asked for Officer Duarte. Again, she placed me on hold. I massaged the back of my neck with my free hand. Silence continued, so complete that I was aware of the ticking of the John Wayne poster clock on the far wall. Then: "Officer Duarte, here."

After identifying myself, I got right to the point. "Are you sure you checked everything?" I asked, pacing the length of the bar. "Skid marks, road conditions, possible witnesses?"

"I can assure you that the evidence we found supports the driver's statement that he lost control."

"But how do you know that he didn't lose control on purpose?" A pause. I heard a rustling of papers. "Are you aware, officer, that my friend, the deceased, had loaned Mr. Ronelli a large sum of money? Or maybe she'd loaned it to him. Or whatever." Stop babbling. "I mean did your investigation take into consideration a possible motive? This could be a homicide." I hammered my last words down with conviction. Another pause. More paper rustling.

"Ms. Hayden," he finally said in a patronizing tone. "The Mt. Rose Highway can be extremely dangerous in freezing temperatures. Unfortunately, over the years we've had a number of similar accidents on the summit. Nothing about this accident seems either unusual or suspicious."

"What if I had proof that Mr. Ronelli owed my friend a substantial amount of money?" I asked. "Wouldn't you be required to at least question him?" I wanted to climb through the phone and shake him.

"If you have any hard evidence that might lead to a motive, I'd be happy to look at it."

I sighed and called him an asshole, but only after I'd hung up. I had to find that damn will.

The harsh ringing of the telephone startled me. I rushed to answer it, hoping it wouldn't wake Julie.

"This is Dave Brenner calling," a deep voice said.

"Dave? Dave, Tahoe-Dave?" I asked. So many people had called since the obituary had appeared in the paper; it was hard to place them all.

"Yes, Dave the Dumb Dentist," he replied, sounding very formal. I couldn't stifle my laugh.

"Oh, Dave! How nice to hear from you," I replied. Karen had stayed in touch with him over the years. Although he'd been married for decades, he kept a place in his heart for her. I remembered this now with a pang of kindness.

"I spoke to Karen last week," he said. "We'd planned to go skiing next Monday. I just can't believe it."

"Neither can we, Dave."

"Is that who I think it is?" Gidge interrupted, rushing up behind me, her hair wrapped in a towel. "Let me speak to him," she said, reaching for the receiver. The hot shower had restored her feistiness.

I covered the mouthpiece with my hand. "Just a minute, please," I said between my teeth. I went on talking for an extra long minute before giving up the phone, just to annoy her. She gave me a look. I gave her one back.

"Dave, is that you?" she asked, practically jumping through the phone.

I ambled over to the breakfast bar, and pawed through the cards and notes of condolence that were piling up. My fingertips brushed over an envelope addressed to me in familiar handwriting. The New York postmark caught my eye. In another two weeks (fourteen days!) Sam would be permanently ensconced in his new residence. It had been a perfectly inescapable fact at home, yet the certainty of that fact had still to penetrate my reality here. Until now. I tucked the card into my pocket, next to the plastic wallet insert I'd picked up in Karen's bedroom.

"How is she?" Rosie asked, nodding toward Karen's bedroom where Julie was sleeping. We were sitting at the table with Jo and Gidge. Arlene was still asleep upstairs.

"Pretty upset," I said, reaching for a piece of toast. Rosie clicked her tongue.

"How do you expect her to be, Rose?" Gidge asked.

"I know," Rosie said. She nibbled at her lower lip.

I glanced over at Jo, whose chair was pushed back from the table. Her hands were heavy and loose in her lap, and her face looked pensive. I wondered if she was identifying with Julie, reliving the pain of losing her own mother.

"She looks great, though," I added. "It's hard to believe she's almost forty."

"She always looked young for her age," Gidge remarked. She leaned forward and picked up her coffee cup. "How else could she have sustained a successful modeling career in this youth-obsessed society of ours?"

"It's impossible for me to believe our kids are grown up," Rosie said.

"I know," Gidge said over her cup. "It seems like only yesterday that Joey took my diaphragm to school for "show and tell." Jo snapped to attention.

"Oh, I'd forgotten that," she said. The thoughtful expression I'd seen on her face earlier seemed to have disappeared. Jo had never had children. Nonetheless, she loved them; ours particularly. "I'll never forget when your Nathan stuffed half a meat loaf up his nose," Jo said to Rosie. "His little face was swollen up like a pumpkin."

Rosie shook her head at the memory. With four boys, Rosie had had the most medical emergencies. She'd learned that certain Lego's will pass through the digestive tract of a four-year-old and that garbage bags don't make good parachutes.

I was glad Arlene wasn't present for this conversation. Talk of our children never failed to remind her of Timmy. She'd pick at her fingernails, or find some other distraction to cover her inability to meet our eyes.

"Thank Goodness those days are over," Rosie said, raising her eyes heavenward. I wasn't so sure I was happy to have them over. With Sam gone, having my children around would have helped stave off my loneliness.

"I've got to check my messages," I announced, rising up from my chair.

In the privacy of my room, I retrieved the envelope from my pocket. I took a deep breath and opened the flap, being careful not to tear it, as if it might become a precious keepsake. On the front of the card was a picture of the ocean. The afternoon sun was low on the horizon, and the world seemed enveloped in a soft golden haze. With luxurious slowness, I drank in the scene, reminding myself that such beauty did exist in a world that for me had turned ugly.

I opened the card. The sentiment inside was short and simple. Thinking of you. Love, Sam. I traced the letters of his name with my fingertip.

I sank down onto the bed. The discovery that someone you thought you could count on was suddenly not there was like leaning on what seemed to be a good strong shoulder and feeling it go all mushy and strange. I was stupid to think Sam would always be there. Stupid.

I reached for the phone. Three new messages. My heart lightened. Surely, one was from Sam telling me he'd changed his mind about leaving. The possibility was almost too thrilling to contemplate.

I heard my former assistant Rita's voice first; informing me that Warren needed to speak to me right away. The next message was also from Rita. The last message was from

Warren himself, leaving me his direct dial number in case I'd forgotten.

I hung up the phone both puzzled and intrigued. What could Warren possibly want that was urgent? Maybe Mr. Glick had ratted on me for not finishing my stint at the outplacement center? No, he wouldn't care about that.

I punched in his number.

"Warren Steadwell's office," Keri answered, sounding bored.

"Hi, Keri. It's Elizabeth Hayden."

"Oh, thank goodness," Keri said. "Hold on, please." I heard a click.

Nestling the phone at my cheek, I turned and looked out the window above the bed. The morning was bright, clouds of fluff blowing in the sky. Karen was up there beyond the clouds, beyond the blue.

"Hello Elizabeth," Warren said. I pictured his slicked-back hair, the faint sprinkling of dandruff on the shoulders of his thousand-dollar suit. For weeks, his face had decorated the wanted poster in the post office of my mind.

"Hello Warren," I said. "I understand you wanted to speak to me." Over the next few minutes, Warren explained that, while the HR Director in Atlanta was "extremely competent," he just didn't seem to have the "skill set" needed to handle the job and, therefore, "the company" would like to offer me my old job back.

Music floated up from downstairs.

"Well, I-I don't know," I said when the silence had lengthened.

"I'm sure we can come to some mutually beneficial agreement," Warren said, sounding like the attorney he was.

I stood and walked over to the mirror above the dresser. I lowered my head and turned it a little to one side to give a more commanding look, the face I'd given myself in mirrors many times before entering into important business negotiations. Drawing strength from my image, I said, "I have several other opportunities in the works at the moment." I kept my eyes riveted to my reflection.

A pause set in. I leaned closer to the mirror. My eyebrows needed plucking.

"Well, it might help to know that due to the increase in the size of our employee population, the position has been upgraded to a Sr. VP level with a commensurate salary and bonus plan."

I allowed myself a small smile.

"And stock options?" I asked.

"A generous award with expedited vesting, of course."

This was fun.

I walked back to the bed and sat down on the edge, my back straight, legs crossed. "There are a couple of other important stipulations," I said. "I must have a guarantee that the position will remain in San Ramon. And, of course, I'll need my former assistant back." He didn't reply. Don't say anything. Remember the basic rule of good salesmanship.

Make your best offer and then shut up. Whoever speaks first loses. Sam taught me that.

"I think that can be arranged," Warren said. I mouthed "yes" and slapped my hand on the bed. "Do I have your verbal acceptance?"

"Yes."

"Good. I'll send out an offer letter detailing the terms and conditions we've discussed immediately. Welcome aboard."

I hung up the phone and fell back on the pillow. Oh, my God. I'd never known Warren to be so compliant. Stan must have screwed up big time. The little weasel.

I jumped off the bed and practically skipped to the shower.

We busied ourselves for the rest of the day with the final arrangements. It didn't seem appropriate to celebrate my good fortune with everyone focused on Karen's memorial. Gidge shared the news that Dave had offered us his boat to scatter Karen's ashes on Sunday. Arlene and I finalized the eulogy, Rosie reserved a block of rooms at the motel across the street for out-of-town guests, and Jo straightened up the house. Gidge drove into Tahoe City to order the flowers for the service.

Despite the noise, Julie slept until late afternoon. When she finally emerged, she looked rested and renewed, wearing her mother's white terrycloth robe, her wet hair pulled off her face in a high ponytail. She greeted and hugged each of her Aunties, allowing us to make a fuss over her.

"Are you sure there's nothing I can do?" she asked as we all huddled around her.

"Not a thing," Jo said.

Julie was silent for a moment. Then she said, "My mother would be so pleased to know that you are all here taking care of her."

"We loved her," Rosie said giving her an extra hug.

When the others had gone back to their chores, I said, "Julie, do you by chance know if your mother had a copy of her will somewhere in the house?" She looked confused. "We know she wants her ashes scattered in Emerald Bay, but I just thought if there was a copy around here, we could make sure there wasn't anything else she'd want us to know." Like how she'd loaned fifty grand to her so-called boyfriend and what we should do if she suddenly turned up dead!

"I know she has a copy in her safety deposit box," Julie said.

"Here at the lake?"

"No, at home in Parkerville." Drat! "I could contact her attorneys, if that would help. I'm sure they could send me a copy. Maybe even fax it. "

"I think that would be a good idea. You know, just to make sure."

"I'll call them right now."

I breathed the smallest sigh of relief.

By six o'clock, hungry and exhausted, we set out for the Mexican restaurant up the street. Julie had left a message with the secretary about the will. She opted to stay home.

"What did you bring to wear to the service?" Rosie asked Gidge, as we walked briskly toward the neon sign. The night air was crisp, and a million stars lit our way.

"The only black dress I own," Gidge replied. She had been unusually quiet since returning from her trip to the florist.

"Oh, that sounds nice," Rosie replied, a bit too cheerfully.

"I'm wearing a pantsuit," Arlene added, pulling her collar up around her neck.

"Which one?" I asked, hoping for one that hid her extra pounds. I wanted her to look her best for Fred.

"Navy with brass buttons," Arlene answered. A good choice.

"How many people do you think will come to the house after the service?" Rosie asked for about the tenth time.

"Stop worrying about the food, Rose," Arlene said. I'm sure you'll have plenty."

"I just don't want to run out of anything." In Rosie's family running out of food was a mortal sin.

We walked on in silence. From a distance came a rhythmic canine barking. I tried to rest my mind by listening to the rhythm of our footsteps. I still couldn't believe Warren's offer. Rita would be so pleased to be working in Human Resources again. I'd make sure she got a promotion and a raise, too. I hunched up my shoulders in delight. I may have been temporarily sidelined by life, but everything was back on track now.

The heat of the small restaurant welcomed us as we entered. The smell of hot food mingled with the aroma of mesquite burning tripped my salivary glands. Young families were crowded around simple wooden tables, lots of people leaning toward each other talking, a mixture of Spanish and English in the air. The hostess showed us to a table in the back and asked for our drink order.

"Let's get a pitcher of margaritas," Gidge suggested.

"Let's," I said, rubbing my hands together.

The service was fast and our meals arrived quickly. "Their enchiladas here are almost as good as mine," Rosie commented, adding more hot sauce.

"Your mom made the best enchiladas I've ever tasted," Jo said, breaking off a piece of her Tostada shell. "Her cooking made me want to kiss the hem of her apron."

"Now that she has no one to cook for, she lives on frozen dinners." Rosie sighed. "Here, Liz, taste this," she insisted, shoving a forkful in my direction.

"No thanks." I held up my hand. "I have an announcement," I said, shifting gears. "I got offered my old job back today."

"What?" Jo said.

"You're kidding," Rosie said.

"Well, really not my old job. A much better job, actually."

"Are you going to take it?" Arlene asked, a bottle of Tabasco sauce poised in mid-air.

"I've already accepted," I said.

"Are you sure?" Rosie asked. "The people at that place were crazy, working all those hours." She picked up her fork.

"Making a living is not the same as making a life." She hesitated. "I think Maya Angelou said that."

I turned my attention to Gidge who had just pulled her nose out of her margarita glass.

"I'm not good with advice," she said. "How about a sarcastic remark?"

"It doesn't matter. I've accepted and that's that. Let's talk about something else."

Feeling strangely ill at ease, I bumped my chair closer to the table and reached for the half-empty pitcher of margaritas in front of Gidge. I refilled my glass and took a swallow that lasted longer than a double feature. When I sat my glass down, I could see Rosie searching for something benign to say.

"How's your mom doing, Arlene?" she said.

"Yes, how is your mother," I said. I licked some salt from the corner of my mouth. Arlene looked at me for a second, as if deciding whether or not to answer. Then, she said, "Actually, she's doing fine now that she's settled in. The caretakers at this place seem much nicer and it's close enough that I can go visit a couple of times a week."

"Good," I said. "That's good to hear."

The busboy appeared and Gidge began speaking wobbly Español. He had no idea what she was saying. To make her point, Gidge reached across the table for the empty basket of chips. Her hand knocked over Arlene's water glass. Water went everywhere.

"Jesus, Gidge!" Arlene said, scooting her chair back to avoid the overflow. "Maybe you ought to take it easy on the margaritas." People turned to look.

"Maybe you ought to take it easy on the tacos," Gidge replied in a voice sharp as an ice pick, nodding toward Arlene's clean plate. The chill in the air could have re-frozen Gidge's margarita. Check, please.

# CHAPTER THIRTY-ONE

## *March 25, 2000*

Everyone except Gidge was up at the crack the next morning. JoAnn had tried to wake her from her tequila-soaked sleep in vain.

Rose moved expertly around the kitchen, humming to herself, as she finished the last of the hors d'oeuvres she'd started the day before. Julie spent the morning on the phone in her mother's room. We left her alone.

The kitchen counters were cluttered with bowls of various concoctions, and dirty utensils were everywhere. I was washing dishes. The monotony of the task was soothing for it allowed me to examine all the warring thoughts that had raged inside my head since my fight with Arlene.

I thought back to the months after Timmy's death, when she would fix me with a stare so bleak and empty that it was as if she were showing me the void where her heart used to be. She had shoveled everything into that empty place—books, gardening, men—but nothing filled it. It was true, our friendship hadn't been easy; our values couldn't be more different. And we hadn't always liked each other. But Arlene was more than an acquaintance with tenure. After all was screamed and done, I was committed to this relationship. That meant letting my anger go.

At a little after nine, Gidge appeared in the kitchen doorway, squinting and scratching her behind thoughtfully. "Is there any beer?" She yawned and shuffled over to the refrigerator.

"Are you sure you want more alcohol after last night?" Arlene said, as she picked up a dishtowel.

Gidge silenced her with a piercing look, and then said, "You may look like my mother, but you aren't."

"I'm making a protein shake," Rosie announced, pouring some milk into the blender. "You should try some of this."

"Are you nuts?" Gidge replied, turning to look at Rosie. As she did, she hit her elbow on the edge of the refrigerator door. "Son of a bitch!" she yelled, rubbing her elbow. Arlene smirked as she finished drying a mixing bowl and placed it in the cupboard.

"My mouth feels like the U.S. Army marched through it on piss call," Gidge said. I recognized the saying as one of her father's. "Beer and a shot of tomato juice is all I need." When neither could be found in the refrigerator, she closed the door and trudged over to the counter.

Jo's gaze roamed the length of Gidge. "What in the hell do you have on?" she asked. I smiled.

It felt good to take sibling-like snipes at each other. The light-hearted atmosphere helped camouflage, just for a moment or maybe an hour, the pain of what we had to do that afternoon.

Gidge looked down. "Shit, I don't know," she said. Her outfit was comprised of blue plaid flannel pajama bottoms and a pink cable-knit pullover sweater, over which was an oversized T-shirt with the slogan "I'm Out of Estrogen and I Have a Gun" printed on it. "It was so fucking cold last night, I just kept reaching down next to the bed and pulling clothes out of my bag." Looking back at Jo, she added, "Hey, you'd better be nice to me, or I won't be around to empty your bedpan." She shook her finger in the air.

Jo poured herself a cup of coffee.

"What is all this shit?" Gidge asked, gesturing toward the bowls and trays on the counter.

"It's the food for after the service, silly," Rosie answered. She flipped the switch on the blender. Gidge grabbed her head with both hands and grimaced. When the noise stopped, she continued to peruse the variety of mixtures in various stages of completion.

"Jesus, Rosie, you're like Julia Child hopped up on Fibercon, or something," Gidge said.

Rosie snorted. "You're the one who's always constipated."
Touché.

"You got me there, kid," Gidge said, pulling her sweater sleeves down over her hands for warmth. "At my age, getting a little action means I don't have to take a laxative."

"Can we please not talk about bowel movements this morning?" I said, pulling a face, as I took off my apron.

Within the next hour, we were dressed for the service. Jo was wearing a chocolate brown St. John knit dress, which surprised me. Before she got wealthy, she, like Gilda Radner, based most of her fashion choices on things that didn't itch. Arlene looked quite trim in her navy pantsuit, the long jacket hiding her hips as she re-positioned the photo albums on the table behind the sofa to make room for the food. Without thinking, I had packed the black suit I'd worn on my last day at work. Now, it seemed only fitting. Two days of equal doom. If only Karen could come back to life the way my job had done.

Rosie was pacing the floor. The knee-length skirt of her gray suit showed off her muscular calves. "I don't know where Jay and the boys could be," she said, checking her watch.

"Quit being such a worry wart," Jo said, securing her diamond stud earring. "We have plenty of time."

A car door slammed. "I'll get it," Rosie called as she hurried down the hall.

"Look who I found," Rosie announced moments later, her arm hooked through Ricky's. His smile curled up at the corners of his mouth, and his eyes twinkled.

I felt a slight aftershock, the trace effect of whatever it was that visited me the other day when I first saw him; love, tenderness, nostalgia.

"Would you like a cup of coffee?" Rosie asked.

"No thanks, Hon." He used to call me hon.

Gidge was the first to make a move, rushing at Ricky and practically tackling him. She stood on tiptoes and threw her arms around his neck. Ricky let out a laugh. "Hey, how the hell are ya?" she said.

"Fine, fine," he replied, hugging her back.

Jo and Arlene followed suit with more restraint, but with genuine glad-to-see-you vigor. Ricky greeted each of them warmly, pressing his cheek to theirs. I was reminded that one of the reasons I'd fallen in love with Ricky was the way he'd made my friends his friends.

I got up from my chair, sucking in my stomach and smoothing my skirt.

"Could I speak to you for a minute, Liz?" Ricky asked looking over at me.

"Sure," I said. "Let's go out on the deck." As we walked toward the sliding glass door, the girls scattered.

Arlene had spent the previous afternoon planting pink azaleas surrounded by white sweet alyssum in clay pots, and placing them in groups on the wooden deck. Each bouquet-like arrangement resembled puffs of cotton candy trimmed with lace. The fresh scent announced the arrival of spring, along with the promise of better days.

I wrapped my arms around myself.

"Cold?" Ricky asked. He, of all people, knew I was always cold. When we were married, he had complained about my feet feeling like blocks of ice against his bare back at night.

Without waiting for my answer, he shrugged out of his sports jacket and draped it over my shoulders. I uncrossed my arms and pulled it close, fingering the soft wool.

"Thank you," I said.

"I was wondering if you'd like me to drive you to the service?" he asked. His thick white hair was shaggy around his ears, giving him a boyish look.

"Thanks, but I'm going with Kevin and Kristen," I said.

"Ah," he said with a nod. His face grew solemn. I thought about telling him he could come with us, but I said nothing.

"You've done a great job with the kids," he said. Our eyes locked. His looked sad, as if his long eyelashes were too heavy for the lids to hold up. He reached for my hand. His hand, rough with years of hard work as a pipe fitter, engulfed mine in a familiar warm clinch.

As I stared at the man to whom I had lost my virginity, I felt my eyes fill with tears.

"Hey, I used to make you laugh," Ricky said. He let go of my hand and reached into his pants pocket. "Out loud. Until you got hiccups." He offered me a folded white handkerchief, a tiny gold sticker still glued to the corner.

"We were a lot younger then." I sniffed and dabbed at my eyes. "There was more to laugh about."

"You're right," he said. We were quiet for a moment. I fingered the hanky in my hands. Ricky looked like he wanted to say something, but was holding back.

"What?" I said.

"I wrote you a letter."

"I never got it."

"I never mailed it."

"Oh."

"You know how bad I am talking about my feelings," he said. "I thought if I wrote them down… Anyway, I just wanted, I mean, do you think there's any chance that you and I could start over?"

His face was so innocently hopeful I couldn't look at it. All I could think of was how for the longest time, I would have given anything for Ricky to ask this. I had brooded on the fantasy of a second chance for us, absolutely certain that it would be the answer to everything. Now, when I searched my feelings I found nothing there to guide me, only confusion and self-doubt.

I drew a ragged breath. "This really isn't the right time, Ricky."

His shoulders slumped. My initial impulse was to try to comfort him. But I knew if I so much as touched him, I'd be in his arms and sobbing, my tears soaking his shirt as I cried over all that had been lost: our marriage, Sam, Karen.

With an unsteady hand, I removed his jacket from my shoulders and offered it to him.

"You're right," he said again, this time with a slight hesitation in his voice and a distinct averting of his eyes. He slipped on his jacket, adjusting the collar of his shirt underneath. "I'll give you a call when you get home."

When he kissed me on my cheek, I let his lips linger for a heartbeat before pulling away. His features jumped into a bashful smile, the kind that used to make me jelly-kneed. Then he turned and left.

After he'd gone, I tipped my head back so that the tears that had filled my eyes wouldn't spill over.

Back inside, Rosie was at my elbow. "So?" she asked.

"He wanted to know if I'd like a ride to the service," I said. I found it hard to keep my voice from thickening into a sentimental husk.

"That was sweet," Rosie said, turning back to arranging the flowers on the dining room table. She knew there was more, but she was willing to wait.

As the time for the service grew nearer, the mood was not quite somber, but there was a sense of purposely-good behavior. Even Gidge treaded lightly in her talk.

Rosie's boys, Matthew, Jeff, Nathan and Jay, Jr. arrived first. They looked so mature in suits and ties. I caught sight of the little bald spot on top of Matt's head. How could this little boy be losing his hair? But then, remarkably, he was turning thirty-eight this year.

When Kevin and Kristen arrived, Julie greeted them with a little two-note song of hello, and pecks on their cheeks, which made Kevin flush crimson. Karen and I always thought that Julie and Kevin would have made a cute couple.

It was difficult for me to believe that this nice man with a neat haircut, an upbeat attitude, who was polite to older people, and who attended services at the First Presbyterian Church every Sunday, was my son. His teenaged experimentation with drugs and shoplifting had made me think he would end up in prison.

"Jeez, Mom," Kevin complained, as I kissed his cheek for the third time.

Kristen stood next to him, unaware of her body or her physical image: tall, solid as a totem pole, even features. Her hair cut in a broomstick-blunt bob flattered her heart-shaped face.

It was so good to see these faux-cousins all together, going around the room shaking hands or giving each other awkward hugs.

"Look at them," Jo said, stepping up beside me. "They're all grown up."

"The only one missing is Timmy," I said. I scanned the room for Arlene. She was standing in the far corner of the dining room, talking with Gidge's daughter-in-law, Wendy. "I can still picture her sitting in Fred's recliner clutching Timmy's size-twelve tennis shoe tenderly to her cheek."

"So sad," Jo said.

I swallowed hard.

"Remember when we used to fish for crawdads off the end of the pier?" I heard Kevin ask one of the boys. They were standing in a loose circle in front of the fireplace, hands in their pockets, rocking back on their heels like grown men do.

"And then you'd chase Julie and me with them," Kristen said, punching her brother on the arm.

Karen had bought each of the boys a fishing pole, which was kept at-the-ready in the hall closet. I wondered if they were still there.

"I remember the summer Timmy and I went to Camp Parkerville together," Nathan said to his mother, who was hovering nearby. Rosie licked her fingers and stood on her tiptoes to smooth his hair. Across the room, Arlene cocked her ear to listen.

"You came home with a permanent ring of chocolate around your mouth and poor Timmy must have had a million mosquito bites," Rosie remembered.

"That's because he kept squirting the bug spray at the mosquitoes instead of spraying it on his body," Nathan explained with a laugh.

I glanced over to see Arlene's soft smile. I sauntered over and laced my arm through hers. Eyes distant, she gave my arm an appreciative squeeze.

We stood together, listening to their reminiscences. A lump of fear lodged in my throat. Is this their fate? To bump into each other at funerals and be amazed that they are the same children who ran around outside with towels tied around their necks, pretending to be Batman, while spraying each other with imaginary bullets—the same close friends who slept two-to-a-sleeping bag, while their mothers stayed up all night talking downstairs? I could only hope their memories were as precious as mine.

# CHAPTER THIRTY-TWO

## *March 25, 2000*

I rode with Kevin and Kristen. Rosie and Gidge went with their families. Arlene and Jo had gone early to attend to the last minute details. At Julie's request, we decided against having the ashes at the service.

The small gravel parking lot was almost full when we arrived. It had been brilliantly sunny and fresh most of the week, but today the sky was the color of steel and heavy with clouds, as if the heavens were as sad to see this day come as we were. As I gazed out the window from inside the warm car, the little chapel sat lonely and cold amongst a group of leafless trees. Two men I didn't recognize were standing on the cement steps, smoking.

Kevin pulled into one of the last parking spaces. I could feel a sharp sickness rise, the one that comes when you realize the worst that can happen has. There was no turning back. Stepping out of the car, a wave of nausea came over me. I bent over to try to get some blood to my head. As I stood bent in two breathing deeply, footsteps rushed toward me.

"Are you okay, Mom?" Kevin asked.

"I'll be all right," I said, staring at my knees. I could see Kristen's long legs behind me. "Just give me a minute." Slowly, I raised myself upright and took a couple of tentative breaths. The nausea subsided. Kristen's big hazel eyes brimmed with tears. I reached out and stroked her cheek with my index finger, allowing myself the remembered pleasure of touching her when she was my property and I was hers; the days when I dressed her for school; the days when I licked my thumb and rubbed a smudge of dirt off that same soft cheek.

I twined my fingers through hers, holding on tight, and the three of us set off across the parking lot.

As we entered the little foyer of the chapel, I was relieved to see how cheerful the inside looked. The stained glass windows of bright blue, yellow and red seemed to glow, despite the lack of sunshine. The wooden floor, freshly polished, gleamed richly in the light from the windows. At the altar, white candles, brightly burning, filled a table, their flames reflected in the glass of a silver frame. Jo had snapped the picture at Karen's birthday party last year. She looked radiant leaning against the deck railing at the Tahoe house, the colors of the sunset behind her. Gidge had ordered a massive spray of white roses, Karen's favorites, which cascaded over the edge of the table. The scent of the flowers was sweet and sorrowful.

Everything was perfect. Karen would approve.

I counted six rows of pews, most of them filled. People were greeting each other in whispers. I felt comforted seeing others who came to share our grief and to seek solace for Karen's loss.

I found myself scanning the group for Greg, but didn't see him. Maybe he couldn't face this. Maybe the guilt was too much. I caught a glimpse of the back of Julie's head, her long dark hair tied at the nape of her neck with a simple black ribbon. She was in the second row sitting next to Rosie's husband, Jay, who had his arm protectively around her shoulders. We had reserved the first two rows on the left for family. We girls would sit together in the front row, our families behind us.

"I'll walk you up, Mom," Kevin said, offering me his arm. His carefully barbered light brown hair shone soft and baby fine in the glow from the window, and his wide-set brown eyes sparkled with worry. I turned and saw wet streaks down Kristen's face.

As we took the short walk up the aisle, a wonderful sense of quietude and peace settled over me. We had planned everything. The ceremony would be short and simple, as Karen would have wanted.

I squeezed in between Arlene and Rosie just as the minister appeared at the pulpit. He was a tall man with silver hair, a pleasant face and the biggest diamond pinky ring I'd ever seen. Strange for a man of the cloth, I thought.

I leaned forward to smooth my skirt under me and glanced across the aisle. There, not ten feet away, looking right at me, was Fred Heflin, Arlene's ex-husband. His once strong jaw line was now loose with jowls, and his warm brown eyes looked sad. I knew he must be thinking of Timmy. I was barely able to resist the impulse to rush over and give him a reassuring hug. I smiled back instead.

Behind Fred sat Dale Terry, one highly polished cowboy boot sticking out in the aisle for all to admire. On his right was Harry Krupman, and next to him, Ricky, eyes downcast, hands clasped in his lap as if he were praying.

I opened my purse and retrieved the handkerchief he'd given me back at the house. As I picked at the gold sticker on the corner, I thought how with one word, I could have changed everything. When he walked down the steps and turned to leave, I could have called his name and he would have come back.

"Let us pray," the minister said, his voice echoing in the high-ceilinged space. I bowed my head, closed my eyes. Such comforting words. I had noticed that my occasional excursion into church, for a wedding or funeral, would elicit a strong emotional response. Maybe I'd start going again? Kevin would like that. A chorus of Amens.

"We are gathered here today to celebrate the life of Karen Ann Christensen," the minister began. We girls had been at a loss as to which surname to use, so we opted for Karen's maiden name. "I did not have the privilege of knowing Karen personally, so I am pleased to have one of her most cherished friends, Ms. Arlene Shoren, assist me in delivering her eulogy." A smile fluttered at the soft corners of his mouth, as he acknowledged Arlene with a nod. She blushed and lowered her eyes.

"Born in Gold Run, Oregon, the only daughter of Sara and Gunther Christensen," the minister continued in a slow, deliberate voice, enunciating every syllable. There would be no mention of Karen's birthdate. We didn't want her to come back and haunt us.

Rosie took a delicate lace handkerchief from inside her sleeve. Gently, she touched the underlid of each eye, being careful not to smear the make-up she hardly ever wore.

When it was Arlene's turn to speak, I was impressed by her composure as she climbed up the steps and stood at attention at the pulpit. Since Timmy's death she had become a master at sidestepping feelings.

She unfolded a single sheet of paper and began.

"I did know Karen Ann Christensen. She was my dear friend. We knew each other for over forty years. Even when we weren't speaking, we were friends." Arlene cleared her throat and went on in an unruffled voice. "I never stopped being amazed that despite knowing me better than just about anybody, she loved me just the same." She brushed us with her eyes.

"I learned a lot from Karen. When I was fifteen, she taught me how to curl my eyelashes and after my son's death, she taught me to keep going long after I thought I could." Out of the corner of my eye, I saw Fred dab at his eye with his handkerchief.

As I listened to Arlene, I realized how much I, too, had learned from Karen—and from Jo, and Rosie, and Arlene, and even Gidge. Grateful for a past littered with helpful lessons, I was less interested in passing judgment or assigning blame than in accepting each of them for who they were.

Filled with a rush of affection toward my friends, I reached over and squeezed Rosie's hand.

When Arlene had finished her speech and returned to her seat, the minister recited the 23rd Psalm. He ended the service with, "May God be with you." A few regular churchgoers responded, "And with you."

Most of the people were silent and stiff as they pressed up the aisles and out the main doors. They moved as if the calm and orderly escape from this place had become the one great necessity of their lives.

Outside, a swollen dark cloud hovered directly overhead, but there were also promising patches of sun. People were gathered in small groups, blotting their noses with tissue, talking quietly. As I searched the crowd for my children, I found it strange that I should feel so content and settled, as if something inside me had softened or reconciled.

My reverie was interrupted by the sight of Gidge taking long strides, the heels of her new shoes clacking on the cement. Members of the congregation turned to look.

"Where's she going?" Arlene asked from behind me.

I caught sight of Greg, just before Gidge reached him. He looked ten years older than the other day at the restaurant, standing off to the side like an intruder.

Gidge flew at him. She slapped his face, and then beat on his chest with her fists. He neither flinched nor tried to avoid her blows. Arms at his sides, he seemed to welcome the punishment.

"You bastard! You killed her! You bastard!" she screamed hysterically.

Just then, a man pushed through the crowd and dashed across the concrete like a wide receiver attempting to score the winning touchdown. In the space of a gasp of breath, I recognized Sam's broad shoulders and long legs.

"Let me through, please. Excuse me." I muttered, making my way down the steps as Gidge continued to lash out. When I reached them, I could see her handprints on his cheeks.

Sam grabbed both of her wrists. "Gidge! Gidge!" he yelled into her face. Greg took a step back. Gidge struggled to free herself.

"Virginia Ann!" I said. I brushed Sam's hand with mine, as I wrapped my arm firmly around her thick waist and pulled her close to my hip. The muscles in her jaw were flexing as she clenched her teeth. She turned to look at me. Her eyes were wild. "Stop it," I said, in the harshest tone I could muster. The anger in her face scared me.

The minister appeared. "Let's take her in the back," he whispered, his breath smelling of mint. "Come along, dear," he said, laying his hand on her shoulder. Gidge didn't budge.

"Gidge, come with me," Sam said, not loosening his grip. Again, Gidge turned to me.

"Go on," I instructed, nodding toward the chapel.

As the minister and Sam ushered a reluctant Gidge away, I took a step toward Greg. Part of me wanted to apologize for Gidge's actions; the other part felt he deserved what had been dished out. Torn, I blinked and stood mute, looking at him.

His eyes fixed on mine, and I was filled with a sense of dread; dread that he had indeed told me the truth.

"I'd better go," he said, adjusting his suit jacket. He began sidling toward the parking lot, his rubber soles making squeaky sounds on the wet pavement. Just as well.

By now the mourners had started to disperse, with lots of head shaking and tongue clucking. I turned my attention to the path that led around to the side of the chapel. Sam was back there. He'd known how important this was to me all along, and he'd come.

"Mom?" I turned to see Kristen at my side, her hand on my arm.

"Hmm, what?"

"Do you want us to stay?"

"Oh no, honey, why don't you and Kevin go on ahead," I said, patting her hand. "I'll catch a ride with…someone."

When she'd gone, my thoughts began to swing wildly. Don't read too much into his being here. But why would he come if he didn't really care about me? Because he's a very kind and thoughtful man, that's why.

A long clean serpent of cars was exiting the parking lot, billows of exhaust filling the cold air. I wrapped my arms around my middle and curled my tired toes inside my shoes, looking down at them. From somewhere high and far away came the faint crawling drone of a plane.

I heard his footsteps first. Please God, let him tell me he's not going. No plea was ever more passionate yet more gently carried by a breath.

With a confident, fluid sureness, he walked toward me. A wind rushed in and lifted the front edges of his suit jacket. My hands fumbled with the buttons on my coat.

"She's a handful, that woman," Sam said as he walked up in front of me.

"You know, Gidge. Never a dull moment," I said. Sam smiled; the kind of smile that makes things seem not so bad. My breath slowed down, my heart stopped knocking inside my chest, and I began to regain my senses.

"What made you decide to come?" I asked.

"Let's go inside," Sam said. "It looks like it might rain." The sky overhead had become a dense blanket of gray clouds that resembled bunched-up dryer lint. He put his hand under my elbow and led me back toward the chapel. As we mounted the steps, a modest glow flickered to life within me, like a candle in the night.

Inside, the lights had been turned off, except for the one over the altar that illuminated Karen's picture. We sat down in the last pew. Sam took both my hands in his.

"You know I've always admired your independence. It's one of the qualities that made me fall in love with you."

I opened my mouth, but before I could speak Sam said, "Please let me finish."

I obeyed.

"My point is you've proven you can take care of yourself." He squeezed my hands. "Now, I want to take care of you."

"Warren offered me my old job back," I said in a rush.

"Well, I'm glad he realized his mistake, however belatedly."

"And I've accepted." I expected Sam's face to register shock of some kind. But he looked calm, almost introspective, as if evaluating what I had said.

"So unaccept," Sam said matter-of-factly. "What counts is our being together. No job, yours or mine, is more important than that."

At his words, I felt something take hold in me, something to do with risk.

"We can do this," he added, kneading my hands in his. Outside, raindrops began dripping from the eaves producing a light ding-ding-ding sound.

"What do I do…?" The past few weeks seemed to catch in my throat. I swallowed hard. Then started again. "What do I do with all the fear stored up inside me?"

"Being afraid isn't the end of the world," Sam said gently. "Everyone's afraid in his own way." I blinked. "It's okay to be scared."

"This scared?"

Sam let out a gentle laugh. "Okay, maybe we'll have to find you a psychiatrist in New York. I hear the place is loaded with them." I couldn't help but smile. "Come with me, Liz."

I quickly backtracked to Warren's startling offer of re-employment. What was it about the prospect of returning to work that made me happy? I pictured myself sitting at my desk frowning into the telephone, spewing forth advice I knew wouldn't be heeded, while email messages piled up on the screen, and stacks of manila folders filled with paper and arranged in order of importance by Rita, competed for my attention. Is that what I really wanted?

"Your heart knows the answer," Sam said gently. "Listen to it."

I took a long breath and waited to hear the familiar sirens blaring, red lights flashing—stop, turn back, dead end. But they were silent.

I turned toward the altar for one last look at Karen's picture. Bathed in a puddle of lamplight, her easy smile was encouraging. I could almost hear her saying sure things don't exist. Sam definitely does. Take him for as long as it lasts.

When I looked back at Sam, I saw the man I had fallen in love with; the man who helped me let my storms die. In his eyes, I saw a soft place to fall.

"Yes," I said, my voice barely audible.

"Yes?" Sam repeated. Even in the uncertain light, I could see delight dawning across his features.

"Yes." I looked at Sam. Something wondrous passed between us. He pulled me to him and kissed me as if it were the very first time.

The rain shower had stopped by the time we left the chapel. I wished I could sit close to Sam in the rental car—I wanted him to hold my shoulders while he drove, but the console was in the way. He held my hand instead.

With a flowing smoothness, one-handed, Sam steered the car out of the parking lot and onto the hard clean straightaway of Highway 89. I gazed out the window, appreciating every tree and cabin that came briefly into sight as we drove by. My thoughts drifted back to Ricky. I realized I'd been holding him accountable for a long-standing emotional debt. But that was only part of it. I held on because I thought there was still something between us, remembering what it was like to be in love with him. After seeing him, that magnetic pull had weakened to a faint plaintive tug that I labeled as familiarity and nothing more. I could see now that dwelling endlessly on the past had kept me from tackling the terrifying future.

I turned to look at Sam's profile, a faint smile on his lips. Never before had elation welled more powerfully inside me: a heady mix of hope, surprise, disbelief, anticipation and gratitude, all crushed into one. Never was I more sure that the past could dissolve at my will. My heart lifted at the thought.

# CHAPTER THIRTY-THREE

*March 25, 2000*

Only a handful of cars ringed the circular drive of Karen's house, which didn't surprise me based on the mourners' reactions to Gidge's outburst.

Sam had come back to me, and I wasn't ready to let him go and return to the sad business of burying my best friend.

"When do you have to leave?" I asked, gripping his hand.

"I have a 3:30 flight out of Reno to New York."

My shoulders sank. "So soon?"

"They're throwing a going away party for Leo tomorrow night at the Pierre." Sam stroked my hair. "I have to be there."

I scowled into my lap, feeling the distance spreading between us.

"I'll be back in the city on Tuesday," he continued softly. He touched my shoulder. I hunched it upward until my cheek was pressed to his hand.

Having said my reluctant farewell, I watched as he backed out of the driveway and turned onto the frontage road. He stopped the car and leaned over to wave to me through the passenger window. I blew him a kiss.

I carried the feel of his warm hand on my cheek with me into the house. The six pegs over the bench were piled with layers of coats and scarves, all except the one that held Karen's white parka. I reached up and stroked the sleeve before placing my coat tenderly over hers. Then I drew in a breath, straightened my shoulders and strode down the hall.

From the hallway, I caught a slice of the living room, the fireplace ablaze. Next to it stood Harry, Gidge's ex, by himself, looking shy and out of place. I knew if I went in to greet him, I'd be forced to circulate. Stalling for time, I ducked into the kitchen.

Rosie and Jo were busy at the counter, their backs to me.

"Well, that went over like a turd in the punchbowl at the church social," I said, borrowing one of Karen's memorable quotes. It was Rosie who reacted first. She turned to me with a look that said, "That may be funny, but shame on you just the same."

"Like it or not, one does have to admire the intensity of Gidge's feelings," Jo said. She licked something off her index finger.

"Gidge is just Gidge," Rosie said in a matter-of-fact tone. Rosie was right. The rest of us had become other people, which I assumed was what was supposed to happen, but it hadn't happened to Gidge. Strangely, I found comfort in my friend's lack of personal evolution. I liked that she remained the same old Gidge.

"Karen always said she had more balls than a Chippendale's review," Jo added, as she reached for the silver ice bucket.

"You must have been surprised to see Sam," Rosie said, her eyebrows held high.

"Yes."

"And…?" Jo said.

"We talked."

Rosie wheedled further: About what? Did I tell him about my new job? What about Ricky?

"I'll tell you all about it later, I promise. But now we should attend to our guests."

"Liz is right," Jo said. She whipped the plastic wrap off a tray of cold cuts with a flourish. "We'd better get out there," she said, marching past me.

The last thing I wanted to do was play hostess. I wanted to put the rest of the day on fast forward, and get it over with. But it couldn't be avoided. With my jaw set in an attitude of brute endurance, I followed Jo, stepping just inside the living room to assess the situation.

Julie was mingling with the guests; introducing herself to people she hadn't met in the same voice she must have used to sell some cosmetic or perfume. She held herself like a young woman who had taken a lifetime of ballet lessons. There is nothing more alluring than good posture. I watched in amazement as she glided from one person to another, hand outstretched, doing a slow step-pause-step, meeting all eyes head on, managing to make every person feel that he or she was the most important one there.

It must have been hard for Karen to have a daughter like Julie, one who is so successful and self-confident that she couldn't possibly give the slightest indication of needing you at all.

I inched forward and did an eyeball sweep of the room, searching for a friendly face. In the corner by the window stood two blond women wearing make-up in jellybean colors and tight clothing that showed off perfectly sculpted bodies. Their abs looked hard enough to deflect bullets. They must be from Karen's health club. I sure as hell didn't want to talk to them.

Helping themselves to the buffet were Karen's nosy neighbors, the ones who threatened to call the police when we set off the illegal fireworks that 4th of July, when our children were small. She was a little bird-like woman with a pinched face and hair the smoky gray of cat fur, and her husband was a doddery old man who looked like the typical villain in a silent movie—the cruel banker who would take pleasure in closing down the town orphanage. I didn't want to talk to them either.

"Such a shock," a voice from behind me said. I turned to see a woman in her sixties stuffed into a Pucci-print dress that was too tight. Every bulge showed. "I'm Helga Helstrom," the woman said with a mouth that looked like it had spent a lifetime whistling. She extended her pudgy bejeweled hand to me. "I own the ski shop on Lakeshore. Karen was one of my best customers." Her hand was hanging out there like a limp flounder, fingernails lacquered in garish red.

"Nice to meet you," I forced myself to reply.

"I'm so sorry," she said, hanging on to my hand.

"Thank you."

"Are you her sister?"

My impulse was to answer yes. Instead I said, "No, just a good friend."

The man from next door joined us. "I just saw her on Monday," he said. "She was such a lovely woman. Such a shame," he added, before popping an hors d'oeuvre into his mouth and wiping his mustache with his forefinger.

I felt my back stiffen. How dare these people speak inadequate words of condolence to me! They didn't give a shit about Karen; not really. They were just here for the free food and a little gossip. Liars! I pulled at the collar of my suit jacket, feeling claustrophobic.

"If you're thinking of having an estate sale, I have some contacts," Helga said. Just then, I spotted the two blonde babes standing at the sofa table, flipping through one of the photo albums, pointing and smirking as if to say, "Get a load of that hairstyle," or "Check out that outfit!"

I could feel my irritation mounting. "If you'll excuse me," I said as I turned and almost ran toward the door.

The blast of cold air burned my eyes as I raced across the deck, down the steps, and out to the end of the pier. Gulping in the fresh air, I waited for my racing heart to slow. It was colder now, and the sky was getting even darker. I paced back and forth, wiping the tears from my cheeks.

I heard footsteps behind me.

"Are you okay?" Jo said, coming up next to me.

"Yeah," I said. "I guess for a minute the whole thing just got to me."

"Hmm." The wind lifted around us. Jo crossed her arms tightly over her chest as if she were battening herself down.

"Where's Arlene, by the way?" I asked.

"She stayed back with Gidge," Jo said. I'd been so wrapped up with Sam, I hadn't noticed.

"I'm used to being stunned by Gidge's behavior, but this time she managed to outdo even herself," Jo said, hugging herself.

"I know what you mean," I said. "She said she was going to kick Greg's ass, but I never really thought..." I took another swipe at my wet cheek. "You really never know what someone will do under pressure." I sucked in another deep breath of cold air. "Do you think Karen was under some kind of pressure we didn't know about?"

Jo uncrossed her arms and turned toward me. Her face seemed pained, her eyes taking me in like she wanted to understand me. "Like what?"

"Oh, I don't know." I frowned at my feet. "I'm grasping at straws, I guess, trying to make sense of it."

She linked her arm through mine. We stood together quietly, arm-in-arm, looking out over the murky water. I felt myself begin to relax as the serenity that Jo always projected flowed into me.

"I'm really glad Sam came. For your sake," Jo said. "He's a good man."

I patted her arm in gratitude.

"I'm going back inside and have a glass of wine. Want one?"

"In a minute." Jo offered me a tissue.

I lingered a while longer watching the sun play hide-and-seek with the threatening clouds and thinking. Sam was a good man. During my children's rough teenage years, he had been my staunch supporter, stepping in when I asked, not as a substitute father, but as the voice of reason. And despite their occasional foot scuffing and eye rolling, he always seemed to get through to them. When each of my parents died, it was Sam who helped me sort through important papers, reading the fine print and making notes.

More footsteps. Faster this time.

"Mom, are you okay?" Kristen asked, a little out of breath. Her face was full of concern. "Kevin said he saw you run outside."

"I'm fine, honey," I said, trying to reassure her. "I just got a little overwhelmed." She nodded. "How are you?"

"I'm fine."

"Are you having any fun?" I asked, tucking a lock of hair behind her ear. Kristen rolled her eyes like a high school sophomore.

"I know, I know," I said. We had agreed that I would no longer suggest she go out and have more fun, in exchange for which she would refrain from complaining bitterly that she was given more household chores to do than her spoiled brother, when they were growing up.

"Your Aunt Rosie said something very interesting the other night at dinner. She said making a living is not the same as making a life." Kristen inhaled appreciatively. "Life is not, after all, just holding down a job. You have to go out. Make friends."

Kristen appealed to me with a look that said, You're preaching, Mom.

"Sorry," I said.

We both turned to face the lake. A ribbon of mist had settled along the opposite shoreline.

"Did you have a chance to speak to your dad after the service?" I asked, keeping my eyes forward.

"Briefly." I wondered what Kristen's reaction would be if I told her about him asking me for a second chance. Probably disgust. While they managed a civil relationship, she never forgave him for leaving.

"I've been thinking," she said, her hand working its way into mine. I was suddenly aware that she was taller than I was. "You should marry Sam." I peered up into her eyes. As an adult, Kristen was the sensible, practical one. If she had been a winner on a game show and she had a choice of a washer and dryer or a trip to Europe, she'd take the appliances. "I mean it, Mother. Kevin and I worry about you being alone."

"That's very sweet, honey. I worry about you, too." It was true. I did worry about Kristen. Her years of fertility and marriageability were passing quickly.

"Besides, you're cheating yourself," Kristen said, sounding profoundly confident.

"Cheating myself?"

"Life is too precious to waste." How did she get to be so smart, this girl I had to hire a tutor for so she could learn her times tables? "You never know when it's going to end." Aha.

Gazing into her anxious face, my expression softened. "You're right," I said. "As a matter of fact, Sam has asked me to move with him to New York." Kristen's mouth dropped open. "I said yes." This hadn't seemed real until I told someone.

I could see tears collecting in Kristen's eyes. I felt my throat tighten a little.

"That's wonderful, Mom," Kristen said, lunging at me for a hug.

"I didn't say we were getting married," I said into her shoulder. Although now that I thought about it, it didn't seem like such a bad idea.

"I don't care. I just want you to be happy."

All of a sudden, I became acutely aware of how much I loved this young woman who was my daughter. "Now, go inside before you freeze to death," I said. "I'll be there in a minute."

"Can I tell Kevin?" she asked excitedly, as if she were five, and I'd just told her we were going to Disneyland.

"Yes, but please tell him to keep it to himself. I haven't told anyone else yet."

Kristen gave me a quick peck on the cheek, turned and practically skipped back toward the house.

Fred Heflin was leaning with his elbows on the deck railing, his back toward me. I charged at him, hugging him hard from behind, my cheek against his back. His jacket felt scratchy and smelled of mothballs.

"Liz, is that you?" he said, loosening my grip and turning around. "How good to see you." He smiled the same charming smile he had when he was nineteen. "You look great, kid!" he said, holding onto my shoulders.

"Oh, you smooth talker, you," I said in a coquettish tone. Fred laughed.

I could tell he had taken special care getting ready. His crisp white shirt was buttoned tight around his neck, and his tie looked new.

"Let's go inside and sit down," Fred said, pulling me toward the door. "I haven't talked to you in so long."

We were in the midst of catching up when Arlene walked into the living room, still wearing her coat. I couldn't help noticing the change in Fred when he saw her. A hopeful expression passed over his face.

"Do you think she'll talk to me?" he asked like a school-boy. All the sweetness of his nature shone through in his question.

"I'm sure she will," I answered, patting his knee, feeling sure not at all.

"I was truly surprised when she called me. She hasn't spoken to me since the divorce was final, you know?" I thought I saw tears beginning to form in his eyes. "She even took back her maiden name." His voice trailed off in an embarrassed way, as if it were his fault. I scratched the side of my nose and thought about how to reply.

"Don't worry," was all I could think of to say.

By three o'clock, the locals were gone. Now that the festivities were over, there was an emptiness in the air.

Half-filled wine glasses littered the living room and un-eaten food soiled Karen's best china plates. Rosie had prepared too much, which would bring her great satisfaction. As I sat in the corner with my stockinged feet propped up on the coffee table, surveying the debris, the echo of the voices filtered down the hall. "So sad." "Such a shock." "I'm so sorry." All of the useless comments that mourners say to the bereaved to make themselves feel better.

Gidge had retreated to the bedroom until Julie retrieved her and insisted she join the rest of us. Since then, she hadn't left Harry's side. She was stuck to him like a wet tongue to a cold pole, taking refuge in his comfort as they sat close together on the couch. Harry had taken on the youthful glow of a new groom.

Fred had stayed out of Arlene's way. He was out on the deck, visiting with the kids. I crept up behind Arlene, who was standing at the window. "He looks good, doesn't he?" I said softly.

"Who?" she answered.

"Oh, come on, Arlene," I said before taking a sip of wine from my glass. The corners of her mouth turned up as she shrugged her shoulders.

"Are you going to talk to him?" Rosie asked, her hands full of empty cups and glasses and her eyes full of anticipation.

"Do you want me to pass him a note in study hall?" Jo kidded from the kitchen. Arlene's mouth curled into a full smile.

"Speaking of talking to someone," she said. "What's going on with you? First Ricky shows up, then Sam."

"Wait a minute," Rosie instructed as she hurried into the kitchen to dispose of the dirty dishes. Back in a jiffy, with Jo close behind, she said, "Soooo?"

"Sew buttons on your underwear," I said, mustering up my best mischievous grin. She gave me the evil eye.

"Okay, okay." I peered over my shoulder at Gidge and Harry cuddled close on the couch. "I don't want Harry to hear me," I mouthed.

"Let's go into the kitchen," Rosie whispered back.

Gathered around the sink, I reported on my conversation with Ricky. When I got to the part about him asking about a second chance, Rosie's hand flew to her mouth.

Arlene shook her head. "Amazing," she said.

Jo gazed at me in disbelief. "After all these years?" she said.

"What did you say?" Rosie asked.

"I told him it wasn't the right time." Jo frowned. "He caught me so off guard, I couldn't think. If you had heard him stumbling over the words…" I shook my head.

Arlene let out a hiss. "What nerve."

"Okay, okay," Jo said, batting Arlene's comment away with her hand. "What did you and Sam talk about?"

"We saw you two go back in the chapel after the service," Rosie admitted sheepishly.

"Boy, nothing gets by you guys, does it?" I said, placing my fists on my hips in mock indignation. Over the next few minutes, they listened and nodded, occasionally emitting the murmuring sounds of comprehension and insight, as I summarized what had transpired. When I'd finished, Rosie said, "You're moving away?" Her voice broke slightly on the last word. She slumped against the counter, her round face in a pout. My mind raced ahead to how much I would miss them all.

"So, I guess you'll be informing Ricky that you're off the market," Jo said. Always a step ahead.

"I plan to call him as soon as I get home." My eyes drifted over to Arlene. "It's hard to let go of your first love," I said. She managed a tight little smile.

Just then, Gidge strode into the kitchen, wineglass in hand. "What's going on in here?" she demanded.

"Liz is moving to New York with Sam," Rosie blurted out.

Gidge didn't startle. She looked me smack in the eye and said, "Good for you!" Raising her hand in a toast, she said, "Here's to all the men who have been brave enough to love us."

"They helped make us who we are today," Arlene added, clinking her glass to Gidge's.

"Husbands may come and go, but friends are forever," I declared. We raised our glasses high and cheered. It was a good, warm moment. Karen would have loved it.

# CHAPTER THIRTY-FOUR

*March 26, 2000*

I awoke early and watched the morning light seep through the windows. Snuggled deep under the covers, I was engulfed in a sense of well-being, as if during the night some diabolical curse had been mysteriously lifted from me. The persistent dull ache that had become a part of me was gone.

Our families had departed the night before. Even the straggling ex-husbands had left, and it was just us girls and Julie again.

Downstairs, Arlene stood at the kitchen counter in her robe and slippers eating Honeycomb cereal out of the box. It was unusual for her to be the first one out of bed.

"Did you have a good night?" I asked, studying her averted face. When I had gone upstairs, Arlene and Fred were sitting kitty-corner to each other at the dining room table talking, their knees almost touching.

"Yes," Arlene answered between mouthfuls, sounding blasé.

"And did you and Fred have a nice talk?" I asked, scooping coffee into the basket. I switched on the pot, leaned back against the counter, crossed my arms and cocked my head.

"Look, we had a long talk, and he's coming down next weekend and we'll talk some more. Is that what you want to hear?" Almost knocking her off her feet, I grabbed her and hugged her as hard as I could.

"Yes," I said. "Yes, that's what I wanted to hear."

A rap on the sliding glass door interrupted our embrace. Outside, Gidge stood hunched over wearing the same clothes she had on the night before, her bed pillow from home under one arm and her other hand shielding her eyes as she tried to see inside.

"I don't believe it," Arlene said, as she went to the door. "You slut. Where have you been?" she asked with a smile in her voice, as she blocked the doorway.

"Oh, shut up, and let me in. It's fucking freezing out here!" Gidge pushed past her.

"Well, well," I said, smugly.

"Okay, fine," Gidge replied. "I stayed with Harry at the motel, if it's all right with you two."

I shot an amused glance at Arlene.

"Don't judge me 'til you've walked a mile in my diaphragm." Gidge brushed past us with her nose in the air.

"Who's she trying to kid?" Arlene said. "She hasn't needed a diaphragm in years."

I laughed. "It seems a lot of old friendships were renewed last night," I teased.

Arlene ignored me and went back to popping cereal into her mouth.

Julie appeared, her dark hair in two low pigtails, her eyes vacant. "What time are we going to scatter the ashes?" she asked. Her voice came out flat and hollow, and I was reminded of how painful it was to say goodbye to your mother, and the private and lasting ways people find to do it.

"You don't have to go if you don't want to," I said.

She lowered her head, as if in shame. I stretched my arm around her shoulders. She released the whimper she'd clearly been stifling.

In truth, I didn't want to go either. None of us did.

By ten o'clock, we were once again gathered in the living room waiting for the boat to arrive. Julie was sequestered in her mother's bedroom.

"I guess this is it," Gidge remarked, assessing the room as if it were the last time she was going to see it. "Hey Jo, you should take our housewarming gift home with you," she suggested, as her eyes fell upon the John Wayne poster clock.

"Wait a minute," Rosie said, grabbing Jo's arm as she made a move to get up. "That was from all of us. Why should Jo get it?"

"Because I was the one who found it at the flea market in the first place, that's why." Jo kicked off her shoes, and climbed up onto the couch. She grabbed the sides of the frame and lifted the poster off its hook. As she turned to step down, something white taped to it flashed.

"What's that on the back?" I asked, squinting.

"What?" Jo asked, setting the bottom of the frame on the carpet and bending over to look. As I leaned closer, I could see it was an envelope addressed to "The Girls" in Karen's distinctive handwriting.

Jo slid her index finger carefully under the envelope to lift it off. Bracing the poster up against the couch, she held the envelope away from her body as if it were about to bite her.

My stomach lurched.

"Give me that," Gidge ordered, snatching the envelope. I sucked in my breath, afraid she would tear it.

From inside, Gidge removed a letter-size piece of paper, folded neatly in thirds. She opened it and began to read to herself.

"Read it out loud, Gidge," Rosie said, her dark eyes glittering as she curled up cross-legged on the floor near Gidge's feet.

"February 8th, 2000," Gidge began. "Hopefully the fact that you are reading this letter means that you've reclaimed our precious family heirloom. As I told you all when you gave him to me, he was truly the best gift I'd ever received, bar none." A pause. "It also means that I'm no longer there with you."

Rosie let out a mournful groan.

"Now, before anybody gets too pissed off, let me explain." Gidge's eyes scanned ahead, and then her breath caught in her throat, and she started to cough uncontrollably. Jo reached over and slapped her hard on the back.

"Here, let me have it," Arlene said, reaching for the letter. Gidge collapsed on the couch, hacking. Arlene scrutinized the page silently, taking her time before speaking.

"I have breast cancer," Arlene read, the volume of her voice dropping. "Yes, the Big C. It's official. I was diagnosed right after Christmas. The biopsy showed that it had spread too far for either chemo or radiation." Under Arlene's voice, I could hear Karen's reaching out to us. "The only option I was given was a radical mastectomy. Now, you know how I feel about my girls, so ripping my tit off is not an option. I'll just wait it out and see what happens." Arlene gripped the sides of the letter with white knuckles as she continued to read. "Now for the good news. Since one out of every eight women gets breast cancer, hopefully, I got it for all of us."

A warm tear slid down my cheek.

"Please don't be mad at me. I love you guys. Karen. P.S. Please look after Squeaker for me, and tell her I wish I'd been a better mother."

The air seemed to have been sucked from the room. You could choke on the silence.

"Cancer," Rosie finally said softly, as if saying the word out loud explained everything. And maybe it did.

# CHAPTER THIRTY-FIVE

*March 26, 2000*

I don't know how long I sat there, staring into space, blank with renewed grief. We were a group of girls who had been inseparable as teenagers; who once could recite from memory a complete list of each other's boyfriends, records, and mix-and-match outfits; who could finish each other's sentences; whose lives were open books to each other. As adults, we had filled hours with intimate conversations, sharing worries and whispering confessions about our children, our husbands, our own feelings of inadequacy. And yet it was possible for one of us to keep a huge secret from the others. I felt myself sag under the weight of this realization.

It took a long time for the world to rearrange itself, for the facts to realign. As was my custom, I had gone to Karen for comfort when I'd lost my job. Might it be possible that if I hadn't been so selfish and had thought to ask how things were with her, she would have told me of her illness? And if she had, what then? I would never know.

"If no one objects, I'd like to be the one to tell Julie," I said, wiping my cheek with the back of my hand. Jo met my eyes. She regarded me closely before responding, as if she were waiting for me to realize what I was asking. But I had no intention of changing my mind. It was the least I could do for Karen.

"If that's what you want," Jo said.

The sound of a boat motor diverted my attention.

The Harbormaster delivered Dave's boat with a gracious offer to escort us, but we had other plans. As always, Gidge would be our skipper.

Like geese following the lead bird, one by one, we boarded the boat without speaking. Arlene and I settled gloomily into our seats with the chest of ashes between us. Gidge pushed the starter button and the engine roared to life. She opened the throttle, cutting a course for Emerald Bay, and almost immediately we were skimming over the surface of the water at top speed, the wake spreading out behind us like an opened zipper.

Closing my eyes and breathing in the cold air, it struck me that despite our wish that the center of our lives will hold firm, it never does. We go along in one direction until an unforeseen obstacle like a lost job, a reckless driver, or cancer appears, and we have to swerve. Suddenly, stunningly, we're in a different life. But Karen didn't swerve. She chose to crash instead.

Gidge cut back on the throttle and made a sharp turn, causing Rosie and Jo to grab onto the side railing to keep from sliding off the slippery leather seats.

"Jesus, Gidge!" Jo exclaimed. Gidge ignored her.

The water in Emerald Bay was a brilliant shade of green. Shards of sunlight danced on the surface, creating a reflection much like cut crystal.

"God, this is beautiful," Jo said, shading her eyes. "No wonder Karen wanted her ashes scattered here."

"I want my ashes sprinkled over my first ex-husband's omelet," Gidge said, slapping her hands together as if brushing off dirt. "What do we do now?"

Arlene got up and walked to the front of the boat. She turned and spread her feet to keep her balance as the boat rocked in its own wake.

"I think we all should say something," she said, circling the group with her eyes.

"What?" Rosie asked, looking uncomfortable.

"It doesn't have to be anything fancy, and if you don't want to say anything, that's fine," Arlene said.

"Wait a minute," Gidge interjected, taking something out of her coat pocket. "I thought it would be nice to put this picture of all of us in with Karen's ashes."

"Let's see it," Rosie said.

"It must have been one of Karen's favorites. Jo found it in her Treasures of Truth Chest," Gidge said, handing the photograph to Rosie. When the snapshot got to me, I could see by my Dorothy Hamill haircut and shiny lipstick that it had been taken in the late seventies. The six of us were standing on Karen's dock wearing jeans, T-shirts, and cowboy hats, our arms slung around each other's shoulders. Gidge had a cigarette dangling out of the corner of her mouth and Karen was waving a bottle of Cuervo Gold in the air, her mouth open, laughing.

"I remember that weekend," I said fondly.

"I do, too," Rosie added, with furrowed eyebrows. "I thought we were all going to jail."

—◊—

We girls were visiting Karen and Charles on a bright, summer afternoon, when some business associates of Charles' dropped by to show off their new boat. As we sat on the deck making small talk, Charles' demeanor changed. Suddenly, he became king of the castle.

"I think Frank needs a refill," Charles said, glancing over at Karen. Spittle had collected in the corners of his humorless little mouth, making him look like a mad dog. Karen got up, turned and left like an obedient child. "While you're at it, could you bring out some more cheese, Babe?" he called after her.

A tug of resentment pulled at my stomach. Were his legs broken? I took a sip of my drink to keep from asking the question out loud.

Before long Karen became fidgety, flashing her fake smile, like the smile she'd give on command for a camera, and laughing nervously. She wasn't used to having us see her in this subservient role. I could see it made her uncomfortable.

"What a beautiful boat," Karen remarked to Frank, displaying her cleavage for his approval while leaning over to hand him his drink. He looked ridiculous in his plaid Bermuda shorts and silly captain's hat. "Mind if I take it for a spin?" Her white teeth gleamed, as she smiled coaxingly.

I almost choked on the cracker I had in my mouth.

To my astonishment, Frank handed Karen the keys and before he could change his mind, with Gidge at the helm, we were off across the lake to one of our pet restaurants in Tahoe City.

The hot sun beat down on our already-tanned backs as we sat outside on the deck, lunching on shrimp cocktails and tequila shooters while congratulating Karen on her brazen request. Gidge's impression of the look on Frank's face as he gawked down Karen's loose-necked tank top made Rosie laugh so hard that tequila squirted out of her nose.

We ordered another round of shots, and Gidge began telling dirty jokes. Within minutes our waiter informed us that the table next to us had complained that we were "loud and obnoxious."

"Hell, we've been kicked out of better places than this," Gidge announced. She had perfected a withering stare that could make a snooty salesperson, naughty child, or presumptuous waiter fold like an origami swan. He retreated.

"If they can't take a joke, fuck 'em," Gidge said under her breath before knocking back her drink.

When we were safely back on board, it was Karen's idea that we show these people just how obnoxious we could be. Gidge made one very wide slow turn, and as we passed in front of the deck, every one of us except Rosie (who crouched down like a coward), stood in line, pulled down our shorts and "mooned" the diners. The round of applause was deafening.

Lightheaded from the sun and the booze, we collapsed in a pile with laughter.

—m—

I couldn't help but think of all the wild and reckless things we had done over the years, mostly instigated by either Karen or Gidge. But for some inexplicable reason, people still loved us in the morning.

I smiled to myself as I drank in the picture. We would never be together like that again. Somehow I had to integrate this into my sense of identity; adjust to being a new person. There's no guide; everyone has to figure it out for herself.

"May I have it, please?" Gidge asked, jolting me back to the present. She took the photo from my hand and lit the corner with a cigarette lighter she had pulled from her pocket. The snapshot began to melt quickly. She reached down and opened the lid of the metal box and dropped it inside. One last sad little gesture.

"Now, a part of us will go with Karen," Gidge announced, snapping the lid shut. She gazed off in the distance, as if she were trying to think of something appropriate to say. "Karen, you've been my friend most of my life and even though we aged, each time we laughed we were young again." A pause. "I'm thankful for every day you shared with me." I waited for the punch line. There was none. Instead, Gidge gave the top of the box a soft pat.

"I'll go next," I said. I hesitated for a moment. My mind seemed everywhere and nowhere. I rubbed my temples and tried to focus. "Karen, you gave me so much: your hospitality, your humor and most of all, your love." I took a breath. "When we were teenagers, we used to joke about dying together in a kind of murder-suicide thing, remember?" I felt a tremor of a smile at the memory. "But in truth, I always hoped I'd go first so I'd never have to live a day without your friendship."

An unexpected surge of anger came over me. "I wish you would have reached out when you found out you were ill. I would have helped you; we all would have helped you through it." If Karen were there I would have shaken her silly. But then, who was I to criticize? I had my own history of not asking for help.

"I love you," I said, my heart seized and aching. I sank back in my seat.

"Say something, Jo," I said, poking her with my elbow. She thought for a moment, and then she sprang up and shot her right arm up in the air, her fist in a black-power salute.

"Seize the day; put no trust in the morrow!" she yelled, eyes heavenward. Her voice reverberated off the giant rocks that surrounded the small bay. She waited a beat. "When Karen and I lived together, we vowed to live each day to the fullest," she explained, looking meaningfully at each of us, one by one, eye to eye.

"Okay, I'm ready," Rosie informed us. "But I need to be next to Karen." Moving in close to the metal chest, she placed her hand lightly on the lid and closed her eyes. "Karen, we always relied on you for a joke or a laugh. You said 'you don't stop laughing because you grow old; you grow old because you stop laughing.' The other day when we were all sitting around your living room talking and laughing, I swear I felt you there. I could smell your perfume." Rosie stopped, bit her lip and began to choke up. Tears rolled down the sides of her nose. She fished a wad of tissue out of her pocket and blotted her face. "Oh, and by the way, don't worry, Jo found your vibrator and put it in the trash compactor. Amen."

Rosie made a final honk.

Arlene hadn't moved from her place near the cockpit. Her face was clamped down into a deep frown.

"Arlene?" I called, "Did you want to say something?" I knew this was why she had asked us all to speak. She had something to say; something that she would not have said at the chapel in front of strangers.

Slowly, she made her way to the back of the boat, her arms outstretched for balance. Grabbing the railing, she sat down.

"Karen, life hasn't been easy for either of us," she began in a small voice, her hands clasped tightly in her lap, as she stared down at the box next to her. "But I want you to know that I couldn't have made it this far without you." Rosie sniffed. "We vowed never to let a man come between us." She shook her head in a sign of defeat. "And yet we did." No one dared to breathe. "I'm sorry I slept with Casey, even if it was after your divorce."

There it was laid open and exposed, the crux of the matter, the reason they hadn't spoken in months. I sneaked a look at the others. No one seemed shocked. I must have been the only one who hadn't known. Too preoccupied with my stupid job, no doubt.

"I had no right to do such a thing," Arlene said. The water made lapping sounds against the boat. "Please forgive me." She kissed the tips of her fingers and gently touched the top of the chest. A single tear edged itself out of her right eye, and she thumbed it away; the first I had seen her shed all week.

"Are we ready?" Gidge asked, her words cutting through the tender moment like a buzzsaw.

"Give us a minute," Jo said, through clenched teeth.

Slowly, Arlene stood up. "That's it," she croaked, looking embarrassed, as if she had forgotten she wasn't alone.

"That was beautiful, Arlene," I said, hoping her final plea for forgiveness would ease her pain. She made an effort to smile. I reached into my pants pocket. "I thought you might like to have this," I said, offering up the yellowed "In

Case of Emergency" card with her contact information on it. She knitted her brow in puzzlement. "It was in with Karen's personal things."

She took a moment to study the card. "Thank you," she whispered.

"Okay, let's do this," Gidge said in her no-nonsense style, an echo across the decades. She bent over the brass box. We gathered around and, together, lifted the box and began to shuffle across to the starboard side of the boat. Despite the fact that we were all lifting it, I could feel the weight of the contents. Rosie was right; cremains were heavy.

For a split second, I didn't want to go through with it. I didn't want to let go of my friend. "Wait," I said, stopping in my tracks. The others followed suit. Suddenly, I understood why people kept the ashes of loved ones on their mantles. I gazed out at the water in quiet motion, the light floating on top like bits of angel hair. But that wasn't what Karen wanted.

"Never mind," I said, shaking my head.

Clustered together at the side of the boat, we opened the lid. I was shocked to see a variety of shapes and colors: pebbles of light and dark gray, black, white, cream, in various sizes, mostly oval or round but some long and pointy, sharp like bits of bone or teeth; just like Rosie had described. I shuddered.

When I looked overboard, I was surprised to see that the water had become so still, I could see the bottom. We tipped the chest forward and watched the contents fall down to the water. They lay there on the surface, in the harsh sunlight, gently swaying with the ripples of the water, as though Karen were giving us one final wave goodbye.

# CHAPTER THIRTY-SIX

## *March 26, 2000*

No one spoke on the ride back. It was over. All I could think of was how we never for sure know ourselves; who we'll sleep with if given the opportunity; who we'll deceive under the right circumstance; whose heart we're willing to break.

As the boat approached the house, I saw Julie waiting for us at the end of the pier, ready to help secure the tie line. I had one last thing to do.

"I need to talk to you," I said. Julie furrowed her brows and blinked. "Let's go inside."

Once again, we were seated across from each other, in front of the fire in Karen's bedroom. Julie's face was clean-washed, and she looked very thin in her designer jogging suit.

"Your mother was a complicated woman," I began. "But the one constant in her life was her love for you." I wanted to believe this with all my heart.

Tears began to spill from Julie's eyes, and her face clouded over with renewed sorrow. The sight of her made me want to stop, say a few more comforting words, and run. How could I lay another burden on this young woman's already grieving heart?

Summoning my courage, I leaned forward and took both her hands in mine. "What I'm about to tell you will be difficult to hear," I said. Julie's dark watery eyes fixed on mine with an intent stare. "Your mother was quite ill," I said as calmly as I could. I paused.

"I knew something was wrong," Julie said in a low voice.

"Terminally ill," I said. Julie drew a sharp breath and tried to pull her hands from mine. I held on tight. "None of us knew. She didn't want anyone to know."

For a long moment, I pondered what to say next, knowing the importance of choosing the right words.

"The last thing your mother wanted was for you to have to watch her suffer a long and painful death. So she…" My words trailed off, but my meaning must have been plain enough, for a spark of recognition lit up Julie's eyes. In a voice much stronger, she said, "So, she killed herself."

The roaring in my ears was from my pounding heart. The gasp trying to escape from my throat would not let me speak. Instead, I reached into my pocket, retrieved Karen's letter and placed it carefully in Julie's hands.

I don't know what I expected Julie to do, curl up and whimper like a newborn or rant and rave about her mother's selfishness. But she did neither. She sat quietly, reading the letter by the light of the fire, seeming to memorize every word. Over and over, her eyes traveled down the page.

After some time, she looked up at me and said, "Thank you, Aunt Liz. I know this must have been very hard for you." She spoke in a soothing voice.

I took this in in silence, feeling weak and relieved, as if a fever had broken.

—⟋⟋⟋—

Bags packed, we were seated around Julie in the living room. She'd asked to speak to us one last time before we left.

"First of all, Aunt Gidge, I want you to know that I don't blame you for what happened after the service yesterday," Julie said, sounding sincere.

My stomach knotted up at the terrible injustice Greg had suffered.

Julie measured Gidge for a beat or two. "You were obviously upset."

"I plan to call Greg and apol—"

"Wait, please listen." Julie made a gesture with her small delicate hand. "There's something I want to say." She took a deep breath. "You were my mother's closest and dearest friends. You were her family. You are my family." Her bottom lip began to quiver. She paused. "My mother was happiest when she was here with all of you. She looked forward to your visits more than you will ever know." It sounded like Julie had prepared this speech.

"I've given it a lot of thought, and it would mean a lot to me for you to have this house." My head snapped back in surprise.

"Oh, my God," Rosie said, making the sign of the cross.

"Don't be ridiculous," Arlene said, waving her hand.

"No, I'm serious, Aunt Arlene."

"Honey, you've been under tremendous stress," I said, going to Julie and wrapping my arm around her shoulders. "Shouldn't you take some time to think this over?"

"I've thought it over," Julie said, in a stern voice. "On the plane and ever since I arrived. With my schedule, I rarely have time to spend at my own place, let alone here."

"You could put it up for sale," Jo said.

"Will you please let me do this?" Julie said, ignoring Jo's suggestion. Quizzical looks made the rounds.

"Could you give us a few minutes to talk about it?" Jo asked gently.

"Sure, Aunt Jo." Julie turned and walked out of the room.

When she was out of earshot, Jo asked, "What do you guys think?"

"Shit, I don't know what to think," Gidge remarked, running her hand through her windblown hair. Her face was still red from the cold.

"I think it's out of the question," Arlene said, pacing nervously. "I mean, how could we accept such a gift? This place must be worth a million dollars."

"It's worth a lot more than that," Jo said under her breath.

"How would we take care of all this?" Arlene asked, gesturing around her.

"We'd keep the existing caretaker," Jo suggested, sounding practical.

Arlene shook her head and turned away. We were finished talking. You could almost hear the hum of our brains at work.

I stood up and walked to the window, my eyes drawn to the end of the pier. I dreamed my way back in time, back to that first weekend, to those fresh, clean faces, the smell of baby oil mixed with the fragrance of pine and the sound of laughter. Strange that now, from a distance of over forty years, this memory was still so vivid.

In the background, I heard their muffled voices start again.

"Gidge, it's different for you," Arlene was saying. "This property used to belong to your parents. For you, it would be like coming home."

Home. The word hung in the air. Home to me had always meant family, and for as long as I could remember, the word "family" had meant these women, my sisters.

All at once, something clicked and everything came clear. "All of you, come here for a minute, " I said, not turning around. "Look out there. What do you see?" Their gazes followed my finger.

"What?" Rosie asked, standing on her tiptoes to see over my shoulder.

"There, on the end of the pier."

"I don't see anything," Arlene said, sounding impatient.

"I see a group of bright young girls, from different backgrounds, who met and bonded. When I look at that pier, I see the birthplace of us. Us as a family."

I turned and searched their faces. "Didn't you hear what Julie said? She said we were her mother's family; we are her family, her only family." A light came on in Arlene's eyes. "By giving us this house, Julie is trying to hang on to what's left of her family. How can we deny her that?" I was willing to fight to make my point.

Our unanimous decision to accept Julie's offer was met with tears of joy. "Thank you," she said, embracing each of us more than once. "I'll call mother's attorneys first thing tomorrow."

"It is paid for, isn't it?" Gidge asked, nudging Julie with her elbow. Julie laughed. She had her mother's laugh.

As we climbed up Highway 267 on our way to the Interstate, I was filled with mixed emotions—an emptiness inside my heart and also a feeling of hopefulness at the prospect of reuniting, of carrying on an important tradition. Karen would always be alive here.

"We made the right decision about the house," I said, looking in the rearview mirror.

"I still think it will be weird without Karen," Gidge said, fluffing her pillow, and stuffing it between her head and the car window.

"We did it for Julie," Arlene said from her seat next to me. She had become my ally.

"Besides, Gidge, we can rent a boat and go over and visit Karen anytime we want," Rosie said with anticipation. "We can pack a picnic lunch and—"

"Hell, I'll buy us a boat," Jo interrupted, leafing through her bulging Day-timer, which was the size of a Duraflame log.

"Goddamn it!" Gidge yelled from the back. "There you go again, acting like Miss Rich Bitch."

"Who are you calling a bitch?" Jo asked, turning around in her seat.

"You!" Gidge swung her pillow, hitting Jo in the face.

"You guys," Rosie whined, playfully pushing Jo off of her.

I smiled as I eased onto the Interstate. I was about to embark on a new life with Sam, and my friends were with me. The future seemed much brighter now.

# CHAPTER THIRTY-SEVEN

*April 2000*

On Monday, I called Warren to rescind my acceptance of his offer. While I waited for Keri to put him on the line, I felt a pinch of duty and guilt, but it passed quickly. When I hung up the phone, I danced around the room like a junior high school student on a sugar high. The call to Ricky was harder, but no less liberating.

In preparation for my move, I dove into downsizing with a vengeance, throwing out things I'd clung to for years such as my Girl Scout handbook and the veil from my wedding. I donated my business wardrobe to an organization that helps welfare women get jobs and gave my exercise bike (that I had ridden twice) to the Goodwill. The more I threw out, the freer I felt. With no sentiment, I boxed up years of history, not stopping to read a card or wonder how I'd acquired some useless gadget.

After the last carton had been disposed of, I lay in the dark exhausted, yet exhilarated, unable to sleep. Watching the shadows of the cherry tree dance on the bedroom wall, I realized that life has a rhythm—its own current and flow. I can either choose to go with it, letting it carry me where it will, or I can continue to swim against it, expending every ounce of energy I have, afraid I might drown.

As I surfaced from the tears of loss and reflection, I noted that life had gone on. It always did. That's what you learned as you got older. Time keeps moving. Precious moments pass in a blink and are gone forever. You can't bring them back. Living now, engaged in the present and taking pleasure from even the smallest things: each new bud that popped out on the sweet olive plant on the porch, the scratch of Sam's whiskers when he kissed me in the morning, the aroma of that first cup of coffee—that was the reward of grief.

In the days that followed, I realized that I had spent my whole childhood holding my breath, waiting for something to happen, for my parents' next fight, for my father to leave, for some disaster. As an adult, I had held on to my possessions, my pain and my pride to feel in control. I'd tried to analyze everything. Why did my parents fight so much? Was it because of me? What went wrong with my first marriage? If I married again, would the same thing happen? My brain was worn out.

It would be hard to change myself, to relinquish control, to be open and receptive to life, to love and to allow being loved in return. But it was time to explode my comfort zone one adventure at a time. When I got to New York, I vowed to take more risks, be more spontaneous, let go of the notions of how my life "should be," and just let it be. I'm too old for tattoos or piercing, but why not take a tap dancing class? If they laugh, they laugh. Who cares? I may even wear shorts this summer despite my spider veins. Maybe not.

Greg's words bounced around in my brain. "She let go." The idea of letting go, letting down even for an instant has always scared me to death. For Karen, letting go may have meant giving up. But for me it could mean simply trusting life's currents to carry me where I'm meant to be—finally and at last released.

A friend is a present you give yourself.

— Robert Louis Stevenson

Judith Marshall lives in Northern California. She has won the Jack London prize for fiction awarded by the California Writers Club and is currently working on her second novel, "Staying Afloat," the story of a devoted stay-at-home wife and mother who morphs into a sex-starved adulteress.

For more information, go to
www.judithmarshall.net

Made in the USA
Monee, IL
06 January 2021

56585541R00229